Lost Without You

Heather Thurmeier,
author of *Falling for You* and *Stuck on You*

CRIMSON
ROMANCE
F+W Media, Inc.

This edition published by
Crimson Romance
an imprint of F+W Media, Inc.
10151 Carver Road, Suite 200
Blue Ash, Ohio 45242
www.crimsonromance.com

To my girls,
Be strong. Be brave. Don't ever give up.
Know you are always loved and never alone.

Chapter One

Zoe Oliver stood with her back perfectly straight and her head held high. Half of her hair was combed back into a clip and the rest fell past her shoulders to mid-back in waves like a golden ocean. A slight fringe framed her face giving her that messy-yet-styled look.

She didn't need to look in the mirror again to know her makeup was still evenly applied with a base of foundation and pressed powder, followed by a dusting of bronzer, her favorite light jade eye shadow that enhanced her blue eyes, her usual eyeliner and mascara, and a coat of raspberry shimmer lip-gloss. Once she finished with her makeup in the morning, she didn't dare scratch her nose or rub her eyes until bedtime. Because of that, she rarely had to fix her makeup during the day.

Looking around, Zoe noticed the appearance of the other contestants. It was hard not to. Apparently they'd all gotten some memo about attire that she'd missed. Each of the five clusters of fellow contestants had four members and all of them were dressed as if they were about to go camping, not staring in a reality TV show.

People on reality shows usually dress up and look nice while they're on camera. Even on the last show, *Treasure Trekkers,* people had their hair done and makeup on and wore cute hiking clothes.

Zoe smoothed out the non-existent wrinkles in her mid-thigh length pencil skirt and adjusted the hem of her blouse so it sat perfectly at her hips. She might be in the wilderness, but that was no excuse for a poor appearance.

But this group of misfits must have gone shopping in the sporting goods section.

That's not going to help ratings.

Of course, it was possible their choice of clothing actually made sense, she supposed, given they currently stood at the mouth to a trail leading off into the Montana wilderness. If anything said camping, it was the lush evergreen forest surrounding them and the birds chirping in the branches. If she wasn't mistaken, she could even hear a babbling stream nearby, just out of view through the trees.

Zoe frowned. She didn't like camping. Or the wilderness. Or the outdoors. She liked it even less while standing around with a bunch of people she'd never met before.

And, taking a second look, why were they all standing in groups of four? She was the only person without an entourage. Huh, weird.

Was she expected to team up with a bunch of strangers to compete in this show? She didn't care for the sound of that at all. She didn't work well with people she knew, so how would she be able to team up with people she'd never met before? With people who dressed like that girl with her brown hair in a tight bun, no makeup, and a pair of the most unflattering cargo pants Zoe had ever laid eyes on. The girl could probably store an entire Macy's catalogue worth of items in those pockets.

Surely Chip knew better than to expect her to dress like that too. He absolutely had to know that sticking her with a bunch of strangers had "bad idea" written all over it.

Chip Cormack, the show's producer, stood off to the side, talking to one of the production assistants with a seriously heavy looking clipboard. Zoe had met Chip for the first time when she went on a dating reality TV show called *The One*. That had gone pretty well. Until she made it to the final two and bachelor Brad had chosen Miss Goodie Two Shoes Cassidy instead of her. How that man had made his decision, she'd never understood.

That wasn't important anymore. She hadn't really loved Brad. She'd been caught up in the moment, enjoying the limelight and attention from him. But she hadn't actually loved him. She just hadn't wanted to be rejected by him, or anyone else, on national television.

How could she love someone who spent his days surfing the waves and expecting her to as well? Zoe didn't swim. Ever. That relationship would have been destined to fail. Not that Brad stayed with Cassidy either, since she'd fallen in love with her cameraman on the show, Evan. Now the two of them were at home, cozy in his little cabin in the woods with their new baby.

Zoe bit the inside of her lip.

And then there was Miles and Paige. "Madly in love and ready to take everything to the next level!" they'd told her recently. Probably making babies at that very moment.

Zoe scowled at the thought of it. She didn't want that life anyway. Why would she? Not that it was even an option for her anymore. Never really had been an option. Well, not since she was fourteen.

She bit down on her lip until the familiar coppery taste trickled into her mouth and forced her thoughts away from where they'd suddenly traveled. All that stuff wasn't important anymore. What was important now was what the heck she was doing here alone when everyone else had come with a group.

Zoe wandered over to Chip and tapped him on the shoulder, not waiting for him to be done speaking with the PA. "Chip, we need to talk."

Chip dismissed the assistant to carry on with her tasks. "Zoe, it's lovely to see you again." He smiled one of his famous Chip smiles—the ones that always made her feel a little lightheaded.

She'd noticed how cute Chip was while filming *The One*. She thought his dark brown messy, spiked hair, which probably took great time and product application to achieve, looked stylish and put together. His eyes reminded her of chocolate—her one indulgence.

When she'd filmed *Treasure Trekkers* last summer and had hurt her ankle, Chip had been at the hospital with her. He'd seemed so sweet and so genuinely concerned for her well being when no one else usually cared. She'd liked his attention. She'd liked him.

Now, seeing him again, standing with him so close to her, she couldn't stop her heart from pounding against her ribs. Damn. She needed to get her emotions under control around him if she was going to make it through the whole show without having a coronary.

"Chip," she started, "I don't understand why I'm the only one without a group. It seems like all the others have teams formed already. Is there something you haven't told me?"

She knew the answer without asking the question. Where Chip was concerned, there was always a surprise. And not necessarily a good one.

"So you've noticed."

"I'd have to be blind not to."

Chip put his hand on her lower back, the heat of his palm making her knees suddenly feel like pockets of gelatin rather than joints filled with bones, ligaments, and cartilage. She forced her shoulders back and demanded her knees behave. She wasn't about to become a pile of gooey hormones over a guy, even if that guy was Chip.

"Why don't we join the others and I'll explain everything?" Chip smiled at her and her anxiety slipped away. Funny how he had a way of doing that to her. That was probably the reason she kept agreeing to be a part of his silly reality shows.

Well, it was certainly one of the reasons anyway. The money he'd guaranteed her this time didn't hurt either.

Together they walked back to the waiting groups, but when Zoe tried to leave Chip's side to join the contestants, he held her back.

"What's going on? I deserve to know," she said quietly, imploring him with her eyes to let her in on his secret. She hated not being in control of a situation and she most definitely was not in control right now.

Chip leaned over and whispered in her ear. "Trust me." His fingers rubbed up and down her arm as he spoke. She suddenly found it hard to concentrate on what he said as everything except the sensation of his fingers on her arm and his breath on her earlobe ceased to exist. "I promised you a payday. Let me make that happen."

She nodded when he pulled away from her. Her skin prickled with goose bumps where his hand no longer touched her. Odd. She hadn't felt this much reaction to Chip on either of the last shows. Although, she'd never been so close to him during those productions either. Maybe Zoe liked more than just his smile.

Chip turned to the others. "If I can have your attention, please?" he started as the familiar business tone in his voice returned. "I have a couple of details to share with you before we get started with our filming."

Everyone focused on Chip.

"I trust that each of you have now been seen by one of our onset medics, correct? I know you completed some health forms and all of you should have had a full examination by your own doctors. This was just a quick evaluation by our medics as an extra check to make sure you are in top physical form to be able to safely compete in the challenges you'll face during filming, and also to establish a baseline to judge any future evaluations you may need as the show goes on."

The contestants nodded nervously. Zoe hadn't been told to complete any medical examination before coming on the show and she couldn't remember having filled out any health forms. Maybe Chip already had those on file for her because of the mountains of paperwork she'd filed for the other shows.

"Now," he said, "I'm sure you all recognize the woman standing beside me. In case you haven't watched any of my other shows— shame on you—this is Zoe Oliver. She was a contestant on both *The One* and *Treasure Trekkers* as well as another show on a different network, though we here at Chip Cormack Productions try not to hold that other one against her." He laughed. The others chuckled. Zoe narrowed her eyes at him.

What the hell was he up to?

"You may have also noticed that Zoe is here without a team. That's because Zoe isn't here to compete with all of you on the show. Zoe is here as your host." Chip clapped, the sound loudly echoing around them.

What did he just say?

"Chip, I…" Zoe started, her voice soft with surprise.

"In a few minutes, we'll get started with our filming. Zoe will introduce the show and give you details about the rules and how the show is going to work." Chip carried on as if he hadn't heard her.

I will? How? Don't I need to know those things to talk about them?

"After that, you will be on camera twenty-four hours a day until filming concludes in one month. Now, please give Zoe and me a few minutes to go over some last minute details and then we'll get started. If anyone needs to use the indoor facilities, I suggest you make it quick."

The contestants scattered off to the restrooms inside the park office but Zoe stood her ground. What had Chip just said? Host?

She turned. He smiled as if he'd just told her how to stay young and beautiful for eternity. But he hadn't. She was pretty sure he'd just said she'd be on national television as a host. She wasn't a host. Hosts were usually charming and charismatic and friendly with everyone. She was none of those things.

"Care to explain to me what the hell is going on?"

"I promised you a payday and the only way I can do that is to pay you a salary. Isn't that what you want?"

"No. When you guaranteed me a payday I thought you had a way to rig the show so I'd actually win this time and finally redeem myself. I didn't know you'd brought me on the show to be some lame host."

"I can't rig my shows for the outcome I want. It doesn't work that way. Hosting is the perfect way for you to redeem yourself and walk away with an easy one hundred grand."

Oh. That was money worth considering. That was enough money to pay off not only the bills already piled on her kitchen counter, but also the ones that would come in the mail for the next several months. That was enough money to finally pay off the last of her hospital bills that had been accruing interest since her stepfather had left her mother two years after her accident and had taken his money with him, leaving them broke and in debt.

"Sorry I didn't tell you earlier, but I didn't think you would come if I did. I figured you'd be too nervous to agree to come on camera as the host, but if you do it, I know you'll be the best host I've ever had." Chip took a step toward her, closing the small distance between them. Since when was Chip so cozy with everyone? He took her hand in his. It felt warm and strong...and comforting, almost as if she could let down her guard with him. Almost.

"Just go along with the show and being the host. I know it's not what you expected but I really think by the time filming wraps up, you'll be happy you were here. This is going to be an amazing experience for all of us."

She nodded. It wasn't like she could leave Chip without a host now. And the money was too good to pass up. She would do it. Be the host of the show. Maybe Chip was right. Maybe America would see her differently after this. It couldn't hurt to try, could it?

"Okay," she said. "What do I have to say? I don't really know anything about the show so how can I start us off?"

Chip squeezed her hand. "I knew you wouldn't disappoint me." He let her hand go and pointed over to another production person who held giant pieces of white poster board. "I've made up cue cards so all you have to do is read them. We'll do it this way for as long as you need to, then when you're comfortable hosting, you can wing it without the extra help."

That didn't sound so terrible. At least she wouldn't have to worry about sounding like a moron. She swallowed her nerves while the contestants gathered back in front of her, the person with the cue cards standing right in the middle behind them where the camera couldn't see.

"Welcome to *Wild Expedition*," she started, her voice a little shakier than she wanted. "A show that will take our contestants out of their comfort zones and into the wild."

She paused, her gaze darting to Chip quickly. How wild exactly?

She cleared her throat and focused on reading the cue cards again. "During the month long expedition, each team of four people will have to complete specific challenges designed to test their teamwork skills, survival skills, problem solving, and personal strengths. This is not an easy game to play, but our five teams are up to the challenge, aren't you?"

The contestants let out a loud cheer. A hell of a lot louder than she would have. She probably owed Chip a huge thank you for not having her as a contestant since this wasn't her kind of thing at all. A whole month of roughing it? No thanks.

"Along the way, we'll have to say goodbye to four of our teams so that in the end, only one team remains to win the shared million-dollar prize."

Wow. A million dollars split between four was still a ton of money for each person. Maybe she should have negotiated with Chip for more salary since she could have made a lot more money as a contestant. Of course, she could play and walk away empty handed too. Again. At least with the salary she walked away with something for her time and effort.

"Each team should have a map in their possession."

They should?

"Your first task is to find your site, set up camp with the gear provided, and survive your first night out in the wild. Tonight I'll check in with each team to see how you're doing. Teams, it's time to get wild! The game officially begins now."

Zoe watched quietly as the teams scrounged in their bags to find the maps that would lead them to their camps. A wave of relief came over her that this time she didn't have to worry about strategy or getting along with the other contestants or any of the other things she'd had to worry about on the previous shows. This time, finally, she wouldn't have to fear water challenges that threatened to remove her makeup in one splash. Sure, she'd always worn waterproof, but there was only so much it could withstand. She might have come across as calm and uncaring at the thought of going out on a canoe to grab a cache with Paige, Miles, and Ben, but on the inside, she'd been a quivering mess. At least this time all she had to do was show up, look pretty, smile, and read a few cue cards. No big deal.

"Ready to go?" Chip asked, motioning toward the trail all of the teams had now started down.

"Go where?"

"To the production camp."

Zoe glanced around at the production trailers that looked pretty permanent by the park office. "Are the trailers going to meet us at the camp or are there some already waiting there?"

Just then a production person handed her a large backpack. The one she'd been told to pack. The one she thought she'd be unpacking soon into a nice chest of drawers in a cozy room somewhere.

Chip shook his head and looked worried for the first time ever in her memory. "Zoe, your job is to be near the contestants to host the show. The show takes place in the wilderness. The trees are too dense for the trailers and there are no nearby roads. I'm afraid the best you're going to get for the next few weeks is a porta-potty and a private tent."

Fear gripped Zoe. This couldn't possibly be any worse. No bathroom with running water. No electricity. No cozy bed to curl up in each night.

"Let me guess," she said through clenched teeth. It didn't matter how cute Chip was, he could really be an annoying little shit when he wanted to be. "You're staying here, right?" No way was Mr. Hot Shot Producer roughing it like she was being forced to.

"No, myself and a handful of other production people will be staying with you in a production base camp. We have tents and a little kitchen and even a couple of camping showers. Don't worry, Zoe, you won't be alone."

"Oh, good, so there will be someone to hear me scream when I get eaten by a bear."

He laughed.

She didn't.

Chapter Two

Chip Cormack laughed at Zoe's comment. He hadn't expected anything less from her. A sarcastic sense of humor wasn't for everyone, and truth be told, he didn't love hearing it from most people. But coming from Zoe, it always made him laugh. It was her feisty personality and her "take no shit from anyone" attitude that had originally made him want her on his shows.

Of course, her headshots hadn't hurt either.

She was damn hot, even if she had built an indestructible wall around herself. Or at least she thought it was indestructible. He was pretty certain that given enough time and determination, he'd be able to break through.

It had only been a couple of years since his first introduction to Zoe, but it felt like a million. His feelings for her had been simmering too long already. He was ready to take things further than friendship or being colleagues with her. He just had to find a way for her to see that she had feelings for him too.

Easier said than done.

Every time she looked at him, he sensed her interest. When they spoke, the chemistry flowed easily. And when he touched her hands or her back…well, it was as if the entire rest of the world stopped existing outside of the two of them. There was something indescribable between them. Except he knew from his own personal experience with her, and from watching her with everyone else, that she had big walls protecting her from letting anyone get too close. If only her damn walls would give just a little then maybe he could find a way to knock them down all together.

As it was, she walked beside him now, her head high, her heels even higher. On the last show she'd worn her heels hiking every day until she'd twisted her ankle and had been forced to wear sneakers. And she never failed to show up in full hair and makeup.

All part of her defense system.

Well, roughing it in the woods for a month ought to fix that.

"We're almost there," he said. "Just a few minutes longer and we'll be at the production camp."

"And where have all the teams gone? I haven't seen any of them since a while back when the trail split in three."

"They're all relatively close to our camp but far enough away that we won't interfere with their survival skills or camp life. And each of the teams is far enough away from each other, or in some cases separated by some natural obstacle, that they can't interact together very easily. I'm not saying it couldn't happen if the teams worked for it, but I've made it pretty hard for them."

"This is a really different show for you," she said, glancing his way and almost stumbling. He reached out to steady her but she righted herself. "Well, *Treasure Trekkers* was pretty outdoorsy, but at least it still had indoor accommodations and common areas."

"It is different. But I wanted something that would really put people to the test in all kinds of ways. I think this show will do that."

"No offense, but won't it get sort of boring for all the teams to be separate all the time?"

Just like Zoe to speak her mind. Another thing he liked about her. He was sick of being surrounded by production people who always said what they thought he wanted to hear. Zoe spoke her mind and it was a relief.

"It might, but I have plans to keep it interesting."

"You always do. I glad I'm not on the receiving end of your surprises this time. Well, except for the whole hosting gig. And the camping twist. Thanks for that, by the way."

He laughed. "You're welcome. Now enough about the show. How have things been with you? I haven't seen you in the tabloids lately."

"Thank God for small miracles. I've had enough of those trashy magazines tracking my every move. Who would have ever thought they'd care so much about a stupid reality TV show?"

"Hey now. One of those stupid reality shows is paying you a nice sum to be here."

"True. You know I used to read those magazines all the time. Now I can't stand to see them in the grocery checkout."

"They aren't so terrible. It's usually good publicity for the shows."

"Only because you're not the one on the cover," she snapped.

"You may have a point there. I've only graced the inner pages, never the front. I don't think anyone would like seeing this mug shot on the cover."

Her lips curled almost into a smile. "I don't think most girls would mind too much."

"Is that a compliment from Zoe Oliver?" he teased. "You really must be feeling out of your element."

They came around a bend in the trail and the pathway suddenly opened into a wider area. Tents of all sizes were set up around the perimeter with three central fire pits surrounded by logs for chairs.

Zoe stopped and took in the site. He pulled on her arm, tugging her gently to one of the two tents set off to the side a little more than the others. His was the outer most tent while hers was right next door, just as he'd planned. He hadn't wanted her to feel alone in the woods by making their tents too secluded, but he also didn't want the entire crew hearing their every move. Strategically placing a film supply tent on the other side of hers meant there would be enough foot traffic to make her comfortable, but also enough privacy that they would have some time alone. Well, if he could finagle a reason to score alone time with her. If not, then at least no one would be around to witness his attempted and failed seduction.

He walked to her tent and unzipped the door, holding it open to the side so she could slip through with her backpack still on her back. As she passed by, he caught the scent of her flowery perfume.

Damn he'd missed that smell.

He'd only had the opportunity to catch a hint of her perfume a couple of times over the course of filming the other shows. But every time he had, the scent made him long to wrap his arms around her and bury his face in her hair. Her scent was delicious, intoxicating…arousing.

"You get settled and I'll come back in a bit to show you around the rest of camp."

"Okay." She nodded, looking around as if unsure of what to do next. "You know where to find me."

He zipped the door closed again to give her privacy. He knew exactly where he hoped to find her someday soon—in his arms.

• • •

Zoe surveyed her room…tent. Hell on earth might be the most accurate description.

Okay, so maybe hell on earth was exaggerating a bit.

Her tent was larger than she'd expected. Feared. Whatever.

She had imagined Chip giving her a tiny popup tent she'd have to crawl into with no room to move around. Thankfully, her tent was not like that at all. It looked to be about a twelve feet by twelve feet, military styled tent. One that could have easily housed a few people instead of just her.

Along one side of the tent, a cot waited for her with a sleeping bag still rolled up with a few wool blankets folded on top and a pillow. Without even sitting on it, she could guess it wouldn't be the most comfortable bed she'd ever slept on, but it was better than the ground so she wouldn't complain. Too loudly.

Beside the bed was a canvas set of drawers. It wasn't big, but it would hold a few of her things, like bras, panties, and T-shirts. On top of that sat a large lantern, a flashlight, and a radio with a clock on the front. She unzipped the inside flap just above the drawers to reveal a screen style window facing out to the lush, dense forest. A ray of dampened light fell across the cabinet, hitting what appeared to be solar panels covering the tops of the gadgets. Good thing they'd gotten here early enough for a few hours of sunshine to come in her window so everything would have time to charge before it got dark.

The last thing in the room was a small cooler. She peeked inside. Instead of finding chilled Perrier and snacks on ice, like she'd hoped, she found a reusable water bottle, a mirror, a bottle of hand sanitizer, some towels, and a few other random things.

Sighing, she took a deep drink from the water bottle. Barely a trickle came out of the bottle. She unscrewed the lid only to find a filter attached to the inside.

Definitely no Perrier around here.

She eyed the cooler. If nothing else, it was another place to put some of her clothes. Although she was going to have to figure out some kind of solution for the things that should be hung, not folded.

"Knock, knock," Chip said from outside her door, startling her.

"Holy crap you scared me," she said, unzipping the door to let him in.

"Sorry. I didn't mean to sneak up on you. You'll get used to listening for sounds outside your tent soon enough. All settled?"

She looked at her backpack, still full. "I guess."

He motioned to the patch of light filtering into the tent from the screened window. "I see you figured out the solar powered gadgets. They need a couple of hours of sun and then they should last you for a few hours of use. If you ever forget to power them during the day, we have extras in an open case beside the supply tent. Those ones will always be fully charged. You can drop your dead one in the case and take a charged one any time you need."

"Great. You've thought of everything, haven't you?"

"I tried. I may have forced you into the wilderness, but even I like a few luxuries out here, like light." He stepped out of the tent. "Come on. I'll show you around the rest of camp so you know where everything is. I don't think living out here for a month will be quite as painful as you feared. As you said, I tried to think of everything."

"Did you think of indoor plumbing? Air conditioning? Spider control?"

"Yes, yes, and yes. But keep in mind there's only so much I can do. We are still outdoors and no amount of preparation is going to cover everything."

"Well an easy solution to that would have been to house us indoors, but I'm sure you already know that."

"I do." He pointed to the fire pits in the middle of the open area surrounded by tents. "Over here, we'll have fires lit each night. Depending on the amount of people who want them, we may light all three or just one."

She followed him to the tent next to hers. "In here is the film supply. You shouldn't need to come in here ever, but there will be crew coming and going as needed throughout the course of the show. I don't think it will bother you at all though."

They wandered deeper into the base camp. "All those other tents are production people's private quarters."

"What about those small tents?" she asked, pointing to a few that were off to the side. They were more secluded than any of the others. Half of them had something that looked like large canvas water balloons above them.

Chip led them over to the closest of the small tents and unzipped the door. A plastic box and a few rolls of toilet paper propped on a branch sticking up out of the ground sat inside.

"My indoor plumbing solution," he said, sounding prouder than he should have in her opinion. Then he opened one of the tents with the canteen looking thingy above it. "And the shower. I would use these sparingly if possible. The bladder only holds so much water even when completely full and although it has a solar heater, it's not exactly a hot and steamy experience."

She peeked over at him and found him looking at her instead of the shower. Maybe it was all that talk about hot, steamy showers, but she suddenly felt hot and steamy herself. Chip's dark eyes penetrated into hers almost as if he felt the same thing. But he couldn't. Could he? Surely Chip didn't think of her in that way. Hell, she didn't normally think of Chip this way either. Of course, she'd always been attracted to him, and being around him had always made her heart flutter a little, but this reaction was probably caused by the excitement of the day. Her emotions were stressed to the max already and her body was on high alert. That had to be it.

Zoe took a step back. "Great," she said, clearing her throat which had gone dry, probably from all the fresh outdoor air. "So I'll be looking forward to the day I get back to civilization again."

Maybe changing the scenery would get the idea of being in a hot shower—with Chip—out of her mind. Picturing Chip naked wouldn't help her be less attracted to him. "What's next on the grand tour?"

"The kitchen and common area." As he walked a few steps ahead of her, she took a deep breath, feeling as if she hadn't been able to a moment before. Then she fell into step beside him.

Inside the kitchen tent there were a few tables with camping chairs set up as well as a kitchen-type cooking area with a couple of butane stove tops and a washing basin.

I hope they cater.

Zoe wasn't the world's best cook on a regular stove, in a real house with proper utensils and pots. A camping stove was well beyond her skill set. She smacked a mosquito feasting on her arm. If the bugs didn't kill her, starvation just might.

"And who exactly cooks in here?" Her expression must have shown her concern because Chip chuckled and put his arm around her shoulders, pulling her close.

"Not to worry, Zoe. I've hired a couple of cooks to help us. You're always welcome to use the equipment yourself if you want something special. But the cooks already have a schedule of meals prepared for the time we're out here so there is no need for you to cook your own meals if you don't want to."

Oh thank God.

"Speaking of food," Chip said, "the cooks will prepare a hot dinner later. Until then, can I interest you in a soda or a bottle of water and a sandwich? I might be able to cook gourmet meals at home, but out here I'm a little out of my league."

Gourmet meals? She'd never imagined Chip to be the kind of guy to cook for himself if it wasn't on a grill, let alone someone able to make gourmet meals.

"I'll take a sandwich and water, thanks."

Chip grabbed them sandwiches and they turned to find a seat. A couple of camera guys she recognized from previous shows sat at one table chatting happily amongst themselves.

"Should we join them?" Chip asked.

Zoe shook her head. She just wanted to relax and settle in. Putting on her happy face and trying to be entertaining wasn't at all appealing right now. "I'd rather not. How about the empty table instead."

For some reason, she didn't feel like she had to put on much of an act for Chip. Maybe because he'd seen her through the highs and lows of the other shows, he'd already seen the worst in her.

Well, maybe not the *worst*. No one saw that side of her.

She'd never let that happen.

"Now that you're here, do you think you'll survive for the month? It's not so bad, right?"

She shrugged. "It's not exactly the Ritz, but I think I'll manage."

"You seemed to do just fine hiking, camping, and geocaching on the other shows. I figured you'd be okay with this too, once you saw you wouldn't be completely roughing it. I did my best to provide some conveniences."

"I appreciate the effort, but I still might hate you a little for dragging me out here. Couldn't our teams have to live in a spa or something instead of the wilderness? Survive the deadly seaweed wrap without fainting from the smell. Or maybe drinking the infamous green smoothie without gagging."

They laughed together.

"I'll keep that in mind for a future show." Chip took a bite of his sandwich while looking at her as if he was studying something.

"What?"

"I've never seen you this relaxed. It's nice."

"It's easier to relax without a camera following me around twenty-four, seven."

Chip seemed to watch her a lot. His eyes were so warm and caring, she couldn't help but let herself melt into his gaze more. He was so different to her now that she wasn't a contestant. Was he like this—warm, friendly, caring—to all his staff, or only to her?

He placed his hand over hers where it rested on the table, squeezing gently. If she thought his eyes were warm, they had nothing on his hands. His touch sent a wave of heat up her arm and through her body, settling low in her belly.

She could really get used to this new feeling she had around Chip if she wasn't careful.

But she had to be careful.

Chapter Three

Chip reveled in the knowledge that he'd possibly just wormed his way into a tiny fissure in the wall...no, fortress, surrounding Zoe. He hadn't realized it would be as easy as a look, a smile, and a touch. If he'd known, he would have tried long ago.

Of course, that would have gotten him in trouble before. Producers couldn't flirt with contestants. But now they were both crew so the rules had changed.

But his feelings for Zoe hadn't changed at all.

He was still as captivated by her as he was the first time he'd laid eyes on her. Still as amused by her as the first time he'd spoken to her. And still as distracted by her as he'd been the first time he'd watched her walk away. Damn, she had a great ass.

"If this is what you're like when there're no cameras around," he squeezed her hand again and dropped his voice low so only she would hear, "I wonder what you're like when there aren't people around either."

She pulled her hand out from his as if it were on fire and picked up her sandwich instead. Her shoulders went back, the softness in her features replaced by hard edges and narrowed eyes.

Wow. He really must have said the wrong thing. Damn it. And right after he felt like he made progress with her. He may have briefly found a tiny crack in her wall, but she'd patched it up with plaster and cement.

"Sorry, Zoe. I didn't mean to make you uncomfortable."

"I'm not uncomfortable." Her voice was confident but he wasn't an idiot. She was lying through her perfectly white teeth.

"Excuse me, Mr. Cormack," said one of the younger production assistants they'd hired from college for the summer. "But I need to put this box of supplies away and no one told me where to put them."

He sighed. Why did he have to do all the work around here? Seriously. If he took a sick day, production would come to a screeching halt, which was exactly the reason why he'd never taken one.

"Well," he started then paused, trying to come up with the girl's name. When he couldn't, he continued. "What kind of supplies are they?"

She set down the box with a *thunk* on the table and pulled a couple of handfuls of cords out. Instantly, the cords unraveled and twisted together. The sight of tangled wires and cords annoyed him like nothing else.

"What are you doing? You're making a mess," he snapped, sounding a little meaner than he'd meant to. But really, how hard was it to pick up a mic pack without completely tangling the cord?

"I..." She blushed and looked at her feet.

He clenched and unclenched his jaw a couple of times. It wasn't her fault she didn't know what she was doing. She was new. He had to remember that.

She fumbled with the mic packs, dropping one. As she attempted to catch it before it hit the floor, the others in her hand slipped, tangling even more.

"Oh for the love of—" He jumped up and grabbed the things from her hands while she bent to get the mic pack from the floor.

"This is how you hold mic packs," he said, wrapping the cord and securing it around the black box. "Not whatever that is you're doing now."

"I'll fix them all. I promise. Just point me in the direction of where to put them."

"We have two supply tents, one for film stuff and one for food stuff. These mic packs and other related film things would go in the—"

"The film supply tent?"

Really? There was still a question in her mind?

"Yes," he answered as gently as he could.

"Okay, thanks. Sorry to bother you." The girl shoved the rest of the things back into the box, heaved it into her arms, and scurried away.

Chip gathered his trash from lunch and Zoe's as well and threw it all in the garbage. When he turned back to the table, Zoe stood, shaking her head at him.

"What?" he asked.

"You'd catch more flies with honey, you know? That poor girl was obviously trying so hard to please you and you were rather rude to her. And here I thought you'd changed by how nice you were to me. I guess you're still the same old Chip I remember from the previous shows."

Without giving him a chance to respond, she walked out of the tent. He followed quickly, not wanting to let her walk away while thinking badly of him. Not that he should care so much what she thought about him, but he did. And knowing she thought he'd acted like a jerk on not one, but many occasions apparently, really bothered him.

They came out into the sunlight just as a cluster of sound people were walking in. One of them stopped and stared. "Zoe Oliver?" she asked.

Zoe smiled as if she was completely comfortable meeting her adoring "fans." Maybe she was. She had been in the spotlight a lot over the last year or so thanks to his shows. And she always seemed to like being the center of attention. This was probably fun for her, having a fan at base camp.

"Hi," Zoe said, offering her hand to the girl. Her voice was sweet and charming. "It's nice to meet you."

"Oh my God, I can't believe it's really you," the girl said, rushing up to Zoe and throwing her arms around her. "I've loved you since you were on *The One!*"

Zoe visibly blanched, all the color draining from her face as the girl hugged her tight. She pulled at the girl's arms, forcing her to let go, and took a quick step back toward Chip, distancing herself from the sound girl.

"That's great. But how about next time you love me from a distance instead of invading my personal space, okay? If you'll excuse me, it's been a long day and I need to prepare for my hosting spot in front of the camera. Some of us actually need to look good and rested each day."

Zoe strode off toward her tent leaving the girl looking like she'd just been kicked in the gut.

"I think she's still in shock from being host and forced to sleep in a tent with no electricity," Chip said to the sound girl. "You know how these princess-types are. Try not to take it personally."

The girl wandered on into the kitchen tent not looking very convinced and Chip sprinted to catch up with Zoe. He fell into step beside her.

"So what was that thing you said earlier about catching flies with honey?" he teased, trying to lighten her mood. He didn't want her to have a bad first day on the show. That could set a bad standard for the rest of filming.

He didn't want to see her upset either.

"Shut it, Chip. You were rude to an employee who was just trying to do the right work for you. That girl assaulted me. She needed to be put in her place."

"Assaulted you? From where I stood, it looked like a hug."

"Well it felt like an invasion of privacy and I'm not interested in having it happen again. So, how about you do me a favor and tell your staff to keep their grabby hands to themselves?"

"Doesn't it seem to you that you're overreacting just a tad to the whole situation?"

They got to her tent and she paused after unzipping the door. She turned to face him. Her entire demeanor had changed from what it had been earlier. First she'd been playful and funny, then rude and hostile, and now...now she looked as if she might cry. Had Zoe always been such a whirlwind of emotions?

"I just don't want people to touch me, okay? Is that so terrible? I'm not one of those touchy-feely girls who likes to be hugged by people. So I'd really appreciate it if you'd tell your staff how I feel or else I'm afraid we may have more incidents like this last one. Got it?"

She disappeared into her tent and he fought the urge to go after her and comfort her. There was more to this situation then some stupid, harmless hug, but following her when she was upset and forcing her to talk would be like convincing the Great Wall of China to scoot over an inch. It just wasn't going to happen.

• • •

Chip clenched his jaw while contestant Rick flirted with Zoe. Again. If he'd known Rick would take such a liking to Zoe— his Zoe—he would have picked someone else to fill the fourth spot on that team. After all, this wasn't a dating show and he certainly hadn't been trying to fix anyone up with Zoe...himself not included.

Zoe was here to host and hopefully fall for him just as much as he'd already fallen her. He'd wanted to be with her for so long. He was tired of waiting for his chance with her and there was no way he'd let some new guy waltz into her life and take away his chance now.

She was definitely not here to fall for some random jerk who got off on fishing and shooting things. Zoe wouldn't go for that kind of guy anyway. She was way too high maintenance for that lifestyle. Being at base camp was even pushing her to her limits. A guy like this one—huge, scruffy beard, and who probably wouldn't miss not having a shower all that much—was not her kind of guy.

And yet there she was with him, laughing at his unfunny jokes and acting like he was some kind of Hollywood heartthrob. It didn't make sense.

It also pissed him right the hell off.

But he was the producer and she was the host who was currently doing her job. Why she had to be so goddamn charismatic on TV at this particular moment, he didn't know.

"Rick, you're too much." She giggled.

She. Giggled.

Zoe Oliver never giggled. The only time he'd heard that sound come out of her body was when she'd been trying to win the affections of Brad from *The One*. Was she trying to win Rick's affections too?

Chip cursed under his breath. Thank goodness he was far enough away from the cameras and never wore a mic pack. He really didn't need that heard by the world.

"You're right, I am too much for most girls, baby, but I think you can handle me. Why don't you come back here tonight and we'll test my theory?"

Holy shit. Really? How did he pass the screening test and why the hell wasn't Zoe bothered by that comment?

"I can't tonight. But I'll keep your offer in mind."

Rick whispered something in her ear. Chip found himself walking toward Zoe on instinct.

"Zoe, we still have other camps to visit tonight before it gets too late. We really should head out."

Zoe pulled back from Rick, giving him a flirtatious smile.

Why didn't she look at Chip that way? He'd been waiting for that look the entire day and nothing. But five minutes with Mr. Wilderness and she was flirting up a storm.

"I've got to go and you've got to start behaving yourself or I'll be kicked off the show and you'll get a new host." Zoe's tone was teasing.

"Well, we can't have that now can we, baby." Rick winked. "I'll be good…until you ask me not to be."

Zoe gave Rick one last look then waved at the rest of the team. "See you guys tomorrow at the new location on the map. Try to get a good night's sleep. You're going to need it."

It was the same way she'd said goodbye at the other camps, just as he'd directed her to before they left base camp earlier. It was the perfect line to lead into the next challenge when they edited the clips together for the show and promo spots.

If only he could think of the perfect line for himself that would lead to him being on the receiving end of Zoe's flirtatious nature.

• • •

Zoe nodded her head and tried her best to look interested while the fifth and final team showed her around their camp. The four men, all rowing buddies on an Ivy League team, were pretty darn proud of the job they'd done around camp. And they had every right to be proud. There progress on setting up camp was amazing.

Like the other teams, they'd made a fire and pitched their tents, but this team had also dug a latrine, organized and stored their food, and started building furniture out of logs and branches to set around the fire.

Zoe had seen all of it for filming, except the latrine. She'd taken their word for the workmanship of that. Then she quietly thanked Chip for providing base camp with a bathroom that at least sort of resembled normal. If she'd had to use an outdoor bathroom like these guys…well, she would have walked off the show long ago.

The only other team that had even remotely set up camp as well as these guys was the outdoorsy team with Rick as their leader. The rest of his team members, his brother and sister-in-law and high-school aged nephew, had done a good job on their camp.

But this rowing team really knew how to work together, and it showed. As did their muscles.

She'd thought Rick was built, but these boys looked as if they'd been sculpted to resemble the perfect male specimen thanks to hours spent on the water practicing their rowing techniques. Obviously, all that hard work building muscles had paid off. They were easily one of the leading teams now on their survival skill alone.

"Looks like you guys have everything covered here." She made a big deal of really looking around. "I guess there's not much else for me to do but give you the new map."

"What new map?" one of the men asked.

"Tomorrow you'll use this map to find your way to a new location where you'll meet up with the other teams and compete in your first team challenge."

"You mean this wasn't the first challenge?" another guy asked, motioning to the camp around him.

Zoe nodded and smiled. "It was. But this game isn't only about surviving. It's also about competing against the other teams. I'll tell you more about the challenges tomorrow with the rest of the teams present. Now, before I leave, do you have any other questions for me? I'll try my best to answer them."

One of the guys who'd been fairly quiet the whole time, standing at the back of the pack as if he didn't want to be noticed, finally stepped forward. "Do you have a question?" she asked him, getting a good look at him for the first time. There was something sort of familiar about him. Probably just because she'd seen him briefly when she'd announced the start of the show.

He shook his head, but narrowed his eyes at her. It made her feel as if she was being evaluated. Inspected. It made her uncomfortable.

"Okay then," she said, forcing herself to relax. "I'll see you all tomorrow. Try to get a good night's sleep. You're going to need it."

She smiled for the camera one last time and fought the urge to roll her eyes at having to say the same stupid line five times. Hopefully tomorrow she'd only have to say things once since she'd be meeting with all the teams at the same time.

Chip and Zoe started down the barely marked path that would take them back to base camp saying nothing for the first few minutes.

"You did great today...with all of this," Chip said.

"Thanks. I feel like I'm just copying what I saw Spencer do when he'd hosted our shows. It feels...weird."

"Well, you'd never know it from how you were today. Every time you had to film something, you seemed really confident and comfortable." He glanced toward her. "And completely charismatic. The camera loves you. The contestants love you. I can already tell that America is going to fall in love with you too."

"I hope you're right."

Maybe I won't be the villain for a change.

"I knew having you host was a good idea."

They fell into silence again, the sounds of crunching leaves and twigs under their footsteps blending with the noises of insects and animals roaming the woods. Her thoughts went back to the last camp and the guy who'd looked at her differently than the others. Why? And why did he seem so familiar?

"What was that guy's name?" she asked, no longer able to keep the questions contained to her head. If anyone could tell her who that guy was, it was Chip since he'd hand selected every contestant.

"Which one?"

"The one with the dark hair and the blue shirt at the last camp. I don't think he told me his name or if he did, I didn't hear him."

"That's Alex."

The name sent off a warning bell in her memory that sounded like an air raid siren, and yet she couldn't put her finger on why. But her pulse responded to the name anyway, spiking up at least a dozen beats faster. Maybe if she had his last name it would bring the memory forward.

She cleared her throat. "Alex who?"

"Alex Brighton."

Zoe's head spun as memories rushed to the surface. No way. This couldn't be happening. She knew he'd looked familiar, but not *that* familiar.

They'd gone to school together from kindergarten until her accident just after she turned fourteen. He hadn't changed much over the years—a lot more muscles, hopefully a bit more maturity—but the same intense eyes, sneer instead of a smile, and ability to make her uncomfortable.

Had he recognized her?

And if he had, would he share her secret with the world?

Chapter Four

Chip stood outside Zoe's tent for the second time wishing he could comfort her in some way and feeling completely inadequate. He didn't even know what was wrong with her. One minute she'd been fine and chatty and the next she'd been closed off, bordering on what appeared to be an anxiety attack.

Twice.

The first was when the sound girl had hugged her after lunch. The second when they walked back to camp and she'd asked about Alex.

As soon as he'd said the name, it was as if a switch went off inside Zoe and she closed herself off to everything and everyone. It was strange. And disconcerting. Why did hearing the name of one of his contestants have that effect on her?

He forced himself away from her tent, not wanting anyone to see him and think he was creeping outside her tent. The last thing he needed was for some rumor to start and Zoe to catch wind of it.

Once he'd zipped himself into his own tent, he grabbed a beer from his private stash and sat on his cot, head in one hand, beer in the other. It was only day one. He shouldn't have put so much pressure on himself to connect with Zoe or have some kind of breakthrough with her on the very first day. Building trust—building a relationship—took time and effort. But she was worth it.

Zoe Oliver was worth any trouble she might cause him—any frustration she might make him endure—even if she didn't know she was doing it. Like right now. Knowing she was only a few feet away in her tent, probably in her pajamas already, if she even wore pajamas, was enough to make his groin tingle with anticipation.

It wasn't just lust he felt for her, though there was a hardy dose of lust in his body right this second, but also a deeply rooted desire to make her happy, to see her smile…to simply be near her.

All this time, over the course of all his shows with her, he'd longed to be able to talk to her as a peer instead of an employer. Now he finally could, and it didn't seem to be going so well when every time he spoke to her, she closed herself off. Well, sometimes she relaxed around him. He loved those moments.

Now he had to figure out how to make them last longer, how to have more of them, and how to keep her from closing off to him again.

Easier said than done.

• • •

Zoe woke from a restless sleep. But her dreams, no, *nightmares*, hadn't even been the stuff of fiction. Nope. What she wouldn't give to have zombie nightmares like everyone else.

It had been a night of reliving her worst days. Days she'd thought were long behind her.

Apparently not. Not with Alex Brighton here.

Several times throughout the night, she'd woken in a sweat then had to take deep breaths to calm the panic smothering her. If only Alex wasn't a contestant then maybe she would have slept fine.

But he was here and he was haunting her.

If he figured out who she really was …

Zoe shook her head. No. She wouldn't let that happen. She wouldn't let him figure out her real identity. She'd spent years perfecting her acting skills when it came to hiding who she really was and she wasn't going to let everything she'd worked so hard for crumble around her because some random guy from her past showed up in the mix.

Chances were he didn't remember her anyway. So what if he'd looked at her funny yesterday. Lots of people looked at her strangely. It was almost as if people thought she was just some character on TV so when they saw her in real life, they sort of acted liked they'd seen a ghost. There was always an element of disbelief.

If, by some fluke, he brought it up and thought he remembered her, she'd tell him it was because of all the press she'd had being on three reality TV shows. A person would have to be living under a rock for the last year to have never heard of her or seen a single picture of her somewhere.

So that was the plan. Deny and distract.

She pulled herself from the bed, stretching to relieve the pinch she felt in her back. That one pesky spot along her ribs that would never quite go away. Not all of her ribs had healed perfectly after the accident that almost ended her life as a teen. She'd never be free of some scars. She hated the discomfort but she deserved to feel it as a solid reminder of the choices she'd made. The mistakes she'd made.

This cot wasn't supportive enough, but it was only a month. She could manage the annoyance as long as it didn't turn into all out pain.

Zoe grabbed her sweater and slipped into it. A serious chill in the air meant it was still probably very early. The sun hadn't had a chance to warm her tent yet. If only she could get a little electric heater. Of course that would involve having a plug in.

Damn Chip for making them film the show so remotely.

She hadn't seen inside his tent. He probably had a luxury suite compared to her accommodations. He probably had the best cot money could buy, solar powered heaters, and any other comforts she lacked. Maybe he was in there right now, toasty warm in his big bed. His naked body heated by a plush duvet.

She swallowed.

Damn Chip for being in her thoughts again.

Why couldn't she stop thinking about him? Sure, she'd found him attractive since the day she'd first met him, but that didn't mean she wanted him invading her thoughts constantly. Certainly she didn't want to be thinking about his naked body lying in a big cozy bed.

Yet here she was, thinking about it. Again.

Precisely the reason why it was great that Rick had started flirting with her. She needed someone who didn't matter to her to keep her distracted. If she let herself give in to the flirting she wanted to do with Chip, nothing good would come of it. Rick, however, was a perfect candidate to give in to a little harmless flirting.

He gave her a flirting outlet.

It was like therapy. Flirting therapy—channeling her self-destructive desire to flirt with Chip into harmless flirting with Rick so that in the end there would be no way she could end up hurt. Rick was never the kind of guy she'd fall for in real life, but he would be fine for a little production fling.

And she'd keep Chip at a distance, just where he needed to stay.

Perfect.

Zoe rose from her cot and opened her makeup bag. Good thing she brought makeup remover wipes with her everywhere she went. They should get her through most of the month without having to go to bed with makeup left on her face like she had by mistake last night. Being on national television—and as a host this time—gave her no leeway for blemishes. Not that she couldn't hide them pretty well with her makeup arsenal, but still. She already had enough to hide. She didn't need to worry about blemishes too.

As Zoe stared into her tiny compact mirror and started to apply a layer of foundation, she finally relaxed a little. She knew what she had to do today. And once she had her makeup applied, she'd be ready to take it on.

•••

"Hi, Chip," she said, breezing past him on her way to the kitchen tent to grab a bagel for a quick breakfast before leaving. She only had a few minutes until they were supposed to start their trek to the location of the first challenge. A bagel and an orange juice was all she had time for.

She definitely didn't have time to stop and chat with Chip.

Although telling her body that was a different story. As her brain registered the scent of his cologne drifting on the wind while she walked past him, her footsteps slowed. She closed her eyes and breathed deep. The scent of him sent a wave of liquid fire into her belly. Her knees went weak.

"You okay?" Chip asked, falling in beside her and holding her elbow to steady her. "You look a little wobbly all of a sudden."

"I'm fine," she lied.

No, she wasn't fine. The exact opposite of fine, actually, since her body currently ignored her earlier wishes to distance herself from Chip and forget about her attraction to him. The heat already smoldering in her belly turned to lava when he slid his hand down her arm and took her hand in his.

"No offense," he said quietly, "but you don't look fine."

"Gee, thanks." She feigned annoyance. She knew exactly what he meant and she wasn't offended in the least, but maybe if she pretended to be annoyed, she'd stop being aroused. If only he'd let go of her hand and take about five steps away from her…and stand downwind so she wouldn't be able to smell him anymore, then she'd be able to clear her head and steady her knees. "I'm just hungry. I haven't eaten yet and since there's no room service in this dump you've trapped me in, I have to come and scrounge for my own food on an empty stomach. Next time you'll probably make me kill something and cook it for dinner."

Chip laughed so hard she thought she saw tears in his eyes.

"It's not funny," she said, trying to pull her hand from his, but he squeezed it tighter, not letting her go.

"It is funny." He cleared his throat a couple of times until he stopped laughing enough to speak again. "You're funny. I never understood why the other contestants on these shows didn't know you were joking when you said stuff like that to them. Everyone always got so bent out of shape about it, but they shouldn't. You're hilarious."

She set her jaw. He saw through her sarcasm? How? She laid it on thicker than cream cheese on a New York bagel. Why the hell was he so damn perfect? Couldn't he not get her humor and think she was a total bitch like everyone else did so her life here would be easier?

Now she'd have an even harder time ignoring him. And her growing attraction to him. It wasn't everyday someone actually "got" her. Of course Chip had to be that someone.

Damn it.

"Well this hilarity is going to come to a screeching stop if I don't get food before the show."

"We can't have that, now can we?" His hand still gripped hers, his thumb tracing a line across her wrist, sending tingles down her fingers. "Every show needs a happy host, not a hungry one."

"Then I suggest you drop my hand once I get my breakfast or you're at risk of losing a couple of fingers."

"I'll keep that in mind."

But her threat must have fallen on deaf ears since he held her hand the entire way. When he finally let go so she could get a coffee, her head started to clear. Thank God she had to spend the better part of the day playing host. She would have her mind on other things, like the game and Rick.

Chip would be forced to stay on the sidelines. It would be even better if Chip would stay at camp, but she knew he'd never do that. He oversaw every aspect of the show, including filming.

Hopefully his overseeing didn't include more handholding or she could end up being completely incoherent on camera.

Chapter Five

Zoe waited while the teams filtered into the clearing from various trails. The cameras were already rolling to catch which team would find the clearing first and which one would be last. Another way to determine the strongest of the pack.

The first team to arrive was no surprise. A big grin spread across Rick's face when he saw her. But it was the cocked eyebrow and the suggestive expression that really caught her off guard. This was a guy who knew what he wanted and went after it. And apparently he wanted her.

Of course, there was the small matter of staff and contestants getting together being against the rules. She wasn't very good at following the rules, but she'd try.

A coughing fit from off to the side of the clearing pulled her attention away from Rick and his obvious invitation. Chip pounded on his chest when she looked at him then took a big gulp out of his water bottle, an expression of guilt on his face.

Sure, coughing. That's believable.

Chip might be able to see through her sarcasm, but the transparency between them went both ways. He wasn't fooling her. She'd noticed how Chip's expression had changed last night when Rick flirted with her at his camp. She'd have to be blind not to see through his little charade now.

If Chip didn't want to watch her interact with Rick, then it was just too bad for him. She had to host and Rick had to be a contestant. They'd be working together until Rick's team either got booted off the show or until it ended. Either way, Chip was going to have to get used to seeing them flirt because she didn't plan on stopping any time soon. Not when it was such a fun distraction from everything else, including Chip.

She turned away from Chip as the last team wandered into the clearing. "Welcome to your first team challenge here on *Wild Expedition*," she said without wasting any time. The guy with the cue cards stood far enough behind the teams that he couldn't be seen on camera, but thankfully, the writing on the cards was huge so she could still read it. "And good news, you all passed the first part of the challenge just by finding your way here."

The teams cheered, obviously ready to do something more exciting than survive around camp for a change. These challenges were their only source of entertainment.

"Today is your first challenge and you need to do your best because the team who comes in first will win the best prize." Zoe motioned to a row of boxes off to one side, ranging in size. "The team who comes in first will get the biggest box. The team who comes in second will get the second biggest box. And so on and so forth until all the teams have been rewarded."

The teams nodded and cheered again. Excitement about what was actually in the boxes built. Zoe hadn't a clue what was in them. She'd have to wait and see like everyone else. Even as the host, she felt a little shiver of excitement shoot up her spine. There was just something so fun about being on these reality shows. It almost made her regret not being a contestant this time.

Almost, but not quite.

"Now," she said, reading the next cue card, "on to the challenge itself. Each team will have to prove they have what it takes to live in the wild."

Not my idea of fun.

"Each team will have to hunt, forage, and scrounge whatever food sources they can find. You'll each have thirty minutes to track down food, then you'll have another thirty minutes to prepare a meal using the fire pits and cooking utensils you see here."

She looked around, noticing for the first time the fire pits and very basic cooking gear stacked beside each. It had been easy to miss the cooking areas at first since each was tucked into its own alcove of rocks. The surrounding trees and bushes made natural barriers between the different areas, which would provide the teams with privacy while cooking.

Zoe glanced to Chip who stood there smiling, clearly enjoying this challenge he'd designed. Chip really had done her a favor not putting her on the show. She would have failed horribly at this challenge. And at surviving around their primitive camps too.

She looked back to the contestants still waiting for the last of their directions before they were given the green light to get started. She forced herself not to stare at the camera directly in front of her. She'd always been fine as a contestant not looking directly at the camera. She knew not to do that. But as a host, sometimes she had to talk to the camera and other times she had to talk to the contestants. Getting the right balance of both was trickier than Spencer Daley, the host for her shows, had ever made it look.

"After you prepare your meal, you'll dish it out onto five plates then set your plates over here to be judged. Everyone will taste the other team's offerings, but no one will know which team cooked which dish. Each team will then pick their top two favorites as well as their choice for least favorite meal."

She paused for a moment while the production person flipped cue cards. "Are you curious to know what's inside the boxes?"

The teams cheered louder than before.

She smiled. "Then let's get this challenged started so we can pick a winner. Teams, your thirty minutes of prep time starts now."

The teams each took off in a different direction, almost as if they'd been told which way to go. Rick's team sprinted off ahead of him, but he walked past Zoe slowly, smirking at her as his eyes traced a path from her hair to her toes. She couldn't stop herself from smiling in response to his evaluation.

"I'm gonna cook you up something real nice, baby. It'll be like our first date, out here, in the wild…It might even make you want to get a little wild yourself." He walked off with a wink and she burst out laughing, climbing down from the tree stump she'd been perched on while hosting. He was too much.

"Do girls actually fall for lines like that where you come from?" she asked him.

He turned back toward her. "Their panties certainly do."

Zoe felt her cheeks burn at his words as he walked off into the woods after the rest of his team. Her panties weren't dropping for him because of one meal…or for any other reason actually. Maybe Rick was more of a player than she'd realized when she'd started her "harmless" flirting with him.

She glanced over to where Chip stood, well within hearing range of that little conversation. He looked as if he was studying a production clipboard, but if the expression on his face was any indication, he was rather pissed at a production note. More likely, he'd just heard Rick's comments too. And if she wasn't mistaken, he seemed more turned off by them than even she was.

"Everything okay, Chip?" she asked, hoping she sounded casual.

"Fine. Why?" he asked, not meeting her gaze.

"You seem a little annoyed at your clipboard."

"I'm fine, Zoe. Nothing to worry about, just a little hiccup in the production schedule to work out on the fly." He scribbled a few notes in the margin then handed it back to one of the assistants. He pushed his hands into his pockets as if they were hanging out, waiting for a movie to start instead of standing in the middle of the woods waiting for teams to return.

Maybe he hadn't overheard Rick's comments. Or maybe he had and he didn't care if she flirted with a contestant. Hell, he would probably encourage it. He'd probably say it was good for ratings for Zoe to hook up with Rick, what with the drama and spectacle it would certainly cause.

"While we have a second, I should point out that I do think it would be best not to fraternize with the contestants so much," he said, turning to face her straight on and finally meeting her gaze. "You do remember how that all worked out for Cassidy on *The One,* don't you?"

Was that a threat?

"Of course I do. I was there for your big scandalous reveal at the finale."

"Then you should already know that a crewmember getting involved with a cast member usually isn't the best idea."

"Well that's good, because I have no intentions of shacking up with Rick. It's a little harmless flirting."

Chip crossed his arms. If she wasn't mistaken, he almost looked a little jealous. Maybe there was more behind his warning than he let on.

"So talking about your panties is nothing to you then? Just casual, everyday flirting to you? Good to know."

"I wasn't talking about my panties, he was."

"Well that makes all the difference, now doesn't it?"

Zoe felt her pulse race as she took a step closer to Chip. "Listen, I don't know what's gotten *your* panties all in a bunch, but mine are fine—" Her voice strained as the heat passing between them spiked at the mention of her panties.

Her chest heaved as she struggled to talk around her hitched breathing.

Focus!

She swallowed, her throat feeling dry. "And I don't plan on dropping them for *anyone* any time soon. Got it?" she finished, her voice stronger than it had been but still rather pathetic and unconvincing.

He smiled, letting his gaze flicker down to the area in danger of "droppage" for a moment before meeting her eyes again. "Now that sounds like a challenge if I ever heard one," he said quietly.

She suddenly felt the panties in question moisten under his gaze.

What was that thing she'd just said about not dropping them for anyone? How was she supposed to follow her rules when he looked at her like that—when her body reacted to him this way?

Before she could wonder too long, he stepped away from her and started walking toward the other crewmembers milling about waiting for the action to start again. He stopped a few feet away, giving her a sideways glance over his shoulder.

"Oh, and nothing's in a bunch for me, sweetheart. I prefer commando."

Oh, so good then. No bunching panties for anyone.

Well, she couldn't, in good conscience, let him have the last word, now could she?

"And so we're clear about the whole Rick business," she started, feeling more confident now that Chip stood two feet away instead of two inches. "I'll talk to whomever I want, whenever I want and no one, not even you, is going to stop me. You of all people should understand me well enough to know I don't respond to bullying very well."

He stopped and looked back at her, the teasing out of his expression. "I wasn't trying to bully you. I guess I was trying to look out for you, but that was silly of me. I know you can take care of yourself."

Damn right she could, and it was nice someone finally recognized that.

She didn't say anything else as he walked away. What could she say? She didn't know what to think about Chip. Was he being nice and looking out for her? Or was he being jealous and trying to tell her how to live her life?

Zoe grabbed a bottle of water from one of the coolers and sat on a tree stump. Pulling her compact out of her pocket, she quickly checked her makeup and reapplied a little powder where she'd started to look shiny even though she usually didn't like to mess with her makeup during the day. Being in the harsh, outdoor elements made her question her makeup's ability to function under pressure. Luckily, her foundation and the humidity were still getting along well. If that changed, she'd have to start bringing her makeup bag to these things for hourly touch ups. Hopefully it wouldn't get any worse than that since she'd already turned away the makeup person supplied by the show saying they weren't necessary, and she didn't like the idea of humidity forcing her to take back her words. Makeup was necessary, but they could keep the person who applied it. Zoe was the only one who touched her face or her makeup and she planned on keeping it that way.

Zoe hadn't let anyone touch her since the car accident. During her long recovery, she'd had more doctors and nurses poke and prod her than she could count. Sure, their expertise had fixed her worse scars and damaged areas, but they'd also made her extremely aware of the location of every remaining bump and crease of her skin. She couldn't let some gossipy makeup person see her without makeup, touch her rough skin or learn the secrets of her extensive surgeries she'd kept hidden from everyone for so long.

Clicking the compact closed, she looked up to find the first set of contestants coming back with supplies. Most seemed to have done well with arms full of berries, leaves, and roots. Hopefully they knew which ones were edible because Zoe certainly didn't.

Rick, on the other hand, came back to the clearing with something that looked suspiciously like a fish.

Good luck to whoever has to actually eat this stuff.

She couldn't imagine being on this show as a contestant. First of all, foraging for her own food consisted of grabbing an apple from the fridge and that was enough for her. Secondly, if she had to catch a fish, she could, but that didn't mean she actually wanted to eat it. Her father had taken her fishing almost every Sunday afternoon growing up, but he knew better than to make her eat it after they caught it.

Zoe got up and wandered over to the first cooking area. The team made up of two dating couples was just getting started with their items. The men on the team were attempting to get the fire lit while the women on the teams organized the items they'd found into different pots.

"How's it going over here?" Zoe asked. "Have you decided on what you're making for your meal?"

One of the women, Tammy if Zoe remembered correctly, shrugged. "Not really. We're going to taste stuff and then see what we think goes together well."

"Sounds like a good plan. I'll let you get to work. You have twenty-five minutes left to cook."

She walked to the next station. They didn't look much further along in their process.

"How is your meal coming along? Did you find enough things to cook with?"

One of the girls from the all-girls team answered. "We found some really great edible wild flowers that will make a tasty salad along with a warm berry dressing."

Zoe was impressed. That almost sounded like a normal dish you'd find on the menu of an up-scale restaurant. "Wow. I can't wait to see how it turns out. Since you have everything under control, I'll leave you to it."

Zoe made her way to the rowing team's station next. Jared, the guy who clearly came off as the team leader, told her all about what they'd found to cook. They too had managed to catch a fish like Rick's team and were in the process of filleting it. Just another reason why she preferred not to eat the fish she caught. Fish guts were not appetizing.

While Jared spoke too animatedly about the process, Zoe felt a shiver of uneasiness run up her spine. Alex stared at her from his spot near the fire, eyeing her. The experience made her extremely uncomfortable.

The look he gave her reminded her all too clearly of the way he used to look at her back then…like she was a blemish on the earth, scum not worthy of his presence. *You deserve what you got,* his words echoed in her mind, stirring up guilt she'd worked so hard to squash.

As soon as Jared was finished, she wished them well and moved away from their cooking area.

The sooner she put a little distance between herself and Alex, the better. By the confusion and concentration on his face, he hadn't figured out why she was familiar yet, but he could at any time. It was either that, or he eyed her that way because he was a sociopath plotting a way to kill her.

She wasn't sure which was worse: secret revealed or sociopath stalking.

Zoe almost sighed with relief as she walked away from Alex and wandered into Rick's cooking area. He greeted her with a big smile and fish guts smeared across his chest—his bare chest.

Apparently Rick didn't believe in cooking with clothes on.

Beyond the fish guts and blood, a ripple of perfect abs and pectorals flexed as he waved. *Day-um.* Rick was built for this kind of thing.

"I've got some meat that might satisfy that hunger in your eyes," Rick said with a wink and wave of his hand down the length of his torso as if he was showing off a fine piece of art instead of his body.

"Rick, that's enough. Give the poor girl a chance to get her thoughts together before you start hitting on her again," Pam said, shoving him.

"Watch your woman, Roger, or I'll have to give her a big old hug before I go wash off the guts."

Pam shrieked and ran away when Rick made a move for her. He laughed and got back to work, finishing up with the fish quickly then handing the fillets over to his nephew Todd.

"So what can we do for you, Miss Oliver?" he said, moving closer to her. Despite the smell of fish guts, Rick was strangely appealing. Or maybe not so strangely when she took in the sight of his abs up close.

She cleared her throat, hoping it would clear her mind too. "Just doing my hosting thing and coming by to see how you are all doing with your meal. What have you decided to cook today?"

"Fish," Rick said simply.

"I see that," she replied just as simply with a smirk.

"And it's going to be so delicious, you'll be begging me for a dinner date around the campfire."

Zoe looked to Pam and motioned with her head toward Rick. "Pretty confident, isn't he?"

Pam laughed, shaking her head. "You don't even know the half of it. Wait until the show airs and you get to hear all the wonderful stuff he's been saying about you around camp. If you don't date him by the end of the show, I'll want to kill him."

Really? She might have to go bribe the cameramen to find out exactly what he'd been saying. All good hopefully. But why was he trying so hard? It wasn't like he was an unattractive man who would be starved for female attention. Maybe he was just bored at camp.

"What's his deal with me?" Zoe asked quietly when the cameraman was filming the boys frying the fish instead of her conversation.

"I don't know, but I keep telling him to stop coming on so strong. Sorry about him. My brother-in-law might be acting like an idiot right now, but I assure you he's normally very nice and respectful. I wish I knew what had gotten into him."

"It's fine. I know how to handle guys like Rick. And I know he's your family and all so you don't see him this way, but he's not so bad to look at or flirt with either."

"I don't know how you can see anything past the fish guts."

As if he knew they were talking about his appearance, Rick got up from the fire and grabbed the bottle of water from Zoe's hand without asking.

"Hey," she started to protest, but her voice got stuck in her throat when he opened the bottle and upended it over his head and shoulders.

Rivers of water cascaded over him, washing away the fishiness from his body and leaving behind only a canvass of sleek, glistening muscles waiting to be wiped dry. Zoe suddenly wanted to take the shirt off her back and dry him. Of course, that would leave her in a bra, but somehow, she didn't think he would mind too much.

"Better," he said, handing her back the empty bottle. "You wouldn't happen to have a towel handy would you, baby?"

"Here you go," Chip said, throwing a towel in Rick's direction. It landed across his face. Chip didn't seem to care as he grabbed Zoe's arm and steered her away from the team's cooking area. "If you'll excuse Zoe, she has other teams to film before we run out of cooking time."

Zoe pulled her arm back out from Chip's grip and stopped behind a particularly thick cluster of trees.

"What are you doing?" she demanded.

"I was serious. There's only ten minutes left and you still haven't checked in with the last team."

"I have plenty of time. It takes two seconds to ask 'whatcha cooking in there?' so I want to know what the hell that was really about. You threw a towel in Rick's face for no reason."

Chip tried unsuccessfully to hide a smirk. "What? He asked for a towel. It's not my problem he can't catch. Besides, I needed to get you to do your job and stop hanging out with the contestants like they're your best friends. That's all."

"Really? It didn't have anything to do with the fact that Rick was flirting with me again? While shirtless."

The edge of Chip's jaw bulged then relaxed as he plastered the fakest smile she'd ever seen on his face. "Nope. I hadn't even noticed. Was he shirtless? Huh. Interesting that you feel the need to bring it up."

She eyed him for a moment and wondered if it was worth her time and effort to call him out on that blatant pile of bullshit he'd just spewed. He glanced at his watch, again motioning for her to head over to the last team. She glanced over too. They were getting out their plates and organizing them on the ground near their fire. If she didn't hurry, she really would miss her opportunity to speak with them before the cooking segment was done.

Confronting Chip on why he was acting so strange would have to wait until they were done filming and on their way back to camp.

"Fine. Let's get this over with."

Chapter Six

Chip held in a laugh as Zoe obviously tried not to gag on the food the teams had put in front of her. Her attempts at tasting the first few plates had been much more convincing. Now he was worried that she might actually get sick on camera. Good thing he could edit that out if needed.

He couldn't blame her really. Only so much could be done with leaves and berries found in the wild. Although the fish Rick's team cooked smelled damned good and the other teams seemed to enjoy the dish as well.

Too bad. He would have loved something to take Rick's opinion of himself down a peg or two. Hopefully the first elimination challenge would be too much for his team. That was the one that really mattered, not this silly food challenge.

"That was...interesting," Zoe said, taking a big drink of water from her third bottle.

He didn't want to be the one to tell her that she should cut back on the liquids a little. She probably wasn't going to like it much when she realized how far away from base camp she was. She'd like it even less when her only option for a bathroom was "this bush or that one" along the trail on the way back.

"Okay," Zoe said standing from her makeshift table of a fallen log. "Now that we've had a chance to taste all of the dishes, it's time to vote for your top two favorites and your least favorite. Then we'll tally the votes and see who wins and who loses. Everyone write your votes down on the paper provided and then return them to me."

The teams sectioned off into their cooking areas to decide on their votes in private. While they did, Chip joined Zoe. "You did great tasting all that food. I was a little worried we might have to censor some sickness in editing but you really powered through it."

"Yeah, thanks for the wonderful competition today." She rubbed her hand across her stomach as if it was sore from the food. It probably was. "Remind me to cook you dinner sometime as payback."

Dinner with Zoe? Hell, yes. Sign me up.

"I'll find a way to suffer through your cooking, I'm sure. How about tonight?"

"I was only kidding. I can't cook, even to torture you."

I wasn't kidding.

Chip kicked at the dirt with the toe of his shoe, suddenly feeling nervous. "Well, then I'll cook for you and you can tell me if my food is torture or not."

He held her gaze. She didn't accept his offer but she also didn't turn him down. He would take that as a yes, since the twinkle in her eye gave away her interest in him even if her lack of verbal skills didn't.

"So, you ready to announce the winners? Any questions about how it works before we film this last segment and head back to base camp?" Best to change the subject before she found her voice and told him no to dinner.

"Actually, I have no idea how I'm going to do this."

"Why? It shouldn't be much different than what you have been doing."

"True, but normally I don't have to remember all of their names. Now I have to call out twenty people by name and I only know about four of them. I'm screwed."

Zoe looked genuinely concerned and nervous. More so than he'd ever seen her before. His thoughts of getting Zoe to have dinner with him disappeared and the only thing he cared about was how to make her feel better in this situation. He didn't like seeing her uncomfortable or worried. It bothered him. Deeply.

"Wait right here one minute," he said, walking away. Finding the sound equipment backpack, he searched through it until he located the things he needed. Then he returned back to Zoe.

"Did you tally the votes?" he asked, setting his new things down on the ground beside her so he could unravel the cords and sort out the pieces he needed.

"Yep. I have the order of the winners, but I still can't remember all their names. What am I going to do? Call over Team Dating Couples instead of calling for them by name? I'm going to look like a total idiot on national television." She sighed.

She looked down at him and he was struck by the expression of fear on her face. Looking less than her best really was an issue for her, even if her physical appearance was flawless. Well, he wasn't going to let that happen today.

Chip put his hand on her knee, rubbing it. Her shoulders drooped slightly and the creases across her brow lessened.

"I promise you will never look like anything less than the amazing woman I know you are while you're on my show." He smiled and she returned it.

She placed her hand on top of his and squeezed. A rush of affection filled him. He wasn't lusting for her, though of course he always felt attracted to her physically. It was impossible not to. But in that moment he simply wanted to make sure she felt safe with him and with the show. He never wanted her to question his motives. More than anything, he wanted her to trust him since it seemed like trust wasn't something she gave over easily.

He grabbed an earpiece attached to a neutral colored cord and reached up, gently fitting it to her ear. He tucked the cord under her hair at the back of her neck and handed her the attached battery pack and belt for her to secure around her waist.

"What's all this for? I'm already mic'd for sound."

"True, but in a second I'm going to be mic'd too—but my audio will only be for you." He attached his own battery pack and mic then switched it on. "Can you hear me?"

"Of course I can, I'm sitting a foot away."

He laughed. "No, smartass. In your ear. Can you hear me through your earpiece?"

She shook her head, looking panicked again. "It's not working."

"May I check it?" he asked, motioning to the battery pack already fastened around her waist.

She nodded.

He slipped his hands under the black box at the small of her back, his hand brushing against her skin. Skin so soft and warm, he would have loved nothing more than to slide his hands up her back, massaging away her tension. Instead he focused on the task and immediately found the problem. She'd forgotten to turn it on.

"That should do it," he said, forcing his hands out from under her shirt.

"Oh," she said, excitement filling her voice. "I heard you that time."

"Great. Now all you have to do is read your cue cards as usual. When it gets to the part where you call the teams to announce the winners of the challenge, I'll say the names into your earpiece and you can repeat them. You won't have to worry about forgetting any of their names."

"You're the best." Zoe reached out, squeezing his hand tightly before letting him go again. "Thank you."

The happiness and confidence in her attitude was all the thanks he needed. Of course, feeling her hand on his wasn't too bad either.

"My pleasure." Chip quickly jotted down the winners then went to his post alongside the action.

The teams took their places in front of Zoe as they waited to find out their ranking in the challenge. He took the opportunity to speak to Zoe one last time before they started filming again.

"You're going to do fine. Just relax. I've got you." He spoke quietly into his mic, not wanting to startle her since she still wouldn't be used to having his voice in her ear.

She kept her gaze straight ahead as if waiting for the signal for filming to start. He watched her shoulders rise and fall with each of her deep breaths. She was so professional and focused. It was amazing this wasn't her full-time gig. Her confidence on camera was awe-inspiring. He might be the brains behind the scenes, but he'd never have the guts to be on camera like she was. She constantly surprised and amazed him.

"One last thing before I give the signal," he whispered into the mic. "You are absolutely breathtaking."

She glanced toward him, a mix of emotion playing on her face, but when her gaze met his, she smiled.

He gave the signal for the cameras to start filming.

• • •

Zoe tucked her earpiece back into the sound equipment bag and zipped it closed. Now she had to wait for Chip to finish giving his notes to camera crews as they changed shifts, then they could head back to base camp.

She watched as he gave his recommendation for the shots he wanted the cameramen to focus on getting while at camp as well as what they already had enough footage of for right now. She liked seeing him do his job. He was very good at what he did. He had a real knack for getting people to do exactly what he wanted and to the best of their abilities. Sure, he could be a little harsh with people once in a while, but it was all because he wanted to make the best show he possibly could.

And she also knew from having seen him work with other film crews before, that while he may be harsh and demanding during filming, he rewarded people for their hard work afterwards. With the success of the last show, she'd heard the crew had all been given bonuses for working so hard.

Knowing he could be firm when he needed to be but also kind enough to reward others for their hard work was really something she admired about him. Often she felt as if she didn't have the people skills to do what he did, which was why she'd been so surprised he'd put her in this hosting role. She wasn't exactly what someone would call a "people person." But she was trying to be for him. For the show.

Maybe even a little bit for herself, if she was being completely honest.

It might be a nice change of pace to be the heroine for once instead of always the villain. Have viewers fall in love with her, not send her hate mail.

She watched as the teams went through their boxes of winnings. The team with the least amount of votes—the dating couples—had received the smallest reward box. In it they'd found rice and beans. Not very tasty, but it would help them have enough energy to keep competing and at least they wouldn't starve.

The other teams who'd placed in the middle—the all-girls team, the rowing team, and the team of doctors—had all received progressively larger boxes, filled with a bigger selection of foods. Rick's team was the winner and their box was the largest. When they opened it, she'd been surprised to see how much variety was inside. Not only had there been rice and beans, but also a few canned goods, spices, coffee supplies, and even a little fresh fruit. That team would be set for a while if they used the supplies carefully.

Of course, they also had the heaviest box of goods to carry back to their camp. Their reward wasn't without its punishment. Good thing they had Rick and Roger on the team to carry the majority of the bulky, heavy items. Some of the other teams might have struggled more if they'd won that reward box.

"Ready to go?" Chip asked, coming up beside her.

They started off down the path that would take them away from the team camps and back to base camp, walking silently for the first half of the trip.

When she couldn't take the silence anymore, she said the thing that had been on her mind since the challenge. "Thanks for the earpiece earlier. You really saved me back there. And for everything you said too. It—um, meant a lot to me."

He nodded without saying anything, making her wonder if he'd meant it when he'd said she was breathtaking or if he'd only said it to make her feel better in the moment. An ache in her chest proved how much she hoped he'd meant it, which was weird since she was trying so hard to ignore the spark of feelings she felt toward him.

"I'm sure you said it to be nice so I'd feel more comfortable, but I appreciate it nonetheless. I mean—" She coughed, her throat feeling parched even after all the water she'd drank today. "Not that I wouldn't have been able to do my job without you saying that stuff to me…well, the names I actually did need. It was that… other thing…that I didn't need. But not that I didn't like it."

Shit.

Why couldn't she say what she'd planned in her head beforehand, instead of rambling on like a complete moron?

"I—" she started again.

"It's okay, Zoe," he said, stopping and placing his hands on her shoulders. "I know what you're trying to say and you're welcome. I'm happy I was able to help you with the names. Just say the word and we can do that again if you need."

He paused, staring into her eyes while his hand slid up her skin to rest at the base of her neck. He leaned toward her and her breath hitched in her throat, making her struggle to fight the restriction.

"And I meant what I said about you being breathtaking," he said, pulling her toward his lips. Soft-looking, supple lips she couldn't help but want to feel touching hers. "Not just today, but always. Every time I see you, you steal my breath."

His lips pressed to hers. She let her eyelids flutter closed, savoring his kiss. Her mouth parted slightly, inviting him in. He accepted, tasting her, teasing her with his tongue. Just as she felt herself melting into him, he stepped back, pulling away from her. He took her hand and started back toward base camp again.

She shook her head, trying to dislodge the cotton suddenly filling the empty space between her ears. She could think of nothing but his lips on hers, his hand in hers. It took everything she had to walk in a straight line without falling over from dizziness. If he thought she took his breath, what had he done to her? It was as if she'd been deprived of oxygen for days, not seconds. She was thankful he had a good grip on her hand so he could keep her from falling if she stumbled. This lightheadedness he'd caused was unnerving. And sort of wonderful.

Had any man ever given her such a reaction before?

No. Never.

No man, no matter how hot or sexy or amazing he'd been, had ever given her this kind of feeling of euphoria before. And all this from a simple thirty-second kiss? Holy crap. What would happen if he kissed her longer, deeper, harder? Her head spun again thinking about it.

Chip stopped walking and a spark of hope for another kiss shot through her. Then she realized he'd stopped because they were outside her tent. How she'd gotten back, she hadn't a clue and yet here she was. And now she had to say goodbye to Chip, which was about the last thing she wanted to do.

"I'll pick you up here at eight, okay?" Chip said, letting go of her hand.

She attempted to force her thoughts into some kind of order. What was he talking about? Why was he coming back to pick her up?

"Are we doing another competition tonight?"

"No."

"Are we going somewhere?"

"Yes. Dinner. My place. You agreed to let me cook you dinner sometime. Sometime is tonight."

Oh. Dinner. His place. His lips kissing a trail down my neck to my collarbone. His hands...

"Okay. I'll be ready."

His gaze penetrated hers. "I will be too."

Ready for dinner or something more? She'd completely forgotten why she'd convinced herself that staying away from him was a good idea. Distance made it hard for his lips to find hers.

Distance was bad.

Close was good. Close could mean his lips on hers again. And even though she knew it went against everything she told herself she wanted, she couldn't help but hope that dinner alone with Chip would lead to another kiss.

Chapter Seven

Zoe paced in her tent and checked the time again. Five minutes until eight. Five minutes until she had to make a decision about whether or not it was a good idea to have dinner with Chip, the man she was supposedly trying to distance herself from.

The man who had removed all the oxygen from the atmosphere during their thirty-second kiss.

The man she could see herself giving up oxygen for all together if he'd just kiss her like that again.

Damn.

Canceling and staying in her tent, alone, for the evening was really the smart thing to do. But being in Chip's tent, with him, was way more tempting. After all, it was only dinner, right? It wasn't as if he'd asked her over for a booty call. Just dinner. A little harmless dinner. And perhaps a teeny tiny bit of flirting. Possibly a tiny kiss to end the night.

No. No more kisses if she wanted to keep Chip at arm's length. But did she really want to?

On one hand, Chip was amazing and being with him felt like breathing clean air after living in smog her whole life. She couldn't think clearly when he'd kissed her earlier. On the other hand, keeping people at a distance was what she did. It was how she survived. If she let down her guard with Chip, he could find out about her scars...about what really happened the day of the accident. If he found out the truth—if he saw the real her, hidden under all the makeup and pretty clothes and perfect hair—he'd never think she was breathtaking again.

Her answer changed every few minutes. She couldn't seem to make the two conflicting sides of herself come to any kind of mutual agreement about what to do with this whole Chip situation. If she didn't make a definitive decision soon, she feared she'd walk around in a state of confusion for the rest of the show.

She was only going for dinner since he'd insisted on cooking for her. It would be rude not to go. And didn't she still need to eat dinner tonight? Her growling stomach said she did.

The bubbling pit of lava deep in her belly said she needed something else a lot more desperately than food.

She'd just drink a bunch of water and force that lava to cool off. It was dinner. She could totally have dinner with him while maintaining her distance. Besides, out here in the wilderness, it wasn't like she had anything else to do.

She could call someone except her cell phone had long since lost its battery, not that they'd have let her contact the outside world anyway. Chip's productions always came with an outside world blackout period. Possibly her least favorite part of production. She needed to be connected to the grid.

Not that she really had anyone in her life to call anyway. Putting distance between herself and everyone else had made sure of that.

So what better way to pass an evening than dinner with Chip?

Of course, she could always go to the kitchen tent and socialize with the other production people. But that would involve her being cheery and trying to get people to like her. Did she really feel like putting in that kind of effort tonight? With Chip at least she felt like she could be herself. He'd seen her in some less-than-her-best situations already and it didn't seem to tarnish his opinion of her, whatever that was.

With Chip, she didn't feel like she had to put on some kind of show or be anything other than what she felt like being at that particular moment. There was something very freeing about that.

And dangerous. Feelings like that could get her in trouble with the whole "keeping her distance plan." She would have to be very careful in this situation tonight.

"Knock, knock."

Chip's voice filtered into her tent, sounding so close, he may as well have been standing inside. She took a deep breath and unzipped the tent. The scent of his cologne hit her even before she saw him, making her lightheaded all over again.

Damn it, she had to stop that from happening every time she was around him or she'd be totally screwed. Well, even more screwed than she already was.

"Hi," she said, holding the tent flap open. Chip stood on the other side. She was glad she'd changed clothes after the challenge since he'd apparently done the same. He cleaned up really nice. Every hair was in place and his shirt was crisp as if he hadn't gotten ready in a tent. In short, he looked damned good.

Chip's gaze slid down her body from her tight fitted shirt to her skinny jeans and finally to the Jimmy Choos she'd strapped to her feet. They weren't practical for wearing around camp, but she wanted to look good and feel good and Jimmy fit that bill perfectly.

"You look stunning as always." Chip held out his hand to her. She accepted it.

Slipping through the opening, she zipped it closed behind her. "And you are a sweet talker as always."

He shrugged with indifference. "I just call it like I see it, that's all. And I certainly like what I see in front of me tonight."

Her cheeks grew hot with his words. She was used to people saying nice things about her, but for some reason, his words seemed more genuine than the ones she usually got. Sure, he was still feeding her a line, but it felt like there was truth behind it instead of some empty bid to get her into bed.

"Thank you," she almost whispered while she waited for him to open his tent. She was strangely excited to have been invited inside. It felt as if she were entering his sanctuary. Like he was letting her into his life more than he allowed others. Maybe he was.

Stepping through, she was surprised to find the space so different from her tent. He had a similar cot to hers, with similar bedding and canvas bedside table, but that's where it ended. The other things in the room were completely different. He had a makeshift wardrobe with a rod, which explained his crisp shirts. A much better solution than her way of laying clothes out and turning them over each day to keep the wrinkles from setting too deep.

In the center of the room, a picnic area was set up complete with a glowing lantern in the middle. A couple of other lanterns were positioned near the tent walls giving the whole area a warm amber glow, almost as if they stood in front of a roaring fireplace instead of inside a tent.

"This is so amazing. How did you do all of this so quickly?"

"It wasn't difficult and I was highly motivated to make tonight special."

"Oh, why's that?"

He led her to the blanket and motioned for her to sit. "I wanted you to have a good meal after all that crap you were forced to consume today on behalf of my competition."

"Feeling a little guilty about your challenge choice?"

"It sounded like a good idea in my head, until I saw what they scrounged up and made you eat." He laughed and poured her a glass of wine before pouring himself one. "I was feeling pretty sympathetic when your gag reflex kicked in."

She laughed too. "Not my best on-camera moment."

"To better moments to come," he said, raising his glass in a toast.

"To better moments," she echoed, clinking glasses with him and taking a sip. Just what she needed, a little liquid relaxer after a long day filming in the woods. The only thing missing was air conditioning. Although even cool air probably wouldn't cool the heat she felt radiating from Chip.

"How did you manage to find wine out here?" she asked, enjoying the crisp, lightly fruity flavor.

"I may have brought my own secret stash of supplies in case of emergency."

She giggled. The wine must be going to her head already because of her empty stomach. "I've never heard of wine emergencies before."

"Hey, it could happen. Never say never." He peered at her over his glass of wine, a twinkle in his eyes she hadn't seen before. Mischievous somehow. Or maybe the better description was devious.

"What are you up to?" she asked. "You look like you're plotting something."

He feigned offense. "I am not plotting. More wine?"

She laughed. "Oh, I get it now. Load me up on alcohol then take advantage of me. I'm on to you, Mr. Cormack, and your games are not going to work on me."

"I don't know what you're talking about. I just thought we could share this nice big bottle of wine and then maybe you'd feel a little more relaxed."

What will happen if I get tipsy?

"That's all? No ulterior motive?"

He nodded and took another sip of his wine. "Why don't we eat? It will help soak up all the wine I'm forcing you to consume. Maybe then you won't be so suspicious of me."

He removed the lid covering a platter in the middle of the blanket, revealing a dish of pasta. Circling the platter was a ring of what looked like garlic cheese bread and a tossed salad sat in a bowl to the side. He served her a plate, then made another for himself.

She took a bite. "Oh my God. You made this? Out here? From scratch?"

"I did. It's not my finest meal, but it was the best I could do with the limited resources available. Most of my first choice ingredients wouldn't keep in these conditions."

She wiped her mouth with her napkin. "This is amazing. I can't even make a sandwich and here you are making all of this on a camping stove. You really shouldn't have gone to so much trouble just for me."

"You were worth every second I spent in the sweltering heat of the kitchen tent this afternoon." He smiled, his eyes crinkling around the edges slightly. "I'm glad you're enjoying it. So tell me what your specialty is. Everyone has something they can cook."

She shook her head. "Not me."

"One dish. I know you don't eat in restaurants every night. And there's only so much you can order in. So what's your go to meal of choice?"

"You think I'm kidding, but I really can't cook. Nights when I stay in and don't want to order, I usually eat cereal or yogurt or some other easy food. I don't cook. But I do love to bake."

"Really? You must not eat the things you bake." His eyes drifted down her body. Heat radiated along her skin in his wake.

"I do eat it actually. Most people think I must be anorexic or something, but trust me, I have a very healthy appetite. I also have a high metabolism and I try to workout when I can." She shrugged. "It seems to work for me."

"I agree."

The silence around them was comfortable as they ate. For once in her life, she was on a date—*Just dinner, remember!*—and wasn't completely nervous about doing the right thing or saying the wrong thing. It was refreshing.

"So how do you manage to keep looking so incredibly put together all the time when you're out on these crazy locations filming and eating whatever your cooks make for you that day?" Zoe asked. She knew other people, tabloids mostly, had made fun of Chip and his very "metrosexual" appearance. But she didn't mind it at all. She liked a guy who took care of himself as much as she did.

Not that she was vain, regardless of what others might call her. She believed in looking your best to feel your best. If you go out into the world, why not do that with your best foot forward?

Chip grinned. "I like to work out too. Maybe we should work out together sometime."

With Chip in the woods. Hot and sweaty. Muscles bulging from the workout. Yes, please.

"You even work out here? What do you do, bench press a tree?" She laughed at the thought of it.

"Mostly I jog around camp. I'm surprised you haven't heard me running past your tent each morning. I also do pushups and crunches. But I'm not opposed to bench-pressing something, although fallen logs are kind of messy. Perhaps you'd like to fill the position for me?"

I can think of a few positions I'd like to fill.

No. Stop.

"I'm not sure I want to be bench-pressed."

He chuckled. "Okay so maybe no bench-pressing. But you are welcome to come for a jog with me any morning you like."

"I'll keep that in mind. Though I do like my sleep more than I like being out in the chilly morning air getting sweaty." She took her last bite of pasta then wiped her mouth with her napkin and leaned back against his cot. She rubbed her stomach. "I'm so full. Remind me to have you over for dinner at my place. You can show me how to use my stove for more than baking brownies."

"Absolutely, but you have to promise me one thing."

"What's that?" she asked, her curiosity piqued.

"I'll cook dinner for you, if you bake dessert for me."

While she pretended to think about it hard as if there was any question in her mind, he took the opportunity to lean against the cot beside her, his arm lying along the edge of the bed right behind her shoulders. His hand stroked a path up and down her upper arm, making it harder for her to reply than it would have been if he'd stayed seated where he had been.

"Deal," she practically whispered. It wasn't as if she had to speak loudly since he was suddenly so close to her, but she wouldn't have been able to make her voice louder if she'd needed to scream her response. Her voice seemed to have vanished with his close proximity. "What would you have me bake?"

He rested his other hand on the inside of her knee and the pool of lava that had been simmering in her belly since their kiss earlier flared to life inside of her again.

"I don't really care what you give me as long as it's warm and soft and makes me want more." His voice was lower than usual, his eyes heavy lidded as he leaned toward her slightly.

Oh. Well then. She cleared her throat.

"Are we still talking about baked goods?" she asked.

"Of course we are. I don't know what else your mind could possibly be thinking of in relation to those things." He smirked and cocked an eyebrow at her, challenging her to admit the dirty place her mind had decided to take up residence.

"Good. I have a delicious recipe for molten chocolate lava cake. It fits your description perfectly."

Not to mention went exceptionally well with the lava now boiling in her belly.

"It's a sweet chocolate cake," she continued, trying not to drool at the thought of him eating it. At her place. Naked. "Served warm so the middle melts when you press into it."

His smirk fell from his face as she felt his hand leave her arm to snake up into her hair instead. "That sounds delicious. You look delicious. On the way back to camp, you tasted delicious."

She licked her lips at his words. Holy hell. Who knew Chip could be so sexy?

"I...you..." she started, trying to find words. Hard to do when it felt as if a vacancy sign had been posted in the spot where her brain used to live.

He silenced her need for words with his mouth on hers. His hand tangled in her hair, tilting her head so he had a better angle to explore her mouth.

She kissed him back, giving in to the need she'd felt since their earlier kiss. A need she'd been trying so hard to ignore. And had failed at miserably.

Chip's other hand squeezed her inner thigh, now much higher up on her leg than it had been a few minutes ago. How had that happened without her noticing?

His tongue mingled with hers again and the answer was clear. He stole her thoughts, her reason, her self-control with his kisses. Damn, he was a great kisser.

He bit her lower lip gently and she melted into him. How could he make her throw away all her hesitations with just a simple kiss?

But when he pressed his lips against her mouth again hungrily, claiming her, she knew it was more than just a kiss. This—with Chip of all people—was amazing. She'd never felt this deep seeded need to be with someone so much as she felt the need to be with Chip, right here, right now.

You can't. Stop.

Her internal protest fell mute as his hand slid the rest of the way up her leg, stopping just short of brushing against the junction of her thighs. She whimpered involuntarily as a wave of desire shot through her. She hadn't been touched by anyone in so long. And certainly the last man she'd been with hadn't caused any kind of reaction like Chip did.

His lips left her mouth and traveled along her jaw in a series of little kisses.

Right along the ridge of her scar. The one covered with foundation, hidden.

She stiffened.

No.

She rolled away from him, from his kisses, from his hands and got to her feet.

Her heart pounded against her ribs as the realization of how close she'd come to giving in to Chip started to set in. She couldn't. No, she wouldn't. She wasn't ready. Not now.

Maybe not ever.

"Zoe, what's wrong? What did I do?" Chip asked, climbing to his feet, reaching for her. "I'm sorry. I really thought you wanted this too. I wouldn't have…if I'd known…"

She backed away, suddenly feeling like a cornered bear. "No. Don't. I can't. I have to go." She quickly unzipped the tent and bolted out into the cool night air as he came up behind her.

"Zoe, please talk to me. Tell me what the hell just happened."

She heard the pleading in his voice but didn't turn around. She couldn't explain this to him without telling him the truth about her life and that wasn't something she was willing to do.

Especially not now that she had to admit to herself she had some kind of feelings for him.

Once she told him the truth, he'd never look at her the same way.

And she couldn't bear to see a look of pity on his face.

Chapter Eight

Chip's chest burned as he sprinted the last quarter mile back to base camp. He welcomed the sensation. At least this was a feeling he recognized. A feeling he understood.

Not like all those feelings he was still trying to deal with from having dinner with Zoe last night.

What was it about her that got his blood boiling and his groin aching all at the same time? One minute she was kind and sweet—and willing—then the next she was closed up tight, insecure, and off limits. Damn.

He came to a halt at his tent and slipped inside quickly to grab his bathroom supplies and a towel then headed straight for the shower. If he was lucky, he had time to rinse off, clean up, and still stop in for breakfast before the cooks closed up shop for the morning. Usually he didn't have to rush, but after a sleepless night thinking about Zoe, he'd slept in and started his run late. All the more reason to hurry and make sure he got breakfast. Being tired and hungry would make filming today long and painful.

Seeing Zoe again today would be torturous enough.

If only he could figure out what was up with her. He knew she had a history of pushing guys away. The dating history she'd filled out on her application for *The One* had been all the evidence he'd needed to draw that conclusion. The question was why she pushed so hard.

Sure, there was her past to consider, but there had to be more to it than that. Did one traumatic incident really scar a person so deeply for life? Not many people knew that Zoe had been in a terrible car accident at fourteen that had left her scarred and forced her to undergo many corrective surgeries. But he knew. He just didn't understand why one event in her life seemed to have such a lasting impact. People got into car accidents all the time and didn't let it still affect their lives years later. Had the accident really bothered her so much? Why?

Chip strolled back toward the shower area, hoping that everyone else was already done for the day and that there was still some warm water left in one of the solar bladders. If not, he'd have to waste even more time filling it himself.

A river of sweat dribbled down his forehead, narrowly missing his eye. He swiped at his forehead with the end of his towel, briefly covering his face. Good thing he already knew the route to the showers by heart.

He eyed the solar-heated bags above them, trying to decipher which stood the best chance of having enough warm water left in it to get him clean in the least uncomfortable way. After a quick inspection, he concluded the second was his best shot.

Walking past the first door, a mumbling came from inside as he passed. He paused, straining to hear if the person inside was okay and just particularly vocal that morning, or if someone was actually in need of help. Although what you could possibly need help with in an outdoor shower was probably something he wasn't interested in finding out.

He stepped toward the second again, deciding it was best to mind his own business. He didn't want to be privy to anything that happened at the showers unless it concerned him specifically. There was only so close a boss needed to get to his staff and he definitely drew the line at shower help in all forms.

"Damn it. Ouch."

Chip paused again as the voice from shower one continued to mutter, louder and with distinctly more colorful language.

When the f-bomb dropped, he found himself drawn to the shower by the sound of a now familiar voice.

"Zoe?" he asked cautiously. "Is there something wrong that I might be able to help you with?"

She cursed again. "No. I'm good. Thanks though."

He smiled. She was a terrible liar. Best to call her out and not beat around the bush for longer than necessary. "I know something is wrong. I've heard you cursing and ouching for the last few minutes. Why don't you open up and I'll help you. I have a towel handy if that's the problem."

He didn't know if he hoped she was in the need of his towel or not. Just the thought of Zoe standing naked on the other side of a thin piece of material was enough to make him need to go for another sprint to burn off steam. Although he could think of a few other ways he'd rather use up his pent up energy—and all of them involved Zoe.

She sighed. "Fine. You can come in." Her voice sounded sad and defeated.

She really did hate having to admit she needed help. Well, he'd try his best not to rub it in her face.

He took a deep breath, steadying his excitement about what he might find concerning Zoe and a shower. His thoughts ran wild.

Slowly, he opened the shower. And found Zoe wrapped tightly in a towel, covering her from just above her breasts to just above her knees. Damn.

He sagged a little with disappointment. He really had hoped to find her in the nude. Guess that would have to stay a fantasy for now. Still, seeing her almost naked was pretty awesome. His workout pants grew tighter as he attempted to casually lean against the frame of the shower stall.

"What seems to be the problem in here?"

He couldn't see any obvious reason for the cursing and need for help. She looked like she was in one piece standing with her back against one of the walls. In fact, for coming out of the shower, she looked pretty damn put together. Sure, she was naked, a point he couldn't help recognizing in his mind over and over again, but she had her makeup fully applied and her hair fell loose around her shoulders in soft wet waves. Give the girl a dress and she could be ready to go on set.

"I, um, seem to be a little stuck." She bit her lip as shifted her weight as if she was uncomfortable.

"You don't look stuck. I'm not even sure what's in a shower stall to get stuck on...to...in." He chuckled. "How exactly are you stuck?"

"It's my hair."

"Your hair looks fine Zoe, not to worry about anyone seeing you," he teased.

"It's not that," she said, swatting him on the arm, annoyed. Quickly, she pulled her arm back and wrapped it across her chest, gripping the edge of her towel in white knuckles as if she were worried it might suddenly vanish. Not that he'd mind.

"So what is it then?"

Her gaze darted out the door and back to Chip. Her hand snaked out again and slipped around his bicep, pulling him into the tiny shower, barely a few inches separating them now. "Quick, close the curtain. I can't have you lingering in the doorway like some kind of peeping Tom."

He pulled the curtain closed behind him with his free hand, not wanting to draw attention to the fact that Zoe was now almost naked, almost pressed up against him, and still had her hand lingering on his body. His heart pounded in his chest again, but not from jogging this time.

He opened his mouth to speak, but his breath caught in his throat when he looked down at her. From this angle, he could make out a hint of cleavage plunging below the edge of her towel. The sight was distracting. He forced his gaze to meet hers. That didn't help to dislodge the dirty ideas in his mind about how much nicer it would be to get clean with Zoe in his shower.

"If I'd known I was going to be in your shower this morning, I would have skipped my morning run. I'm afraid I'm a bit of a mess and not at all the knight in shining armor you might need right now."

She licked her lips. "You're exactly the person I need right now. And I hope I'm right thinking I can trust you."

"Of course you can."

"I also hope you won't laugh at my stupidity when you see how I'm stuck."

He smiled. "I'm incredibly curious."

Sighing, she tilted her head to the side and stepped away from the wall, closing the gap between them. Behind her, a section of blonde hair was tangled with one of the shower frame poles. He couldn't help but laugh a little.

"This is your big crisis? A tangle of hair?"

She squeezed her hand around his bicep. "You promised not to laugh."

"Actually, I didn't." He smiled, glancing down to her. She peered back up at him.

He hadn't realized just how short she was without her regular stiletto heels on. For some reason, whenever they were walking between camp and the filming areas, she wore sneakers but still seemed taller. Even when they'd kissed on that trail yesterday, there'd been slightly more space between them and they'd been on unlevel ground.

Seeing her mouth so close to him, he longed to bend down and kiss her. But he would resist. For now. "You assumed I wouldn't laugh, I never agreed not to."

"Well are you going to sit there and laugh at me or are you going to help me get my hair untangled?" Her voice was clipped and annoyed, her eyes full of fire.

"No reason to be huffy with the only person around to help you. Let's not get your panties all in a twist. Isn't that how you so elegantly put it the other day?"

"Yes, and to quote you, I can't because I'm currently commando."

His vision glazed over in a haze of lust. "I'm well aware of your current status, not to worry."

Her lips parted slightly as she breathed in a ragged sounding breath. Seemed the air was a little thick in here for both of them. He hadn't felt like he'd taken a full breath since he'd entered her shower.

Reaching behind her, he started working on the tangle, gently pulling apart the strands. The urge to push her against the shower frame and kiss her like crazy almost overwhelmed him, but he forced himself to focus on getting her free.

"Do you have a little pair of scissors in your bathroom bag?" he asked, frustrated at his slow progress.

"No, and you're not cutting my hair. I could have done that myself."

"It would only be a tiny snip."

She pressed her hand flat against his chest, no doubt feeling his heart pounding against his ribs. She looked him straight in the eye, pulling his attention away from the knot. "This is not just hair. It's an expensive extension," she whispered. "I'm not about to let you hack away at it for no good reason."

"Being stuck isn't a good reason?"

"Nope."

She moved to rest her forehead against his chest, not bothering to remove her hands from where they still lingered on his pecs. He closed his eyes for a moment, savoring the feel of her snuggled up next to him, touching him…breathing in his scent, if her deep breath was any indication.

Heat flooded his groin and he fought for control of his thoughts. Easier said than done.

Minutes later—almost longer than he could bear—he pulled the last few strands of hair free and raked his fingers through them, smoothing the frayed edges. When he was sure she was fully freed, he raked his fingers through her hair one last time, separating it down the middle and pulling her lengthy tresses in front of her shoulders. Now no hair was behind her to accidentally get tangled again.

He let his hands rest on the rounds of her shoulders. "You're free."

She pulled her head from his chest, her eyes half-lidded. A mere two inches separated his mouth from hers. It would take less than a breath for him to close the distance and kiss her again.

But last night when he'd done that, all he'd succeeded at was fueling the fire in his groin and scaring off Zoe. Whatever the mixed message was she kept sending him, he wasn't going to listen to it anymore—not when listening would only get him pushed further away.

"Thank you," she whispered, licking her lips and tilting her chin up toward him, a clear indication she wanted him to kiss her.

"My pleasure," he said, stepping away from her and the temptation of her lips.

Before she could say anything else, he slipped back out the door and into his own shower. For once, he was happy the water was borderline cold.

• • •

Zoe's shoulders slumped as she collapsed onto her cot in the safety of her own tent. The cold showers were bad enough—*Solar heated my ass!*—but then getting her hair caught and having to be rescued by Chip, well, that just about started her day off as badly as it could be.

Thank God she'd at least had the chance to wrap herself in a towel and apply her makeup before she'd been so careless and gotten stuck. She would have had to cut her extension out on her own instead of being able to allow Chip to help her. There was no extension worth the price of having Chip see what she really looked like without her makeup on.

Not that it mattered anyway. Even in the tight confines of the shower and the fact that she was more than half naked, he still hadn't kissed her. She'd felt the connection between them again, chemistry sizzling like an electrical storm. And yet as soon as he'd freed her, he'd freed himself from her hold and walked away. No kiss. No nothing.

Which should have been exactly what she wanted. Right?

She didn't want to get involved with Chip. She didn't want to get close to him or anyone else. No, she couldn't get close to Chip because if she did, that would mean telling him about who she really was and she couldn't handle that. Not now, not ever.

So why did it sting so badly when he'd walked away from her this morning without even attempting to kiss her?

Chapter Nine

Zoe slipped into the stilettos she'd carried with her from camp, tossing her sneakers to the side near her bottle of water. She hated having to bring two pairs of shoes with her everywhere, but she didn't want to look short on TV and hiking through these woods in heels was a bad idea—her twisted ankle on *Treasure Trekkers* had taught her that life lesson.

"Ready?" Chip asked, coming up beside her.

She stood and wobbled as her foot slipped off a wet fallen branch she hadn't even realized she'd been standing on. Chip caught her arm, steadying her before quickly letting go.

Something sparked between them again.

She brushed off the back of her skirt, trying to also brush off the electric charge coursing through her from his touch. It worked. Sort of. She'd been successful for the last few days since the whole shower incident and hadn't put herself in direct contact with Chip. But on a filming day it was virtually impossible not to be near him. Even with the distance of a few days, she wasn't ready to be so close to him again. Her defenses still weren't strong enough to successfully ignore the chemistry she felt toward him.

"Yes, I'm ready."

"Good. Let's get this over with then," Chip said, consulting his clipboard. "You have to do the opening and directions, then we'll fill in the commentary later once we know how it all turns out. Then you'll have to send one team home."

She nodded. That didn't sound too hard. "Okay. I can do it."

He glanced up from his work and met her gaze. "I know you can. Do you want me in your ear today? It would help if you used their names today since a team will be going home."

The thought of his voice in her ear again sent a shiver of desire down her back. Yes, she wanted him. She needed him. In more ways than she wanted to admit.

"That sounds good. I'd like your help."

"Anytime. That's what I'm here for. And in the shower for too." He whispered that last part before walking away and taking her breath with him.

She wasn't the only one with lingering memories of their closeness in the shower. So why hadn't he kissed her? She sighed. *Probably because I made him feel like a predator when he tried to kiss me in his tent.* It didn't take a genius to figure out that if a girl runs away as if your place is on fire, she probably doesn't want you to kiss her again. She couldn't blame him, but the lack of an attempt kiss in the shower still annoyed her on a very primal level nonetheless.

Stop. This is how I want things to be with Chip. Why couldn't she get it through her thick skull that it was actually a good thing he hadn't kissed her?

He returned a minute later with an earpiece. When she was fully equipped and they'd checked to make sure she could hear him, she found her place and called the contestants over.

"Welcome back to *Wild Expedition*, the show that has our teams fighting to survive in some of the most horrendous conditions." She glanced away from the cue cards to the teams. It wasn't that bad in their camps, was it? "And now you're going to be put to the test again. How well you survive this challenge will mean the difference between staying another week or going home."

Concerns rippled through the teams as they realized this meant it was not another reward challenge but one that would ultimately end the game for one team.

"Each team must again forage in the woods—this time to find the supplies you'll need to build a raft that will hold all team members. Once your raft is built, you'll paddle upstream to find flags. Each team must retrieve one flag and then paddle back downstream. The first team to cross this finish line with their raft intact, their flag in hand, and all four team members present will be our winners. The last team will be going home."

She paused for a moment while the cue card flipped. "Any questions?" she asked.

"Did you want me to kiss you that morning in the shower?" Chip's voice whispered in her ear seductively.

She gasped at the sound of his voice so intimately in her ear as well as because of the question. Her knees suddenly felt weak. Her pulse thumped in her ear along with Chip's voice.

"Shit," he cursed. "I didn't mean to say that out loud. Zoe, ignore me. Ignore my stupid, poorly timed question and finish the intro so the teams can start the competition."

He stood to the side of the filming area as usual, his clipboard still in hand. But at the moment he wasn't focused on it at all. Nor was he focused on what the contestants were doing or whether or not the camera crew was catching the right angles.

He stared directly at her, waiting for her to start talking again.

But how could she read the cue cards when she couldn't even think straight?

"Zoe, say something. The teams are waiting. I'll edit out the long pause, but please say something."

"I don't know. Maybe," she said, unable to take her gaze from his.

"Zoe, listen to me. Read the cue card. Read it. Now." Chip's voice was harsh and demanding.

"You don't know what?" Rick asked. The other teams echoed his question.

Zoe suddenly felt as if she'd been doused with ice-cold water. Holy shit. Had she really zoned out and answered a question aloud that no one but her had heard?

Rick cocked his head to the side. "You alright today, baby?"

She forced a smile to her lips. "I'm fine, Rick. Thanks for asking. What I was going to say was, I don't know about you, but maybe I'm ready to get this competition started." Her voice sounded unexpectedly enthusiastic. Thank God. "I can't stand the suspense any longer. So let's get started. Teams, bring me a flag!"

She held her smile long enough for the teams to send up a loud cheer and rush off into the woods, cameramen trailing after them as quickly as they could. The other production people moved to their positions along the river where they would be able to supervise the teams without getting in the way or in the shot.

Chip rushed to her side as she walked to her next position at the edge of the river where the teams would build their rafts and paddle upstream. "Good recovery."

"Thanks."

She got to her mark and stopped. She glanced into the woods wondering how long it would take for the first teams to make it back to her with their raft supplies in hand.

"You shouldn't be here. The teams will be back any second and I think we've had enough mistakes for one day, don't you?"

Chip put his hand on her shoulder. "I'm sorry. I don't know what happened. I didn't mean to say that out loud. This is my mistake, not yours. And I won't let it happen again."

She nodded, still too stunned with how the start of this competition had turned out to comment.

Chip wrapped his fist around the mic pinned to Zoe's shirt, effectively blocking any audio it might pickup. "The truth is, I haven't been able to stop thinking about you since the other day when we kissed on the trail and then the time I spent with you in my tent. But seeing you in the shower, wrapped in a towel…

the way your head and hands felt on my chest…damn it, Zoe. I haven't been able to get you out of my head all week."

He glanced around them as if looking to see if any of the teams were on their way back yet or if any of the production people were noticing their private conversation. As far as she could tell, no one had noticed anything unusual.

"You should go. The cameras and contestants are going to be back any minute now."

"I know. I'll go. But promise me that you'll talk to me about this later. Privately."

"I don't think that's a good idea. You need to go. I see them coming back." She felt her pulse pick up its pace as the teams neared. She wasn't sure if it was from the fear of someone figuring out that there was something a little different going on between herself and Chip or if she was getting caught up in the adrenaline of the show.

"Why isn't it a good idea?" Chip asked, stepping closer to her and stroking his fingers along the side of her neck. The sensation was enough to make the world around them disappear. "I know you feel this thing between us. Stop pushing me away long enough for us to figure out what it is."

"No," she said, not believing the word herself. "You need to go. I can't talk to you about this now. Or later. I want you to leave me alone. I don't want to be kissed by you or anyone else." She cringed, knowing the words hurt him as much as they hurt her. But she couldn't spend time alone with Chip. She couldn't let him in any closer than he already was.

He dropped his hands to his sides. "I've never wanted to kiss someone so badly as I wanted to kiss you that morning. When you're ready to get over whatever is standing in your way, you know where to find me."

When Chip walked away, Zoe felt as if her resolve to resist him crumbled to her feet. She did want to be with him. She did want to kiss him again. But she couldn't.

And no amount of persistence or guilt from Chip was going to change that.

Maybe the easiest way to make him understand was to show him she wasn't interested in him. And the best way to do that was by distracting herself with Rick. At least with Rick she didn't have to worry about her feelings actually going anywhere dangerous.

• • •

The teams paddled hard down the river in a race to the finish line. Three of the teams were in a deadlock tie on the river while the last two teams wandered about like lost ducks a few hundred feet upstream. Chip held his breath, waiting to see which team would come in first.

So far it looked as if Rick's team was going to win.

Screw Rick and his stupid good-at-everything team.

He'd hoped Rick would lose today and be sent packing so he wouldn't have to look at his smug face while he flirted with Zoe every time he got within fifteen feet of her. But that didn't look like it was likely to happen. With his luck, he'd be stuck with Rick right until the end of the show.

Unless of course he could figure out a challenge that Rick would suck at. But what kind of challenge would that be? The guy seemed to be able to handle anything they'd thrown at him so far. He could survive in the wild so well he could have been raised by animals. He seemed to be able to cook with even the most limited ingredients. And the guy was built like a lumberjack so any physical feat would probably be no sweat off his back. There had to be something the guy couldn't do. Chip just had to work harder to figure out what it was and then maybe he could redesign one of the challenges to capitalize on it.

Sneaky and a little lowbrow, but totally worth it if it sent Rick home.

Just then Rick and his teammates splashed onto shore and dragged their raft and flag across the soft mud to where Zoe stood waiting for them at the finish line.

"Congratulations! Rick…" Zoe paused, her gaze darting to Chip to silently tell him she needed help with the names.

"Pam, Roger, and Todd," Chip said clearly and quietly into his mic so that Zoe would hear him in her ear. "You're doing great."

"Pam, Roger and Todd, you are the winning team!" Zoe clapped for them and looked enthusiastic that they'd won. "Join me over here for a moment while the rest of our teams check in."

The other teams crossed the finish line. Second was the team of doctors. Chip once again said their names for Zoe, which she repeated back to the viewing audience without hesitation. They were getting good at this. She looked calm and beautiful doing her hosting job, smiling at the contestants as they arrived and cheering them all on equally. He'd known she'd settle into the role just fine.

When the rowing team crossed the finish line in third position, Zoe's smile faltered for a moment.

"This stream must be tougher than it looks if the rowing team struggled," she said without malice. It was true. Chip had thought their team would be the first to the finish line today.

"Things aren't always as they seem, are they, Ms. Oliver?" Alex retorted, his voice sharp as if he was pissed off at more than coming in third.

Zoe paled but recovered quickly, plastering her usual smile on her face. If Chip hadn't been watching her so closely, he could have missed her reaction. What was that about? Was something going on between the two of them too like there was with Rick? This didn't seem fun and flirty at all. This seemed angry and suspicious.

"That's true. But more often than not, it's just a person's perception that's off." Her smile looked uncomfortable, not at all genuine.

"Of course, sometimes a person's perception is right on. Sometimes it's best to trust your gut, even if what you see doesn't go along with what you've been told."

Zoe's jaw clenched. She shifted from one foot to the other and narrowed her eyes at Alex. *What's up with those two?* They sounded like they were talking in code.

"In this case," Zoe said, her voice strong and unwavering, "I think rowing a raft made out of logs is much different than rowing one of your usual streamlined boats. So maybe we all perceived the river to be easier to navigate than it actually was on the rafts. I think we all underestimated the strength and power of the stream. Next time we should all tread more carefully, don't you think?"

"You can say that again." Dale laughed, patting Alex on the back. "That raft didn't steer worth a damn and it had nothing to cut the current with. That river was a bitch."

"At least we can use it to keep in shape while we're here since paddling that piece of driftwood was a workout and a half," Jared added.

The boys stepped to the side still chatting about how they would use their new training tool as the last team crossed the line, panting and falling to their knees in exhaustion.

"I'm sorry, girls, but you're the last team to cross the finish line and that means you're our first team to go home."

The four girls climbed back to their feet and hugged each other, then waved to the cameras as they said a few quick goodbyes. A moment later, they followed out one of the production people to be taken back to their camp to collect their things before heading home.

As they passed by him, Chip felt a small amount of remorse for ultimately being the person to send them home and end their chances of winning the money. It was his least favorite part of the job. But someone had to do it. At least they got to go back to the land of restaurants, soft beds, and hot showers. So he couldn't feel entirely bad for them.

"Now to find out what prize our winning team receives," Zoe said, carrying on with her hosting responsibilities. She picked up a small cooler and handed it to Rick.

"Thank you, baby. You want to open it with me?"

"I think your hard working team deserves that honor," she answered with a flirtatious looking smile.

Chip ground his teeth together. Rick couldn't leave soon enough.

The team opened the cooler and found ice and cold drinks. They cheered at their reward.

"After the long, hot days we've had, I'm sure that will be the perfect thing to rejuvenate you." Zoe turned to face the camera straight on. "Tune in next time to *Wild Expedition* to find out if our teams will have to prove their survival skills or overcome more physical obstacles."

"Clear," Chip called to let the entire crew know they were finished filming for the day and could start packing up. Well, everyone except for the cameramen who would follow the teams back to their camps and continue filming until their shift ended at five and the next crew of cameramen took over for the night. He wandered over to join Zoe while she removed her mic pack and earpiece.

"Are you sure you don't want to help me cool off after these long, hot days?" Rick asked Zoe as Chip walked to her side. "I'm pretty sure I can find a few good uses for all this ice if you join me at camp tonight. Or maybe we'd have more privacy if I visited your tent."

"You make a tempting offer," Zoe started.

"Tempting, yes. But she's going to have to decline. Crew and contestants are not to mingle outside of taping segments of the show."

"That right?" Rick narrowed his eyes at Chip.

Chip pulled his shoulders back. Rick might be a tough guy, but Chip was no slouch. He could stand his ground against anyone, especially douche bags like Rick.

"That's right. And I'd remember that rule if I was you or you might leave me no choice but to throw you and your team out of the game. Zoe's off limits, got it?"

"I think the lady can make her own choices." Rick put his hand on Zoe's shoulder. "So what's it going to be, baby? Me or the rules?"

Zoe looked between both of them. Chip held his breath. She couldn't possibly be interested in this Neanderthal, could she? She didn't look at Rick with the same spark in her eyes she had when she looked at him.

"I think you both make my life way more complicated than it needs to be. My job is done here for the day so I'm going back to camp. You two feel free to stand around and beat your chests like monkeys a little more if you want, but I've had enough of your testosterone party for one day."

Chip held his tongue as Zoe strode away from them and back toward base camp, then turned on Rick. "I mean it. Stay away from Zoe or I'll have you and your team removed from the game."

"I get it. You're trying to put the moves on her too, aren't you?" Rick laughed. "Let's just see who gets in her panties first. Game on."

Before Chip could reply, Rick wandered off after his team, disappearing into the woods. This wasn't a game. And Zoe wasn't some prize to be won.

Rick sure as hell wasn't getting anywhere near her panties.

Soon Chip would figure out a challenge to get Rick tossed out of the game and then he'd have one less thing standing in his way of getting Zoe to be with him.

But first he had to go after her and make her realize she wanted to kiss him just as much as he wanted to kiss her.

And this time, he wasn't going to take no for an answer.

Chapter Ten

Zoe stopped at a large boulder off the side of the trail and sat. Her feet ached in the heels she wore. She slipped them off and rubbed her arches. If only she'd changed her shoes as soon as filming had ended. Instead, she'd left in a hurry from Rick and Chip's testosterone fight and had forgotten her sneakers. Hopefully one of the production people would find them when they packed up and bring them back to camp for her. Until then, she was stuck in heels.

Kind of ironic since she'd always been an advocate for wearing heels anywhere. But lately, they didn't seem as appealing to her. Maybe she was getting lazy and ordinary.

Or maybe she was slowly learning there was more to life than sexy stilettos.

"Whoa now," she said aloud even though no one was around to hear her but the squirrels and birds in the trees. "A week in the wilderness must be too much for me if I'm seriously starting to think that sneakers would ever be better than heels. I need a dose of reality soon. This reality show thing isn't cutting it anymore."

Sighing, she strapped her heels back on her feet and started back along the trail. At least the wilderness was good for thinking. She had a lot of that to do right now.

Like what exactly could she do about the men suddenly complicating her life?

First there was Alex who'd acted as if he might have remembered her again today. Why the hell couldn't his team have gone home? He obviously knew she had something to hide, and it was probably only a matter of time before he figured out what it was—*who* she really was.

Then there was Rick. He was good looking and all but totally not her type. She didn't want to be with a gruff outdoorsy guy like him, but it was hard not to flirt with him when he started calling her baby and making sexy comments all the time. But with Rick it was just a fun distraction for her. Should she really carry on with that and encourage his behavior? It probably wasn't very good for the show since she was a crewmember now and he was a contestant. There were rules, whether she liked to follow them or not. But more than that, did she really want to lead him on knowing full well that she was only using him as a distraction to keep her mind—and hands—off Chip?

And then there was Chip.

What could she do about him? She'd been trying her best to ignore him since the shower incident and yet one look from him today and she felt her resistance melting faster than the polar ice caps in a hundred and fifty degree summer. One glance from him and she wanted to sprint across the forest and into his arms.

Hearing his voice in her ear had almost made her lose all hope of maintaining control. It was so deep and whispery and intimate. Having him with her that way was almost too much. When he asked if she wanted to kiss him, her knees damn near gave out on her.

And yet even though her body obviously wanted to be with him, she had to resist so she wouldn't risk him finding out about her past. Beyond the makeup and hair hid a girl who a put together guy like Chip would never settle for. He paid far too much attention to every detail of his appearance to put up with a sub-standard girl like her. Better to keep him away than to let him get close and have him push her away later when her heart would get broken.

Of course, seeing him spar with Rick made her decision that much harder. How could she stay away from Chip when he so clearly wanted her and she wanted him? If she wasn't careful, she'd find herself in his arms again. All the more reason to keep her distance.

Guess she'd get used to walking the pathways alone.

Movement a few feet off the trail caught her attention. A pair of rabbits nibbled on the low leaves of a bush, pausing every few seconds to listen to their surroundings before hopping a little further and eating more.

Life must be pretty simple for a rabbit. Eat, hop, sleep, make bunnies. Not a bad existence.

Holy shit, I'm jealous of a rabbit. I really have been roughing it too long.

A snap of a branch startled her out of her thoughts. A squeak escaped before she could compose herself. The rabbits bolted into the safety of the thick bush at the sound.

"I didn't mean to startle you," Chip said, walking up beside her. "I thought you stopped to wait for me because you heard me coming."

"It's okay. I was lost in my own head too much to hear you. What are you doing here?" Had he followed her to bring up the whole Rick thing?

He smiled and started down the trail. "Heading back to base camp, of course. Isn't that what you're doing?"

"Of course it is." She fell into step beside him. Relief swelled inside her that maybe he wouldn't ask any more questions. It would be nice to have a quiet walk back to camp with a friend.

Sure, a friend, she chided herself. Her pulse had already sped up and it wasn't from Chip startling her. It was from him being only a few inches away.

"I'm sorry I got all hotheaded back there with you and Rick. That guy annoys the ever living crap out of me."

"Really? I never would have guessed," she joked, hoping to keep the mood light.

"Very funny," Chip joked back. "The way he calls you baby all the time rubs me the wrong way. Like you're his girlfriend and he has a right to call you whatever he wants."

"Relax. We're not in a relationship or anything. There's no need to get all bent out of shape over a nickname."

Chip stopped and put his hand on her arm, forcing her to stop too. His grip on her arm was light. She could have pulled away easily at any second. But one look into his eyes and she felt paralyzed. Fire burned bright in his eyes, but not from anger at Rick. No, this fire was from something that burned hotter than anger.

This was the spark of something hot between them that she'd been trying so hard to ignore.

She swallowed, feeling that urge to throw herself at him again. But she wasn't going to.

"I can't take not knowing anymore. I want an answer to the question I asked you earlier. Did you want me to kiss you? I need to know. I'm doing the best I can to control myself around you since you can't seem to send me a clear message of what you want. But I'm not sure how much longer I can go on this way."

She had to pull away now. If she stayed, it would only lead to the place she didn't want to go with Chip. The place she *couldn't* go.

She pulled free of him. "I already told you an answer." She bit her lip and took a tentative step back toward base camp. She needed distance. Thinking with her head instead of her heart was impossible when Chip was so close, when he looked at her like that. "I don't know and that's the best I can do."

He stepped forward, closing the gap before she could put any real distance between them. Stroking his thumb along her bottom lip he said, "Tell me your answer is no and I'll walk away right now and leave you alone. Just say that one little word and I'll stop."

Say it. Say no.

Zoe's eyelids fluttered closed as she savored the feeling of his touch on her lips, knowing that as good as it was, feeling his mouth on hers would be infinitely better. She needed to tell him "no" to spare herself the pain later, but everything inside screamed "yes."

"Say no, Zoe, and I'll go." Chip's breath was warm on her lips. She opened her eyes to find him hovering above her mouth. So close. "Last chance."

She opened her mouth intent on telling him to go, but no words came forward. Instead, she felt the uncontrollable urge to lick her lips, but when she did, her tongue flickered across the end of his thumb.

Before she could apologize, his hand wrapped behind her head and he moved toward her, pressing her against a large tree. The rough bark cut into her back, making her arch against him. The resulting sensation of his hard body touching hers sent a pool of warmth into her belly.

She gasped as his lips found hers, his tongue eagerly invading her mouth. Despite her best effort to resist him, she melted into his kiss, his touch. Running her hands up his back, she clung to him, pressing against him. The hardened length of his desire pressed against her hip.

She wanted more than anything to trace the outline of his length with her hand, to feel him grasped in her palm as he kissed her.

But that was exactly the kind of thing she couldn't let happen.

Zoe turned her head to the side, gasping for breath as if she'd been suffocating. Tears sprang to her eyes. She wanted him so much, but wanting him would never equate to having him fully. He would never have her once he knew the truth.

Chip held her head in both hands, forcing her to look at him, and wiped a stray tear with his thumb as it rolled down her cheek. "Zoe, what's wrong?"

"I can't…I don't want…" She choked on the words, trying and failing to be strong.

"You can't kiss me like that and then tell me you didn't want it or you didn't like it. Kiss me, Zoe."

He claimed her mouth again and she melted into him against her will. Seemed her inner strength was a hussy who wanted a good time in the moment and didn't give a damn about what happened with Chip in the future. But Chip would care. And he would break her heart and leave her in ruins and there was nothing she could do about that if she gave in now.

"No," she said, pushing hard against him. "I don't want this. I don't want you."

"You're lying," Chip said, taking a step back from her, looking as if he'd been hit across the face with a sledgehammer.

"I'm sorry, but kissing you is a mistake."

With that she turned and ran down the path as fast as she could in her heels and didn't stop until she was safely back in her tent.

• • •

Chip punched the tree trunk then cursed as the pain of his stupidity radiated through his hand. The way she looked at him, the desire he saw in her eyes, she had wanted him to act on his feelings for her. He hadn't been mistaken about that. And when he kissed her, he'd felt her melt into him. Hell, he'd felt her grind against the bulge in his pants.

She did want him, no doubt, but she stopped herself. Again.

Maybe she wanted Rick too and that's why she kissed him then pulled away. Getting rid of Rick, sooner rather than later, would eliminate one of the complications keeping Zoe from being with him.

She wanted him. He knew it. He just had to figure out how to make her realize it too.

Or he had to bide his time and sit tight until she figured it out for herself. He knew she would eventually, but waiting really sucked.

At least he had other things he could occupy his time with. Like plotting which upcoming challenge could potentially be the one to send Rick home. To do that, he would need to watch some of the footage taken of him around camp. If Rick showed a weakness anywhere, it would be at camp with his teammates where he felt most comfortable.

And Chip would watch footage until he found Rick's weakness, even if it took all night.

Not like he had anything better to do anyway now that Zoe had run off.

He shoved his aching hand into his pocket and started toward camp. Maybe he'd stop in the kitchen tent and see if he could scrounge up some ice for his knuckles. Every few days the cooks trekked back to civilization to get supplies, including ice for the coolers. Hopefully he'd luck out and today would be one of those days.

Chapter Eleven

Chip crawled onto his cot and pulled the blankets over his head. It would be daylight soon and he didn't want to see it when it arrived. Exhaustion swept over him as he slowly warmed up inside the tight embrace of his bed.

He'd come back to camp determined to find something that would put Rick at a disadvantage. It had taken him almost all night and a few too many solar batteries to scour the hours of footage they had logged from his camp. Half a dozen beers later, he'd finally found it.

Rick's weakness.

A grin split across his lips as he thought about it with smug satisfaction. Perfect. He already had a challenge in the schedule that would put Rick to the test. It was supposed to be the week three challenge, but being producer of the show meant he could change things as he saw fit. And waiting until next week to try and get Rick off the show wasn't fast enough for his liking. Nope. Switching the challenge schedule around a little might help get rid of Rick's team an entire week sooner.

Now he just had to pray that it worked and Rick's team was sent packing.

Of course, there would still be the problem of Alex and whatever his issue with Zoe was. Yesterday at the challenge, it was obvious Alex and Zoe knew each other somehow, but no amount of research had given him the answer as to how.

Chip had compared their files extensively. They didn't live in the same town, they hadn't gone to college together, and they didn't seem to have any friends or family in common either. So how did they know each other? He'd been worried at first that they were exes, but that didn't seem to be the case. Or if they were, they'd kept their relationship hidden.

The only unusual thing he'd come across tonight was the lack of information concerning Zoe previous to her accident. It was as if she didn't exist before that moment, but she'd been fourteen when it happened. Weird. Or maybe not weird. How much of a paper trail did a fourteen-year-old girl have?

Chip yawned, too tired to try and wrap his brain around the mystery of Zoe and Alex any longer. Maybe after he'd had some sleep he'd feel up to tackling that issue again. For now, he was happy he'd been able to figure out a way to hopefully send Rick and his team home.

• • •

Zoe paced inside her tent.

Yesterday had been one giant ball of messiness. Not only had Alex given her a rough time, but Rick had flirted with her, Chip had gotten jealous, and then he'd kissed her.

Hot damn. That kiss.

She wanted to forget about it. She wanted to push it from her brain. But instead, the memory of that kiss infiltrated her every waking thought.

She had wanted to give herself to him so badly in that moment, completely swept away by the man who could kiss her like she was the only woman in the universe. And she'd thought that was all it was, a moment of being swept away.

But then she'd come back to camp and locked herself in her tent all night except for quick trips to the bathroom and kitchen tents, and no matter how hard she tried, she couldn't get that kiss to leave her alone. It wasn't as if she was caught up in the moment anymore either. Nope. Chip was inside her head, under her skin, and quickly burrowing his way into her heart.

She had to put a stop to it.

"You can't let that happen again," she scolded herself. "You can't be with Chip like that. He's a threat to your well-being and you can't let your guard slip with him."

Except just the thought of slipping into Chip's arms again was enough to make her feel weak-kneed. He made her feel something different than she'd felt before. Sure there was the lusty element to her feelings. Who wouldn't want to be with a man who could kiss like Chip? But there was more to it than that.

When she was in his arms, when he kissed her, she felt...whole.

"That was so much more than a kiss." She sighed. It couldn't be more than a silly kiss. She couldn't let it be more.

Zoe heard a noise outside of her tent and twisted quickly in the direction it came from. She still wasn't used to the noises that seemed to be everywhere out here in the wilderness. As she turned, her toes connected with the bottom leg of her cot. Pain shot through her toes and into her foot.

"Ouch. Damn it," she said, squatting down to inspect the damage. Aside from some redness where her toes connected with the metal, there didn't seem to be too much to worry about. "That's what I get for daydreaming about a kiss when I should have been doing something more productive, like paying attention to my appendages."

"You alright in there, Zoe? Do you need me to get the medic?" Chip's voice came through the tent loud and clear and it wasn't even raised.

Damn it.

How could she be so stupid? Why couldn't she remember she was in a flimsy tent and not a hotel room with solid walls? If Chip was standing outside her tent when she'd hurt herself and had been close enough to hear her say ouch, then he'd also been close enough to hear her talk about that kiss with him.

Great. Just fricken great.

"I'm fine," she said, her voice shaky knowing that he'd heard her every word. "Just stubbed my toe, nothing to worry about or call the medic for."

"Can I come in and have a quick look at it to make sure you're fine? I, uh…" He paused. "I promise I won't kiss you since you don't need more things to daydream about."

Even without seeing his face, she could hear the joking tone in his voice and knew instantly he had indeed overheard everything she'd said about kissing him. And he seemed pretty damn happy with himself about the whole thing too.

"Thanks, but I'm fine." She pressed her lips into a tight line in an effort to resist saying anything else. Who knew what she'd say to dig her hole even deeper. Best to keep quiet.

"If you're sure. I'm calling a production meeting in ten minutes in the kitchen tent. Do you think you can make it there safely yourself, or would you like me to wait around and help you? I can't have my host breaking anything important while we're filming."

Zoe rolled her eyes. "I'll be there with all my pieces intact."

"Great. See you in a few."

Zoe held her breath, listening carefully for his footsteps to retreat away from her tent. When she was sure he'd left, she let out a long, slow breath.

Way to go. I'm going to keep my mouth shut from now on.

Deciding that maybe it was better to give her toes some rest after their near death experience, she slipped on her sneakers, which one of the production assistants had returned to her. She took one more peek into her mirror to check her makeup and hair and then left her tent to attend Chip's spontaneous production meeting. Hopefully he wouldn't comment on anything relating to her—or even look directly at her. If he did, she was liable to faint from embarrassment and that wasn't something she wanted to explain to the other production people.

A hush fell over the kitchen tent as Chip stepped in front of everyone. He looked less put together than usual and she could even make out dark bags beneath his eyes as if he'd pulled an all nighter. But why would he? Surely they didn't edit together the segments for the show until they got back to the land of civilization.

"Good morning. I'll keep this nice and short. This afternoon, many of us will be leaving base camp for the remainder of the week. I'll need each of you to pack a bag of essentials bearing in mind you will have to hike with this bag. So please think carefully about what you take with you. We will meet the teams at a new location."

"Zoe." He turned to face her directly and she felt her cheeks blush. "I'll need you to visit each of the camps this morning and give them some instructions and a map to our new location. Your usual cameraman Bill will accompany you to film but I'm afraid I will not be able to tag along today as I need to secure things here. Do you think you'll be alright getting to the various camps and back here in time to pack a few things?"

He cocked an eyebrow at her and she had the urge to pull attitude on him. He was implying she wasn't capable after her stubbed toe incident this morning. He was trying to tease her right here in front of everyone.

"I'll be fine, thanks." She managed to reply without attitude in her voice, a rather large feat given the circumstances. He couldn't resist teasing her at every opportunity, could he?

"Great." He turned back to face everyone as if he'd done nothing wrong. Technically he hadn't, but it didn't feel that way to her. "We'll be out of base camp until we send the next team home in a few days, so make sure you take the things you need. It won't be easy to return to camp if you forget something. And you don't need to worry about bringing food or water or any other supplies like that. That will all be taken care of. You only need to worry about your personal things. Are there any questions?"

When no one spoke up, he continued. "Great. Get packing. We leave camp at two this afternoon and that should give us plenty of time to set up once we arrive at the new site."

The crowd started to wander away when Chip shouted, startling Zoe enough that she jumped.

"Wait. One more thing I almost forgot. Make sure you get cleaned up before we go. The new location is very remote and we will not be able to bring our luxurious bathroom setup with us. This is your last chance for a shower for a few days so use your time wisely."

The production people grumbled as they wandered out of the tent, many of them commenting about fitting in time to shower and pack. Zoe was thankful she'd gotten up early this morning and had already showered. That would save her the inevitable traffic jam the shower tents would see in a few minutes.

It didn't leave her any additional relaxation time though since she had to trek to each of the contestants' camps to hand out maps. She'd have to hurry if she wanted any time to think about what she needed to pack.

• • •

After collecting the specific instructions and the maps from Chip, Zoe had set out immediately for the contestant camps. She'd managed to snag a granola bar and a bottle of water for the trip so at least she was being efficient and eating breakfast along the way.

The first three camp visits had gone relatively easy. The contestants seemed more excited than she'd expected to have a new location to call home for a few days. And they were more than a little thrilled to have new people to talk to during their time at the new camp too. Zoe wasn't surprised. Even with the large crew on this production, seeing the same faces everyday at base camp got a little boring.

Zoe got to the last camp as they were cleaning up their breakfast dishes. What they'd eaten, she had no idea. Possibly some of the rice they'd won at the first reward challenge. Or who knew what else they might have been able to scrounge together from the woods. Regardless, it smelled peculiar and threatened to turn her stomach. She vowed to make this the quickest stop.

"Hey, baby. You're finally coming to visit me?" Rick grinned. "Good thing I finished my breakfast. Now I've got lots of energy to spend on you, if you catch my meaning."

"I do, and I'm not here for that." Zoe called out to the other members of his team, motioning for them to join Rick. "I'm only here for a moment to pass on a production message. Seems we're moving to a new camp for the week. You're to pack up some of your things and follow this map to the new location. You won't return here until after the elimination challenge, *if* you survive it. Any questions?"

"When do we need to be at the new camp?" Pam asked.

"Late this afternoon or early this evening so you have enough time to get settled before dark. Any other questions?"

"Are we going to be out there alone again, like here?" Todd asked, looking nervously between Zoe and his parents.

"No. The production crew and the other contestants will all be staying in the same camp this week." She smiled to try and reassure Todd that things would be fine. Truth be told, she was just as nervous about the new living arrangements as he seemed to be. She'd have to be even more careful to maintain her appearance with all those extra people around. And the lack of an even limited bathroom setup like they had back at production camp wouldn't make her job of looking the part any easier. "Okay then, follow the map and I'll see you all at the new camp tonight."

Zoe turned to walk back to base camp. Rick fell into step beside her.

"What's up, Rick?" she asked, looking down at the trail instead of at Rick. This first section was really rough and she didn't want to risk stumbling as she hurried back to her own camp to get packed up.

"You didn't let me ask my question."

"Oh, sorry. I didn't realize you had one." She stopped on the trail and turned to Rick, wanting to be professional. "What was your question? I'll do my best to answer it."

"Since the production team is staying in the same camp as us, I'm hoping you might stop in and keep my tent warm each night this week." He cocked an eyebrow.

Zoe folded her arms across her chest. "That wasn't a question."

"No, but I'd still like to know the answer."

"Listen, Rick, you're cute in an outdoorsy kind of way and all, but crew and contestants really shouldn't be fooling around. I don't think Chip would like it very much if he knew you were inviting me into your tent tonight. So maybe let's try to keep the flirting to a minimum from now on, okay?"

She hadn't planned on ending her little flirtatious thing with Rick, but hearing him hit on her again after everything going on— or not going on—with Chip, made her suddenly less interested in flirting with him more. It probably wasn't smart to use him as a distraction and lead him on.

"Screw Chip. I don't care what he says. You can't stop people from being together if they want to be." He pulled her close, his arms snaking around her waist, dangerously close to touching her ass. "And I know you want to be with me, baby."

Zoe pressed her hands to his chest to push him away but before she could, his lips were on hers, his tongue forcing its way into her mouth. She mumbled an expletive against his mouth but he must have taken it as something else because it seemed to encourage his exploration of her further. His hands traveled south, grabbing her ass in both palms, pressing her against him. His expected outcome for this meeting was suddenly clear as his hardened length pressed into her.

She gave him a hard shove and he took a step back, his eyes droopy with desire she didn't reciprocate.

"If you can't wait until tonight in my tent, we can find a cozy place right here, baby."

She shook her head and took a few steps down the path, away from Rick. "No. I'm not interested. Not now, not tonight."

He looked confused. "Are you playing hard to get all of a sudden? 'Cause I like a challenge."

"I'm not playing hard to get. You're just not getting me. Period. I'm sorry if you thought maybe I wanted something from you, but I don't."

She had led him on, flirting with him and laughing at his sexual invitations. But that kiss hadn't sparked anything inside of her.

Not like the kisses she'd had with Chip, which had made her melt like candle wax in the desert. No, any question she'd had about flirting with Rick as a distraction for Chip was instantly thrown out the window the second Rick's lips landed on hers. His kiss did nothing for her.

"Is this because of that producer? Did he beat me to it? Has he already been in your pants?" Rick shook his head. "That dog."

Zoe's annoyance spiked. "No, he hasn't been in my pants! Jeez, could you be a little more crass? I'm not interested. Got it?"

She didn't wait for him to reply. His reply could end up being another unwanted kiss. Instead, she hurried down the trail without a second thought to Rick. She'd been wrong to flirt with him before. She knew that now. Not only was she the host for the show, but he also didn't hold an ounce of the attraction she felt toward Chip.

The last thing she needed right now was another man making her life more difficult, so putting an end to the flirting with Rick was the best choice. Then she'd just have to avoid Alex's suspicions and somehow not fall any harder for Chip than she already had. That should be easy enough.

Chapter Twelve

Chip finished packing the last of the extra things he needed into his backpack before shouldering it and leaving his tent. Of course he probably wouldn't need the condoms or his book since getting free time for either activity was unlikely, but he always wanted to think positively.

He had just enough time to pop over to the kitchen supply tent and grab an extra box of protein bars in case the production crew forgot to bring them. He could live without many things in the wild, but protein bars wasn't one of them.

Flipping open one of the chests they used for storage, he rummaged around until he found the box of chocolate, caffeinated goodness he liked best and slammed the lid back down into place securely. A few crewmembers were staying behind to monitor the camp, but you couldn't be too careful. There were a lot of animals in the area and not all of them were friendly or harmless and he didn't want the smell of food to attract any unwelcome visitors.

"How's it going, boss? Do I have time to grab a snack for the road before we head out?" Cam asked. He had his backpack on one shoulder and his production equipment case gripped tightly in one hand.

"As long as you're quick," Chip replied, shoving the box of protein bars into his bag and replacing it on his shoulder.

"Hey, what's with the change of schedule? I thought we weren't doing this one until week three."

Chip nodded. "I figured we needed to mix it up a little bit sooner rather than later. Keep things interesting for the contestants and for the viewers once the show airs. What better way to do that than to stick all the contestants together in a camp that they have to build from scratch?"

Cam took a bit of granola bar and spoke around the food in his mouth. "Good call. Although I think the viewers are already going to have their hands on their remotes to record the show after what happened today with Rick and Zoe."

Chip froze at the doorway to the tent. Adrenaline spiked in his veins. What had Rick done? He clenched his jaw until it ached.

Breathe. Stay calm.

"Oh yeah? Why's that?" he asked, trying to sound casual about the whole thing.

"I'm surprised you didn't hear already." Cam shrugged. "Seems the cameraman for camp two was coming back from a bathroom pit stop and found Zoe and Rick off on the trail in a pretty intense lip lock. Good thing he had his camera with him to capture some of that action, hey boss? You would have killed him if he'd missed it."

Chip forced a smile to his lips. "You're right. I would have killed him for missing that. Was Jackson the one on shift for camp two today? I'd like to check out that juicy footage tonight once we get to the new campsite."

"He was. Ah crap. I think I forgot a few things in my tent. I'm gonna grab them quick and meet you by the fire pits. Don't leave without me or I'll never find my way to that new camp."

"Then you better not take too long." Chip's voice had a harder edge than he'd intended it to. It really didn't matter if they left exactly on time or a few minutes late. And he wouldn't leave anyone in camp who needed to go. But he couldn't keep the anger about Rick and Zoe's kiss out of his tone.

Chip pulled a few deep breaths into his lungs in an attempt to calm his anger. He couldn't go back into camp like this or he'd take his anger out on his crew. That wouldn't help anyone. He'd be better off not listening to the gossip and not worrying about Zoe or Rick until he'd reviewed the tapes.

And if what Cam had just told him was true, then Zoe would have some explaining to do and Rick would be on his shit list. Thank God he'd moved up this challenge. Now maybe he could get Rick tossed out of the game for good. And hopefully he'd be out of Zoe's life then too.

. . .

Zoe eased her backpack off her shoulders and dropped down to sit on one of the stumps they'd turned on its end for a stool. The "little" hike to the new campsite seemed to take forever and had been exhausting. Maybe Chip didn't mind so much trekking into the woods, but she definitely wasn't cut out for this lifestyle.

And she still had to pitch a tent before she could change into her hosting clothes and officially welcome the contestants to their new camp for the week.

All she wanted to do was check into a hotel, soak in a hot bubble bath, and sleep in a soft bed. Why had she signed up for this again?

Oh yeah, the money to finish paying off her medical bills.

She would be free of that debt and maybe she'd finally be free of any connection to her past too. She looked up from her perch and surveyed the surroundings. Alex was hammering a tent peg into the ground. He looked up and caught her eye, sneering at her.

Or maybe she'd always be stuck with her past with guys like Alex around.

Hopefully not. It wasn't fair that she had to live through her past once already. It was even more unfair that she had to keep reliving it with every check she wrote to the hospital. If she also started getting recognized by people she used to know, there'd be no end to her misery over what had happened. She'd be haunted by that accident forever. And it wasn't just the accident haunting her with Alex here. It was the teasing that came afterwards too. Alex had been the worst of the bunch, always first with a comment and always last to stop laughing. How many surgeries had she undergone to stop their taunting? How much time had she spent isolated in a painful recovery so she wouldn't have to face the kids at school again with the same horrifying face...the same guilty conscience? When she'd finished her last surgery, she'd thought she was done with that part of her life forever, never to see any of them again. But apparently not.

Sighing, Zoe pulled herself up from her spot on the stump and reached for her tent. She dumped the contents of the tent bag onto the ground and found the paper instructions, taking a quick glance over them. They looked just as annoying and complicated as the few other tents she'd been forced into building over the years.

Zoe worked tirelessly for half an hour laying out the tent tarps and poles and was finally ready to erect her tent when Chip walked up. The expression on his face was unclear, which was odd since she could usually tell what kind of mood he was in. This time though, it was almost impossible to tell. Part of him looked extremely pissed off, and another part looked flirty and interested in her as usual. Strange. Maybe he was having a worse trek into the woods than she was.

"Need help?" he asked.

"I do. I think I have everything right so far, but I'm not sure I can erect it myself."

He smirked and raised an eyebrow at her suggestively. She felt her cheeks grow hot. "I'll grab these poles and you grab those two. Once we *erect* it, hold tight and I'll come slip the pole into the right spot."

She swallowed hard at the innuendo. Had he meant it to sound so dirty?

They counted to three then lifted the poles at the same time so they arced in the middle creating a dome. It wasn't anywhere near as large as her tent in base camp but it was only for a week so hopefully she could tough it out.

Chip came around to her side while she held the poles steady. He took one from her, brushing her hand with his as he did. The small touch sent a shockwave of tingles up her arm. Once the pole was secure, he squatted down next to her and took the remaining pole from her hands.

"That should do it," he said, turning to face her once the last pole was in place.

He was closer than she felt comfortable with at the moment. Not because she didn't enjoy being this close to him, but because she enjoyed it too much. The urge to reach out and touch him, or worse, kiss him, was overwhelming. His cologne drifting on the breeze infiltrated her senses once more, hindering her judgment.

"Thanks." She stood quickly so she wouldn't be tempted to give in to her impulses. "I think I can get everything else settled from here."

He stood slowly and if she wasn't mistaken, he took in every inch of her with his eyes as he did. By the time he reached her face, her cheeks were flushed with heat at his scrutiny. How could he make her feel this way with only a glance?

It was unnerving and wonderful at the same time. She didn't know how to deal with that mixture of emotions.

"If you need any more help…with anything, just ask me," Chip said, not moving away. "Can I ask you one thing before I go?"

"What's that?"

Chip shifted closer to her and cupped her jaw in his hand, his skin warming hers. For the first time she could remember since her accident, she didn't feel the urge to flinch away at the contact.

Instead, she found herself leaning in to his touch as his fingers gently caressed the side of her neck, right below her ear.

From where they stood, no one could see them. She hadn't realized until that moment how secluded her tent location was because of the trees, but she liked the thought of a little privacy in the crowded camp.

He stroked his thumb across her lips, inching closer to her.

"Did you kiss Rick on the trail this morning when you left his camp?" His jaw bulged as if he were gritting his teeth together as he waited for her answer.

"No," she whispered, barely able to get the word out with him still touching her, stealing her breath with his closeness.

He let out a long sigh. "Good. I'm glad it was silly gossip."

Oh no. She should have finished her thought faster.

She shook her head. "No, I didn't kiss him, but he did kiss me."

Chip's eyes narrowed, he dropped his hand to his side, and pulled his shoulders back. Funny how he could go from sensual and alluring to intense and hardened in a flash. "What does that mean?"

His words held an edge, but not anger toward her. She could tell he fought control over his emotions at her confession of what happened with Rick.

Thinking a little clearer now that Chip wasn't touching her anymore, she was able to fully articulate her thoughts and explain. "It means he put his mouth on mine, but I didn't ask him to, nor did I want him to. And I pushed him away."

"You're telling me he forced himself on you?"

"That sounds a little harsher than necessary. I'm saying he made an unrequested play for me and he was shot down. That's all. No big deal."

"It's a big deal to me and I'm going to make sure he knows it." Chip stormed off toward camp faster than she could say anything to stop him.

She thought about running after him and telling him to drop it, but she didn't want to cause a big scene in front of everyone—production people and contestants were already here and setting up. And honestly, there was a little part of her that was sort of turned on by the thought of Chip going to defend her honor and put Rick in his place. She'd grown tired of Rick's flirting, and now with the kiss, she didn't want to risk encouraging him further. Maybe a little threat from Chip would sort things out for her.

An image of Chip all puffed up on testosterone, his biceps bulging as he threatened Rick, fluttered through her mind like a scene right out of a romantic comedy. She bit her bottom lip to stop from smiling as she dragged her things into the privacy of her tent and zipped it closed. She flopped onto the ground on her back, peering up at the ceiling of her tent, and let the smile spread. Chip cared about her enough to be pissed off that Rick had kissed her. She could count the number of times a man had defended her over anything.

Zero.

But Chip was right now. And the knowledge of that made her feel more cherished than she ever had before.

• • •

Zoe stood in front of the contestants who all looked about as tired as she felt. It had been a long, grueling day and the sooner she was done with this last bit of filming, the sooner she could head to bed for the night.

What she really wanted was a shower, but that wasn't going to happen until they got back to base camp. She hoped the rest of the days they were here in the temporary camp didn't involve as much manual labor, or else there was no way she'd make it all that time without a shower. Not to mention, everyone else would be without showers too. Disgusting.

If only Chip had given them a little clue as to why they had to be in a new camp for a week in the first place. At least then maybe she'd understand. As it was, it felt like a move for no other reason than to annoy the contestants and force them into a situation that made them uncomfortable. It did the same to her.

The cue card person held up a new batch of cards and Chip gave her the hand signal to continue. She'd already welcomed them to the new camp and recapped week one quickly for the viewing audience who would watch the show when it aired in a couple of months.

"This week you'll all be living together in one camp. I know that sounds like fun after living with only four people in your camp for the last week. But be careful how much and with whom you socialize. Alliances can be formed, but so can rivalries. Choose how, where, and with whom you spend your time wisely."

Zoe held her breath. This would be a perfect time for one of Rick's comments about where he'd like to spend time with her. She glanced toward him nervously. His jaw was set, his arms crossed and he watched her with a deadpan expression instead of his usual flirty one. Maybe Chip really had laid down the law this time.

She glanced to where Chip stood in his usual spot along the sidelines of the filming area. He looked smug and satisfied with himself as he smirked at Rick.

Yep. Chip hadn't been bluffing with his promise to set Rick straight.

Zoe forced herself to focus on the cue cards again so she could finish. "We'll have two competitions again this week. One will be tomorrow for a reward. The next will be at the end of the week for elimination. At that point, one team will return home and the remaining three teams will make their way to new camps."

Zoe waited while the cue cards changed. "If there are no more questions, I'll leave you all to finish getting settled in here at your new camp. See you tomorrow for the next challenge."

She smiled and looked at the camera until she saw the red light flicker off. She stepped off her tree-trunk stage as Chip walked over and the contestants started to disperse.

"Can I have your attention, please?" Chip began. Everyone stopped. "I know it's a little unusual for the production people to stay so close to your team camp, but that's how things have to be done while we're here this week due to natural restrictions in this area. Now I know it's tempting, but there is to be no communication between production crews and the contestant teams other than what you're already used to with your cameramen. There will be two separate fire pits and common areas and I don't want to see *any* co-mingling of the two. Do I make myself clear?"

A handful of contestants grumbled responses as they formed back into their team groups and wandered off to finish setting up their tents. Zoe followed after Chip as he walked back toward the "crew" side of camp.

"You couldn't resist pointing out to Rick he wasn't allowed on my side of camp this week, could you?"

Chip gave her a sideways glance but kept walking. "Can you blame me? He made it perfectly clear when he kissed you earlier that he doesn't know where his boundaries are. I thought it best to remind him and everyone else."

"That's all it was then? A reminder about boundaries?" She couldn't stop the little twinge of sadness inside. Maybe Chip didn't care that Rick kissed her as much as he cared about whether or not people followed the rules of his production. It was always about the production and nothing more with him, wasn't it? "It wasn't...personal?"

He stopped for a moment and stared at her. "You know it was," he said so quietly she almost didn't hear him then he walked away.

She wanted to say something back about how she appreciated what he'd done, but it was too late. He was already talking to a few crewmembers who appeared to have questions about where to put things. And she didn't know what she'd say to him anyway. Truthfully, she didn't really understand how she felt about Chip or the things he'd been saying to her—the things he'd been doing to her...like making her head swim with a single kiss.

Chapter Thirteen

Zoe stared, disbelieving, as members of the four remaining teams made their way across rope bridges from one side of a waterfall to the other. What they walked on couldn't even be called a bridge. It was literally one large, corded rope for their feet and another for their hands above it. Together, all four team members had to make it across, grab supplies, and then carry them back the same way.

Terrifying.

That was the only word she could come up with for this reward challenge. Full on terrifying. Once again she wanted to hug Chip for sparing her this challenge by having her as host instead of contestant. She wasn't made for these kinds of tasks.

Of course she knew that if anyone fell from the ropes, they would just land in the pool at the base of the waterfall. And they all wore life vests so it wasn't as if they would drown, but still. The mere thought of being up there on a wiggling rope made her feel faint. The thought of landing in water was even worse.

She cheered for the teams as they made their way back across. Only the team who got back to their platform first and second would get to keep all the supplies they'd carried over. The other two teams would go back to camp with nothing.

As she watched the teams racing as fast as they could to the finish, movement on the furthest rope caught her attention. The rowing team was suddenly swaying and supplies were tumbling off their bodies into the water. A moment later, two of the boys from that team followed in quick succession, plunging into the water below. They came up sputtering and yelling at each other as they swam toward Zoe and the film crews.

"What the hell, dude?" Jared yelled at Alex as they pulled themselves onto the shore. "I can't believe this shit. Now we're screwed and we needed that extra food."

"It's not my fault," Alex retorted, sounding equally as angry. "You're the one who had to swap your supplies from one shoulder to the other. If you hadn't shaken the rope so much, I would have been fine to make it across."

"Whatever, dude. I didn't fall until you went overboard and bounced the rope."

Zoe turned her attention back to the game playing out above her as Alex and Jared continued to argue over whose fault the fall really was. She didn't care either way other than she wished Alex had stayed on his rope because that put him farther away from her.

"The first team to reach their platform is…" She held her breath and paused while the two fastest teams took their last few steps to the platforms. The team of dating couples managed to stumble into their win a few seconds in front of Rick's team. She was thrilled that Rick's team hadn't come in first, but she would have preferred if they hadn't won a reward. "Our team of dating couples wins!"

Chip leaned over and whispered the names of the winning team members. His breath was warm on her earlobe, sending a shiver down her spine. This was even better than using the earpiece as they'd done for the previous challenge. This time she could feel him, smell his cologne, and if she turned her head, she'd be close enough to kiss him. Luckily all cameras were pointed at the action and not at her reaction to Chip.

"Thank you," she whispered back, not giving in to the urge to turn her head. She took a few forced steps forward and waved for the teams to climb down and join her.

"Tammy, Matt, Jane, and Damon, you are our winners today! Congratulations. Let's see what loot you managed to bring across the rope bridge with you."

They took stock of their reward. Rope, tarp, some food, and a few cooking supplies would all go back to camp with them at the end of the week if they stayed in the competition past elimination. Regardless, they could still use the supplies for the remainder of this week at their new temporary camp.

"Well done. That's a great haul." She turned her attention to Rick's team. "Rick, Roger, Todd, and Pam you came in second place which means you also get to take your supplies back to camp. Congratulations."

"I'm sad to say the rowing team and our team of doctors will not be returning to camp with rewards this week. But maybe if you're lucky, the other teams will share their spoils with you while you're at the temporary camp."

"Not likely," Rick said with a snort.

Zoe wasn't surprised. He wasn't the kind of man who would share anything he didn't have to. She cringed. How had she been stupid enough to flirt with him?

"Alright, everyone. I'll see you back here at this same location in a few days for your next elimination challenge, but don't plan on walking the ropes again because this time it will be something completely different."

"Can I say something before we're finished?" Matt asked.

"Of course. What is it?" Zoe asked. Hopefully it wasn't a hard question to answer because there were no cue cards for this unscripted bit.

Matt turned to Tammy and took her hand. He fell to one knee, gazing up at her with admiration and love in his eyes. "Tammy, being out here with you during this crazy adventure has made me realize that you are even more amazing than I already thought you were. I can't imagine doing this kind of thing with anyone else by my side and I can't imagine anyone else I'd rather have by my side for the rest of my life. I know I probably shouldn't do this here, but I can't wait any longer. Will you marry me?"

"Yes," Tammy squealed through her excited tears, falling into his arms and kissing him as if there weren't cameras and people standing around staring at them.

Zoe's hand went to the necklace she wore that had been her grandmother's, rubbing the pendants between her fingers. They had always brought her comfort, reminding her how strong her grandmother had been, but today, biting back tears, it didn't seem to be working. But maybe there was no comfort big enough to fill the void that Matt's proposal to Tammy had just made in her heart.

Matt reached into his pocket. "It's not much and I'll buy you a proper ring when we get home, but for now, maybe you could wear this." He slipped a handmade ring onto her finger. It looked like a tiny black stone had been knotted into a piece of the twine they used to secure their tarps at camp. It wasn't pretty, but the sentiment made Zoe's vision cloudy.

She blinked away the wetness before it could become anything and wished Matt and Tammy well as they stood and rejoined their team with a round of hugs and congratulations from the other contestants.

"On that note," Zoe said, her voice wavering, "I think it's time to head back to camp. I'll see you all in a couple of days."

The light on the camera turned off and she knew her filming requirements were done for the day. Now it was the contestants' responsibility to get back to camp. She turned and tromped through the woods, not bothering with the trail since that would mean heading back with everyone else. The last thing she wanted was to make small talk. Or worse, to have to listen to how much in love Tammy and Matt were.

She swiped the tears trickling down her cheeks as she trod through the forest. It wasn't that she wasn't happy for Matt and Tammy; she just wanted what they had. And she knew deep down inside that she would never get it. She'd never let herself get close enough to someone to find that kind of all-consuming happiness, and even if she did, the person would surely head for the hills the moment they learned who she really was.

She wiped her nose with her sleeve since she didn't have a tissue. Gross, but in the wilderness, she had to make do with what she had.

And she had to face the facts about what she didn't have—what she would never have.

• • •

Chip casually watched Zoe where she sat, separated from the others near one of the fire pits. It had been three days since the reward challenge and each day she'd seemed to become more and more withdrawn from everything, including him. The cameramen were really the only ones working right now since the rest of the crew was waiting to film the reward challenge in another day. Most of the crew seemed to be enjoying their free time around camp, hanging out, chatting, playing cards, and doing a little drinking.

But not Zoe. She wandered around a few times a day and came out of her tent for meals, but other than that, she stayed in her tent. He'd stopped by a few times to see if she wanted to talk, but she always claimed to be tired and asked him to leave her alone.

She did look tired. Maybe roughing it in this new camp was too much for her.

But he couldn't help thinking it had something to do with the proposal that happened at the reward challenge. It seemed too coincidental that her mood changed immediately afterwards. Not that she hadn't been trying to put a little distance between them before too. However, when she had, he could tell it was because she was trying to stop herself from feeling what she felt for him. This time the distance felt different—almost as if she was shutting down and pushing him away completely, for good.

He couldn't let that happen. He knew how she really felt about him even if she didn't want to admit it to herself. The way she kissed him, melted into him, peered into his eyes like she was seeing his soul…There was no way those feelings weren't true. And no amount of her pushing him away was going to make him come to a different conclusion.

As the darkness deepened the crew began wandering away from the fire to go to bed. Chip watched as Zoe followed suit. Without so much as a goodnight to him or anyone else, she left the light of the fire pit and returned to her tent.

It made him so sad to see her this way when she was usually more the life of the party. In the other shows he'd produced, Zoe had always been out and mingling with the other contestants, having a good time, and enjoying the experience, but she seemed completely the opposite here.

Maybe giving her a job as the host had taken some of the fun out of the experience, but it also should have taken some of the stress away too since she didn't have to worry about winning this time. Or maybe it was his fault she was miserable. If he hadn't given in to his impulses and kissed her, then maybe she wouldn't feel so…whatever it was she felt right now.

Or maybe it was Rick's fault for kissing her too. He clenched his fists at the thought of Rick's mouth on Zoe's. He liked to believe this was all Rick's fault better than putting the blame on himself. He didn't want to be the source of Zoe's suffering.

As the last people dispersed for the night, Chip pulled himself to his feet and poked at the embers remaining in the fire pit to make sure none of them were in danger of sparking and lighting anything else on fire. Luckily, the embers were almost out and only smoldering in the very middle of the pit so he felt confident in leaving them to burn out on their own. He trekked off into the woods to relieve himself before turning in for the night as well.

On his return from the woods, he noticed Zoe creeping out of her tent. She paused at the opening, scanning the fire pit area and seeing no one, stepped from her tent, zipping it up behind her. She had something tucked under her arm, but it was too dark and far away to tell what.

"What's she up to?" he whispered.

Zoe disappeared around the back of her tent into the woods, away from the rest of camp. Wherever she was headed, it wasn't the safest place to go at night, alone. She didn't even have a lantern or flashlight with her.

"This isn't good," he muttered, following after her as quickly and as quietly as he could. He didn't want to be creepy and invade her privacy, but her walking off into the woods alone at night couldn't be ignored either. What if she came across a wild animal?

What if she came across Rick while in the dark, alone?

Chip couldn't risk that happening.

Ahead of him, Zoe cut through the trees, not bothering to use the trail. At this rate, she was almost more likely to break an ankle tripping over something in the dark than she was to get attacked by an animal or Rick, who may as well be an animal with how he'd been stalking Zoe this entire show.

Zoe took a right and Chip struggled to keep pace with her. He jumped over what appeared to be a low-lying branch then got a face full of leaves and twigs as he landed hard on his stomach. He'd been so busy worrying about Zoe falling and hurting herself that he hadn't paid enough attention to his own feet. A scratch down the side of his neck stung from a particularly nasty branch.

He struggled to his feet then ran as carefully as he could through the trees to catch up. As the trees thinned, he heard the rushing of water and knew instantly where Zoe had gone—the waterfall.

Chip peered around a tall tree and saw Zoe already in the water, her clothes piled at the water's edge along with a towel. Too bad he hadn't realized this was where she was heading or he could have swung back to his tent and grabbed a towel of his own.

He watched her for a moment, dunking her whole head in the water only to come up squealing from the cold. The waterfall looked beautiful and refreshing, but in truth the water was freezing. Not wanting to be creepy, he stepped out from the trees and announced himself.

"Whatcha doing in there, Zoe?" he called.

She screamed. Not exactly the welcome reaction he'd been hoping for.

"What the hell are you doing here? You scared the crap out of me," she yelled back. He noticed her fold her arms across her chest to cover herself. She apparently didn't realize that all her important parts were fully covered by water, it was dark, and he was a good twenty feet from her.

"I was making sure you didn't get attacked by bears."

"Bears!" she yelped, glancing around.

He laughed. "I'm kidding."

Even from a distance, he could make out her shoulders slumping forward. "Oh thank God. I thought you were serious."

"Nope. You're actually more likely to get attacked by a wolf out here than you are a bear. So no worries."

"Gee, thanks for the reassurance of my safety."

He couldn't keep the smile from his face. He loved hearing her get sarcastic with him. Maybe she was finally letting down her guard. "Your safety is my number one priority."

"Really? I thought making millions of dollars watching innocent people make asses of themselves on national television was your number one priority."

"Ouch."

She was feisty tonight. All that freezing water must be bringing out the bitch in Zoe. Sadly, he liked it. It fueled his fire to hear her stronger and more defiant after the last few days of her sulking around. Hearing her in a more normal Zoe mood made him want to be near her. "Cover your eyes, I'm coming in."

Freezing water or not, he wasn't going to waste this rare moment with Zoe alone, in a decent mood—and naked.

"Why are you coming in here?" she asked, not covering her eyes or turning around.

If she didn't want to cover her eyes, then she was about to get a show since the moon had just broken through the clouds, brightening the darkness. He pulled his shirt over his head and let it fall to the ground beside her clothes. He noted her mouth drop open at his now shirtless form. He grinned. Whatever she tried to tell him about not being interested in him was a lie. The expression on her face gave her away completely. She was far more than interested.

"Because it looks like you've brought shampoo and I could really use a bath. Being in the wilderness doesn't really mix with my usual lifestyle either, you know." He kicked his shoes to the side and peeled off his socks. His fingers paused at the waistband of his jeans. "Last chance to look away and hide your innocent eyes, Zoe."

He waited a moment but she didn't move.

"I was here first. You should go bathe somewhere else."

He ignored her and finished undressing. The cold hit him like an arctic breeze. He was suddenly happy that Zoe's watchful gaze had him at half-mast otherwise the shrinkage in the cold air would have been mildly embarrassing. As it was, he could stand proud of what he had to offer.

Chip quickly grabbed the bottle of shampoo waiting on the shore with her things and waded into the water. When it got waist high, he almost lost his nerve to continue. How the hell was she standing it? If Zoe hadn't been his reward for going in, he would have bolted back onto shore and into his clothes.

Instead, he tried to be tough and attempted to block out the cold. Nearing Zoe helped tremendously as seeing her naked skin glistening in the moonlight was enough to make him forget his own name never mind something as trivial as the cold.

Damn, she was so incredibly beautiful. He'd never seen anyone as captivating.

Chapter Fourteen

Thank God it's too dark for him to see my scars, Zoe thought, forcing the tension out of her shoulders as Chip waded in closer to her. The moonlight offered enough light to see shapes and…sizes—oh there'd been no denying his size—but the moon wasn't bright enough to define any intimate details like scars.

"Was that you I heard making all that noise behind me in the woods? I almost broke my ankle trying to keep ahead of you." Zoe couldn't keep the edge from her voice. It wasn't as if she was mad at Chip for finding her out here, but she sort of wished she wasn't naked at the moment. She sort of wished he wasn't either.

But damn. Chip was even better looking than she'd imagined with his clothes off.

Not that she'd been imagining him naked or anything. *Yeah, sure, right.*

"I was following you, but only because I was concerned about where you'd be going in the woods so late at night. I wanted to make sure you were safe."

"And now that you know I'm safe, you decided to get naked and share my waterfall?" she challenged.

"You noticed."

"Hard not to," she grumbled.

He smirked. "You're more observant than I thought."

Oh shit. Now what the hell could she say to talk her way out of this one? She hadn't meant hard as in *hard,* although his arousal had been obvious. Damn. He wasn't just good looking and muscular. He was…well-built, too.

"That's…that's not what I meant." Her voice came out weaker than she'd have liked it to, but she couldn't keep the embarrassment out of it. She couldn't show weakness around Chip. She couldn't. She had to flip this around so that he knew she was still in control. "Although now that you bring up your…nether regions, I did notice an unusual amount of grooming. I knew you were conscious of your looks, but I didn't realize you took it to such lengths."

He grinned and arched an eyebrow at her. "Noticing my length too. How interesting. I never realized you paid so much attention to your surroundings."

Zoe's cheeks burned despite the freezing water. Why couldn't she stop putting her foot in her mouth with him? "I just meant it seemed like an awful lot of manscaping."

"I don't get any complaints. You might be surprised how much you like a clean-shaven man."

"Oh, and why is that exactly?" she asked impulsively.

Shut up! Why are you still talking about his penis?

"Because the tree is even more impressive when the bushes are trimmed."

She gasped at his comment.

Chip dunked under the water.

Zoe rolled her eyes skyward, cursing under her breath. What the hell was she thinking asking him about that stuff? And why did the thought of finding out how impressive his "tree" was for herself make her feel so hot and bothered? Wasn't she trying to avoid contact with him? This situation and conversation seemed the exact opposite approach to helping her keep that goal.

He resurfaced and shook his head like a dog after a bath. She squealed as the cold water sprayed her. Squeezing a dollop of shampoo into his palm, he handed her the bottle, then lathered his hair.

She never once attempted to look away. The view was too good from where she stood.

Water trickled down his sculpted, smooth chest and off his biceps. She wondered if his skin was as smooth and silky as it appeared. Was he as smooth as he appeared elsewhere too? The question made her head fuzzy and pulse quicken.

He dunked beneath the water once again and came up with his hair rinsed clean. When his gaze met hers, he smiled.

"Your turn," he said, taking another dollop of shampoo from the bottle and handing it back to her. He moved behind her and his hands were in her hair, scrubbing and massaging while she stood there like a deer in headlights, unsure of what do to, or where to run to.

Her pulse raced through her veins at his touch. She'd never had someone wash her hair before. Hell, she'd never had a man wash anything on her body before. She'd never let anyone this close to her when she was naked and makeup-free who wasn't too drunk to remember what she looked like in the morning.

Chip's hands worked her scalp then trailed down her hair to the ends, scrubbing as he went. His fingers brushed against the back of her neck, right near her hairline, and she shivered, wondering if he felt the ripple of scar tissue marring her skin.

His soapy fingers rubbed the back of her neck then moved outward, stroking her shoulders in circles, easing out the tension she held in them like armor. Her head fell to the side when he hit a particularly sensitive spot and she groaned as the pain released with his touch.

Chip's breath was startlingly warm on her chilly earlobe, sending a shiver down her back. "You are so incredibly beautiful, Zoe, I wish I could see you in full light to take you all in."

She stiffened uncontrollably. That would be her worst nightmare. To have a man as gorgeous and perfectly sculpted as Chip see her in full light with all her imperfections exposed.

His lips brushed against her ear and she softened slightly, unable to hide the reaction his touch caused in her.

"Even in the near-dark of the moonlight, I can hardly resist you," he whispered. "Do you have any idea what you do to me?"

"No," she whispered back, not trusting the strength in her voice.

"Then let me show you." He spun her around so she faced him. His eyes were intense, penetrating into hers. "Rinse."

She obeyed, dunking her whole head under water until it felt clean. She popped back up, taking a deep breath of air, but the cold water and the fresh breath did nothing to clear the fog in her brain at seeing Chip still standing there, admitting his desire for her. She desired him too. More than she had desired for any other man she'd been with. But could she really give herself to Chip here, this way, when she was so figuratively and literally naked?

He pulled her against his body and cradled her face in both hands. "You drive me crazy in every single sense of the word and I can't take it anymore."

He pressed his lips to hers urgently, his need for her breaking through his usually calm and controlled demeanor. She opened her mouth against his with a lustful sigh, accepting his tongue and exploring with her own.

Her head swirled with his kisses. Fighting to hold onto reality, she pressed her hands against his bare chest, needing to feel something tangible. All those nights she'd woken from dreams of Chip, covered in sweat and shaking with a need she thought she'd never fulfill, came rushing back to her. She clung to him. Clung to the moment she might only ever get to live through once, because at least out here, right now, her scars were hidden by the darkness.

All the feelings she'd been trying to ignore crashed to the surface and she gave herself over to his kiss. She gave herself willingly to him.

His mouth left hers, trailing kisses along her jaw to her ear then down her neck. For the first time ever, she didn't stiffen at someone's touch. He couldn't see her scars even though all her makeup would have washed off by now. And he probably couldn't really feel them either with the other overwhelming sensations surrounding them.

Finally for once, she was free to give into the moment with Chip without reservation that he'd figure out her secret and bolt from her horrified at what he'd see. Because he couldn't really see her in the dark, he just thought he could. And the feeling of his lips on her skin was simply too good to stop him.

She didn't want him to stop. She needed this moment.

No. She just needed him.

"Zoe, I want you. I need you. Be with me tonight." It was a request she wasn't going to deny.

"Yes," she said simply, running her hands down his chest and wrapping them around his waist. She dropped her hands lower, feeling the swell of his desire for her. Gripping him, the water made him slick, his skin feeling like silk in her palm.

Chip groaned and rested his forehead against her shoulder for a moment, his breath coming out in heavy gasps. "I've imagined what it would feel like to have your hands on me, but real life is so much better. I've been trying so hard to resist you and now, here you are, stroking me. I think I might die."

"Then what are you waiting for?" She ran her hands back up his chest and wrapped them around his shoulders, forcing him to pick up his head and look at her again. His gaze was intense. Needy. She wouldn't pull away from him tonight.

He claimed her mouth again, his intensity almost overwhelming. Her knees went weak and she pressed against him, stabilizing herself. He snaked his hand between their bodies and caressed her breast. She arched her back, pushing her breast into his hand as his thumb flickered across the tight peak.

Chip pulled away from her, his gaze raking down her body leaving her shivering. His face scrunched up, looking annoyed. "I need to get you out of this water." Without awaiting her reply, he scooped her into his arms, his hands clasping her rear. She hooked her arms and legs around him and nibbled on his neck as he carried her out of the waterfall.

He kicked at her towel in an attempt to spread it out then grumbled and cursed and laid her down on her back. The ground was cool beneath her, but Chip's body heat instantly warmed her.

"Stupid towel," he mumbled, kissing a path from her throat to her breast. He sucked her beaded nipple into his mouth, swiping his tongue across it. His mouth felt as hot as fire against her chilled skin. Heat pooled low in her belly and she squirmed under him.

Next he found her center. He touched her in ways she couldn't remember being touched before. Every moment was a tantalizing mix of hot and cold sensations.

"Chip, please," she cried out when she thought she couldn't take anymore of his touch. She needed him. All of him. Every last incredible inch of him.

He rolled off of her and scrounged in his pants for something. After a moment and distinct, "Hell, yeah!" he was back, condom in hand. "I was worried I didn't have one. Thank God my ridiculous need to carry my wallet at all times has finally come in handy for once."

She smiled at his happiness even though she knew they could have done it safely without any protection. There was no risk of her getting pregnant at least, just another of her many imperfections, but she supposed there was always the risk for disease. So it was a good thing that Chip was smart and responsible and not thinking with his penis alone because apparently she couldn't say the same for her rational thought.

He rolled the condom on and positioned himself above her. Zoe moaned as he slid into her heat, his body still chilled from the water. The effect of the two temperatures was mind-blowing. She rocked her hips in time with his thrusts, her legs wrapping around his waist, anchoring him to her.

Chip kissed her again, but this time she didn't just feel lust and desire. She felt something else, deeper, stronger, more passionate. Zoe kissed him back, putting everything she had into this one perfect moment with him.

As she felt herself begin to crest, she clung to him, raking her fingers down his back. His muscles flexing and stretching beneath her fingertips took her over the edge. He was just so beautiful. So perfect.

Her body clenched around his as he called out his release then stilled. His breathing was as ragged as hers when he collapsed down onto the ground beside her. He pulled her into his arms, spooning her while they caught their breath. His came out in soft puffs against her shoulder and she closed her eyes, savoring the intimacy while sheltered by the dark.

She rolled over in his arms and stared at him. His eyes were closed and his chest still heaved, taking in breaths. God, this man was gorgeous. He had strong, chiseled cheekbones and jaw, soft lips, a straight nose, and the most perfectly arched brows. Of course, those were probably perfected in a salon rather than by nature, but she didn't care.

He was stunning. And when he touched her cheek and opened his eyes to peer at her, she saw so much goodness in his gaze. He didn't look at her like she was a beauty queen or a prize to win as some had, nor did he look at her as if she were a monster as she was also familiar with. He looked at her as if he saw the real her—the Zoe she felt like on the inside, even if that person didn't shine through on the outside.

She took in a shaky breath, overcome with the feeling that this was as good as it was ever going to get for her. No one had ever made her feel like this. She didn't feel as if she had simply satisfied a need like she usually did when she was intimate with someone. This was different.

And it was a little terrifying.

She'd never felt so vulnerable in a man's arms as she did with Chip. She'd never wanted to give herself so completely to someone as she wanted to give herself to him, right now. Every time she was with him, actually. If only she could.

But she knew better.

She couldn't stay here in this moment with him. She couldn't give herself to him fully because doing so would mean sharing everything about her life with him. She couldn't do that. She'd worked too hard to make her life as perfect as it could be and telling Chip her history would ruin everything.

No one but her family knew the truth and she had to keep it that way or everything she'd worked for—everything she'd suffered for—would be for nothing.

If she told him the truth, she'd lose him.

Zoe propped herself on one elbow and ran her fingers across Chip's jaw. His skin was scratchy from needing a shave, but she liked the rough feel of it. It was a good reminder that not everything would go as smoothly for them as she wanted it to. She still had a rough side that he'd never understand.

Zoe pressed her lips to his and he opened his mouth, responding to her. She put everything she had into that kiss. Every emotion she wanted to share with him…every ounce of wishing and wanting. When she finally got to the longing of wanting to be with him forever and knowing she never would, she forced herself to pull away. He smiled at her with a twinkle of desire stirring in his eyes that told her he was ready and willing to go again.

She bit back tears, knowing being with him again would destroy her.

"I have to go," she whispered. She slipped into her clothes faster than she thought possible and bolted for the cover of the forest, leaving Chip behind, calling after her.

Chapter Fifteen

Chip trudged back to camp as quickly as he could, but Zoe was faster. By the time he reached her tent, it was dark and quiet. He worried for a moment that maybe she hadn't actually found her way back to camp in the dark. Fear rose in his throat at the thought of her out there, alone.

A sniffle and a tiny crinkle of tissue came from inside her tent. Chip let out the breath he'd been holding, sagging with relief. Whatever had happened at the waterfall to make her flee didn't matter, as long as she was safe now.

"Zoe, I know you're in there and I'm coming in," he said loudly enough for her to hear him, but hopefully not so loud the other nearby tents could eavesdrop.

"Don't," she said as he slid through the tent opening and zipped it up behind him again. "Or completely ignore me."

"Yes, I choose that option." Chip sat on the ground beside her makeshift bed and pulled her blanket down to her chin. "What happened back there?"

"I don't want to talk about it."

"Too bad. You can't sleep with me, which was fucking amazing, I'll add, and then disappear like something bad happened."

She wiped at her eyes with the tissue again. The light was too dark in the tent to see how upset she was, but the sniffling was pretty obvious. Had she been crying since leaving the waterfall?

"I just can't be with you again, Chip. It'll never work out between us. I shouldn't have been with you tonight, although you're right, it was amazing." She took a shaky breath. "But that makes this even harder."

"You're not making any sense, Zoe. You want to be with me or you don't want to be with me, which is it?"

"I *can't* be with you," she whispered.

He leaned forward, hovering over her, desperate to understand. What he wouldn't give to go back a half an hour ago to when he was in a similar position with her but when everything still made sense.

"Did I do something to hurt you?" he asked. His chest burned with the possibility. He'd never forgive himself if he had.

"No," she said, her voice stronger. "It's just…me. I'm not meant to be with you. And contrary to what the tabloids would have people believe, I'm not into flings. I shouldn't have been with you tonight knowing I couldn't be with you ever again."

"I think I should get some say in who I'm with and I want to be with you. I've wanted you since…longer than I care to admit. Whatever's going on, we'll work it out. Talk to me."

"I can't. You won't understand. You think you want me and that you know who I am, but you don't. You don't know anything about me and…and I want to keep it that way. I can't be the kind of girl you usually date. I can't be some trophy girlfriend. Please just leave."

He shook his head. "Trophy girlfriend? What the hell are you talking about?"

"I've seen pictures of the girls you usually date in those tabloid magazines and I know you think I'm like them but I'm not. I'm not at all who you think I am."

He laughed, annoyed. "You keep telling me I don't know who you really are, but you're wrong. I probably know a hell of a lot more than you think. I research my contestants. And I didn't see anything in your file that made me not want to be with you. But this attitude you're throwing at me about trophy girlfriends is just about insulting enough to make me walk away right now. I do care more about the women I date than if they look pretty on my arm. Give me a little credit."

"I'm never going to be the woman on your arm, so let's end this now. I'm sorry if I led you on, but I don't want to be with you again, now or ever. Please go."

Zoe rolled onto her side, facing away from him. He knew he wasn't going to get anywhere talking to her tonight but it still took a few minutes to pull himself up from the ground and out of her tent.

She didn't make sense.

She wasn't telling him something. All that stuff about a trophy girlfriend was weird and out of left field. Did she really think that's what he wanted? Did she really think she didn't classify as a trophy girlfriend if that is what he'd been looking for? She was beautiful, well-spoken, and smart. Any man would feel like he'd won a prize to have her on his arm.

No way was he going to let her be with anyone else but him. Not after tonight. Zoe was the only woman he wanted to be with. Now he needed to figure out a way to make her realize she felt the same way.

• • •

Zoe stood on the edge of the pool beneath the waterfall, facing the contestants who'd lined up in their teams in front of her. It was time for the elimination challenge to start and she was about to read her cue cards, but the only thing she could focus on was that everyone stood where she and Chip had fooled around together. If she looked carefully, which she hadn't been able to resist doing, she could almost make out butt prints still formed in the mud. Thank God the contestants were now marking the area with their footprints so she wouldn't have the constant reminder of her time with Chip much longer.

Her gaze travelled to Chip. The expression on his face said he was reliving their night together too. The thought sent an unwelcome shot of heat through her body. Being with Chip had been more than amazing. It had been everything she'd never thought she'd get the chance to have.

After Chip confronted her in her tent, she'd lain awake in bed thinking. Maybe Chip had been telling her the truth about not caring about having a trophy girlfriend on his arm. She'd been so convinced someone as perfect and gorgeous as Chip wouldn't want to be with anyone less. And while she tried her best to look as perfect as possible on the outside, there was no amount of makeup that could cover everything.

But maybe Chip really wouldn't care that she was flawed. Maybe the tabloids had portrayed him in a way that wasn't a hundred percent true like they had her. If that were the case, maybe they could have some kind of relationship. Possibly, she'd overacted in the moment and panicked when she'd felt so close and comfortable with Chip after being intimate with him.

Of course, she still couldn't tell him everything. But it was possible she could give him the quick version to explain the scars.

He met her gaze and the corner of his mouth pulled up into a tiny lopsided smile.

She rubbed the pendants on her necklace in her fingers, the smooth sensation calming her instantly. Maybe she didn't have to worry about the past so much. Could she focus on the future for a change and forget about everything else?

Chip signaled that it was time to get started. Zoe turned her attention to the cue cards and started reading. "Welcome back to *Wild Expedition*, the show that puts your survival to the test. Today I'm afraid another team will leave us and return home. Let's find out what your challenge is."

The cards flipped and she continued reading. "Behind me is the beautiful waterfall and pool where we had our reward challenge earlier this week. Today you'll be facing it again, only this time you won't be high in the air. Instead, you'll be diving deep to retrieve bags of puzzle pieces from the bottom. Each team member will be required to grab a bag of puzzle pieces, so I hope you all know how to swim."

Zoe paused for a moment, glancing around at the contestants, while she swallowed her own fear. If she'd been competing today, she'd have had to forfeit the challenge. No way could she dive into the lake on camera. Most looked nervous but excited and ready to take on the new challenge. Rick looked pissed off and on the verge of getting sick.

"Each team member will dive and retrieve a bag of puzzle pieces before the next can go. Once all bags have been collected, teams can dump out their pieces and solve the puzzle. The last team to correctly solve their puzzle will be eliminated from the game. Are you ready to get started?"

The teams cheered and stripped down to their swimsuits then lined up on the water's edge in team clusters. At Zoe's signal, the first members of each team ran into the water and dived beneath the surface. A few seconds later, heads popped up to take a breath before diving back down again. Moments later, the rowing team member swam back to shore with his first bag and the next in his team ran into the water.

Zoe eyed Alex, the third of the rowing team members who would dive for a bag. A huge smile played on this face, the biggest she'd seen this whole game.

Rick's team was the second back with their first bag thanks to Todd. Pam was next in line to go for their teams so she tagged Todd's hand and sprinted into the water. Rick still wore an expression of discomfort.

The team of doctors made quick work of the bags, retrieving the first two quickly to tie up with the rowing team while the team of dating—and newly engaged—couples struggled in last place. They barely made it back to shore with their first bag when the rowing team had brought back their third.

The pace of the challenge was furious as all teams tried to dive and swim as quickly as they could. The rowing team made it to shore with their last bag as Rick was heading out for his team's final bag. She heard him grumble something to himself as he ran into the water, but couldn't make out what he'd said with all the other commotion around.

Zoe moved so she could watch the rowing team as they attempted to untie the ropes knotted around their bags. She secretly hoped they'd struggle enough that the other teams could catch up. The sooner Alex was gone, the sooner she could relax a little more. But even as she wished for their failure, they succeeded in dumping out the contents of their bags.

Rick yelled a profanity from the water where he bobbed on the surface, coughing and smacking the water. He was definitely annoyed about this challenge. Apparently there was something Rick wasn't so good at surviving—water.

Zoe laughed at seeing Rick so annoyed. She hadn't seen him be anything but completely cool this whole time. Finally they got to see Rick was human like the rest of the contestants and not some super outdoorsman.

She glanced to the side at the sound of a chuckle. Chip watched Rick flounder in the water with a huge grin on his face as if he thoroughly enjoyed watching Rick struggle. Against her better judgment, she wandered closer to Chip.

"You could try to hide your amusement," she whispered, covering her mic with her hand so hopefully their conversation wouldn't get picked up.

"I could." He smiled. "But I'm not going to."

"Why are you enjoying it so much?"

His gaze met hers, as intense as it had been in her tent. "Because I don't want him hitting on you anymore. You're mine, not his."

She sucked in a breath. She'd never been claimed in such a testosterone filled way before. It simultaneously annoyed and aroused her. "I'm not yours. I'm not anybody's."

"You might think I don't know the truth about you, but I do. I know the truth of how you feel about me, and with Rick gone, it'll be much easier for you to admit your feelings to yourself. So yes, I'm happy Rick sucks in the water."

Zoe wandered back over to the teams, three of whom were now putting their puzzles together. Rick's team stayed at the shore, cheering him on as he finally swam back with their last bag. The rowing team had lost their sizable lead while she'd chatted with Chip. Now the doctors were in the lead, making quick progress with their puzzle.

Rick's team untied their bags quicker than the other teams. Not really surprising since knot tying was one of Rick's survival skills. It stood to reason he'd also know how to untie them. They dumped the pieces on the ground and began putting their puzzle together at an alarming rate. Apparently Pam and Todd were really good at puzzles.

The smile fell from Chip's face as Rick's team quickly closed the gap on the dating and engaged team then passed the rowing team too. Unless something drastic happened to screw up their puzzle at this point, they were no longer in danger of losing.

Zoe heard the unmistakable sound of Chip cursing under his breath. She wouldn't mind if Rick went home, but right now she was more interested in Alex. The more his team sucked at puzzles, the better it was for her.

Team doctors threw their hands in the air and cheered. She ran over to inspect their puzzle. Chip had told her in advance the puzzle would spell out, "Reach deep and you survive."

"Congratulations! Team doctors are our winners. Your team is safe for another week."

Zoe turned her attention away from the celebration to the remaining teams. Rick's team high-fived as they put their final piece into the puzzle, securing their place in the game for another week. She congratulated them quickly then moved on to watch the rowing team and the dating team struggle with the last few pieces of their puzzle.

Zoe said a little prayer the rowing team would somehow screw up right at the end and open the door for the dating team. But her prayer was a little too late as the rowing team snapped their last piece into place, sending the dating and engaged team home.

When the cheering subsided from the rowing team, she joined the two couples, who looked less upset than she expected. "I'm sorry to tell you your team was the last to finish the puzzle, and because of that, your team has been eliminated from the game. I'm afraid you're all heading home today."

They nodded. "That's okay. I think we were all ready to leave," said Tammy. She spun her rope engagement ring around her finger. "We got so much out of this experience. It was really hard and challenging every step of the way, but also a lot of fun. Although after two weeks in the woods, I'm ready to get back to civilization and hot showers."

Everyone laughed. Zoe knew exactly what she meant and suddenly a little spike of jealousy ran through her at the thought of them getting hot water and warm, soft beds. "I think we can all relate to that feeling."

"I know I should be sad we're eliminated and we won't get a chance to win the money anymore," Matt said. "But I can't help feeling like I won regardless. I'm not walking away with the money in my pocket. Instead I'm leaving with the most amazing fiancée I could ever have dreamed of. I'm still a little in shock she said yes."

Tammy playfully smacked him on the shoulder. "I'm still surprised he asked me when I smell this bad!"

Everyone laughed again.

Zoe turned back to the main camera once the laughter had quieted down. "Alright, safe travels home and to the rest of you, go back and pack up your camp because you're moving again. In your tents, you'll find instructions on how to find your new campsite location. So you better hurry because night is coming whether or not you're ready."

The teams headed back toward camp, no doubt all eager to get their things packed and rebuilt at a new campsite before the sunset for the day. She didn't envy the job ahead of them at all. Then a thought struck her. If the teams were leaving their temporary camp, that probably meant production was too.

She groaned and rolled her eyes. Great. Just what she wanted to spend the rest of her day doing, packing up her stuff to take it back to base camp. At least once she got back, there would be a few more luxuries like the camping toilets and showers and an actual tent to eat dinner in tonight. Maybe it wasn't all terrible having to head back.

As her tent came into sight through the trees, Alex stepped in front of her. She startled and staggered backwards a few steps. "Damn, Alex. You scared the crap out of me." She laughed, trying to settle her nerves. "What can I help you with?"

It wasn't uncommon for contestants to ask her questions about what they should or shouldn't be doing. Once in a while, she even knew what to tell them. Hopefully Alex's question would be an easy one.

"I'm tired of always coming in last." He crossed his arms. "So from now on, you're going to give me the inside scoop about the upcoming challenges so I can prep my team."

He couldn't be serious.

"Um, okay. Well that would involve me knowing what the challenges were in advance, which I don't." Alex was going to have to suck it up and deal with the surprise of the challenges like everyone else had to.

"Don't lie to me, *Zoe*."

Something about the emphasis he put on her name specifically sent a chill down her back. "I'm not lying. Chip doesn't tell me about the challenges before they happen. That's why I read everything off those giant cue cards. You must have noticed."

"Well then I guess it's a good thing that you've been getting so close with Chip. Don't think I haven't noticed the looks and quiet conversations while we're filming."

"You don't know what you're talking about. Chip and I talk all the time because we're crew. That's what a production crew does, they work together."

Alex cocked an eyebrow at her. "Does the crew always sneak off to the waterfall together late at night too?"

Zoe narrowed her eyes at him. "So what? We're crewmembers and we can hang out late at night whenever and wherever we want. It's the contestants, like you, who have to keep to themselves, which is why you shouldn't try to force me into telling you something I don't know."

"I don't care what you're doing with Chip as long as it results in finding out the information I need to know to win the challenges. So go get on your knees, or whatever else you have to do, and get me the information before the next challenge."

Zoe's pulse pounded in her throat. How dare he speak to her that way and insinuate she was nothing more than some cheap sex toy. "Listen, you little shit. I don't know who you think you are threatening me this way, but I'm Zoe Oliver and no one threatens me. Now get the hell out of my face before I have you removed from the game for harassment. Don't think Chip won't do *that* for me."

A smile slowly spread across Alex's lips. The urge to smack it off his face almost overwhelmed her. "I knew you wouldn't do me this favor without the right motivation. Now I'm asking you one last time. Do whatever you have to, to get me the challenge information because if you don't, I'm going to tell everyone who you really are."

She sucked in a breath, the heat of anger draining from her face, replaced by cold fear. "I don't know what you're talking about." Even she didn't believe her pathetic attempt to convince him whatever he thought he knew about her was wrong.

"Don't waste your breath. I remember everything, Zoe. Or should I call you Andrea?"

Chapter Sixteen

Zoe staggered into her tent at base camp and dropped her bags on the ground. She zipped the tent closed then laid down on the bed and folded her legs up to her chest. The sobs came quick and hard. She struggled to stay quiet for fear of Chip hearing her and having to explain her tears.

This, she certainly couldn't tell him about.

Maybe she could talk about the car accident she'd survived. Maybe she could even relive the surgeries she'd undergone to fix her injuries...to change her face so she didn't look like a monster anymore. But she couldn't tell him about the rest. She couldn't tell him about her life as Andrea.

Just the thought of her old name made her cringe. How had Alex figured it out? No one from her life then had any idea she was Zoe now. There should have been no way for Alex to figure it out. But that didn't matter now. Because he had figured it out and she was screwed.

She'd agreed to Alex's demands, because she didn't have any other choice, then she'd stumbled back to her temporary tent in a fog and somehow had managed to pack up everything. Her return trip to base camp was a blur, not remembering a single step she'd taken to get back here. All she could remember was repeating, "He knows. He knows," over and over again in her head.

The debilitating guilt she'd attempted to suppress all these years suddenly crashed through to the surface. The pain, both physical and emotional washed over her in a wave, threatening to suffocate her. She'd clawed her way out of this place once before, but she feared she wasn't strong enough to do it again.

The same words chanted in her brain now. *He knows. He knows.* She trembled until the darkness overtook her and she drifted off into a troubled sleep.

When she woke the next morning, she felt like she'd drank two bottles of champagne. Her head thumped as if a steel drum band had taken up residence in it overnight. Dragging herself from her cot, she peered into her tiny mirror and cringed at the mess her makeup and tears had made on her face through the night.

She may not have slept well, but at least she'd come to a decision. Her nightmares of being chased by monsters had returned after all these years but she wasn't going to let them catch her. Nope. She'd do whatever she had to, to put all of this behind her.

Even if that meant getting closer to Chip, and risking the chance her feelings for him would grow stronger in the process, so she could get the information she needed for Alex. The risk of a broken heart was far less painful than the world finding out her story.

• • •

Chip glanced up from his bowl of instant oatmeal, surprised to find Zoe sitting across the table from him. Since their night at the waterfall, she'd been anything but friendly to him. Now here she was, looking better than she had in days and smiling at him like crazy.

Odd.

"What's up?" she said before taking a bite of an apple.

"Nothing. Breakfast."

He knew he should be upset with her for how she'd pushed him away the last few days, but he couldn't bring himself to be rude to her. He liked her company and he was happy she'd chosen to sit with him and talk to him this morning. Damn it, he liked being with her even if she didn't feel the same. But he knew she did. She only had to admit it to herself before she could admit it to him. Maybe she was starting to realize her feelings for him now they'd had a couple of days to cool off.

"What's up with you?" he asked.

She swept her hair off her shoulders and settled back into the chair looking completely at ease, unlike the frazzled mess she'd appeared to be for the last couple of days. Maybe it was that being back at base camp agreed with her more than being out in the temporary camp.

She'd obviously cleaned up in the shower and slept well. She looked refreshed, almost back to how she'd looked on their first day here.

"Not much. Happy to be back in civilization." She laughed. "Is it weird this is civilization to me after that last camp when I originally thought this place was super backwoods?"

Chip smiled, unable to resist the effects of her happiness wearing off onto him. He loved seeing her like this—relaxed, confident, comfortable. It was awesome. He had to find a way to make sure she stayed this way from now on.

Whatever the reason for her change in mood, he planned to ride it out as long as possible and enjoy it to the fullest. This was the Zoe he'd been searching for.

"It's a little strange, but I know what you mean. That last camp was way too remote. I'm happy to be back with cots and showers, even if they are outside and chilly. At least they're warmer than the waterfall."

The words were out of his mouth before he could stop them. He wanted to relive that night with her more than anything, except for the part where she left him with no explanation. The last thing he wanted to do was bring it up now when they'd only started talking again.

But instead of getting upset like he feared she would, she smiled and carried on as if nothing but a regular old bath had happened in the falls. "I know. I took a lukewarm shower this morning and it felt like heaven compared to the cold waterfall."

The thought of Zoe naked in the shower flashed through his mind, making his pants tight. If only he could be with her again. Hell, at this point he'd take another dinner date in his tent where he could spend a few moments alone with her talking.

"So, at the elimination challenge the contestants got a new map in their tents, right? Where are they off to this time?" she asked, taking the last bite of her apple then wrapping the core in a napkin.

"Oh, I stuck them in a new location so they would be forced to rebuild again and this time they'll have to do it without production crews around to help."

"You're a little bit evil, aren't you? You love to torture your contestants."

"Hey now. I always try to play nice, but I also have viewers and ratings to worry about."

"You don't always play nice. That finale for *The One* with me and Cassidy was anything but nice." Zoe eyed him accusingly yet playfully.

He rubbed his hand across his forehead. How many times had he regretted that moment of television history? At the time, he'd wanted to hurt Cassidy and Evan for ruining his show, but in the end, they were really what made it such a huge success. "I wish I would have handled the finale a little differently. I really didn't mean to throw you and Cassidy into the spotlight like that. But it was good for ratings."

"It was. And we both survived. Although I did hate you a little for a while after that." She bit her lower lip.

"Really?" he asked. He wasn't surprised in the least. He'd be pissed if someone had put him in front of a live studio audience then caused a big dramatic spectacle. "I'm sorry you were involved."

She shrugged. "It's okay now. Cassidy and Evan were meant to be together and I was definitely not meant to end up with bachelor Brad. So maybe I should thank you for sparing me the humiliation of actually dating him after the show."

"So you don't still hate me?" He held his breath waiting for her answer.

She peered up at him through heavy lashes. "I think you know I don't."

Relief washed over him.

"So what's the new contestant camp like? Is it full of tarantulas? Do I have to tromp through a swamp to get there? Do I need to fill out my will before the next set of challenges?"

He laughed. "No. You're relatively safe for the next week or so."

Zoe cleared her throat. "What are the next couple of challenges exactly? Just so I'm prepared." She cleared her throat again.

Hopefully she wasn't getting sick. She looked fine. Actually she looked better than fine. But he still worried about her health and the health of the rest of his crew. They had limited medical supplies out here with them, mostly first aid necessities and not a lot of medications that would help with a bad cold or flu. A contagious anything could completely knock production off schedule.

"You okay? You sound like you're getting a cold?" he asked. "Can I get you a tea with honey for your throat or anything else?"

"I'm fine," she answered quickly. "Allergies. I need to drink more water to wash the, um, allergens out." She gulped some water from her bottle. "So you were saying something about the upcoming challenges?"

Why was she acting weird all of a sudden? She'd never cared this much about the challenges in the first two weeks.

"Why are you so interested? Are you worried about something?" It wasn't as if they were a big secret or anything. But he did try to be careful with who he told because some people, while well meaning, had a habit of accidentally letting information slip. He didn't care if production people knew what was happening, but he couldn't risk the contestants finding out about challenges in advance. That would put them at an advantage over the others, and it would take some of the great reactions to the challenge reveals out of the usable footage. And he definitely didn't want to ever be accused of rigging the show.

She looked down at her hands and fiddled with the label on her water bottle. When she glanced up at him again, she appeared a little sad.

"I don't like being in the dark about everything all the time. It makes me feel stupid and as surprised as the contestants. I always thought that the other host knew about the challenges ahead of time. I guess I wish I was privy to the information too."

He considered what she said. It made sense and he felt bad for keeping her in the dark. "I'm making the final notes on this week's challenge schedule later today. Why don't you stop by my tent tomorrow and I'll fill you in on what's coming up?"

"Sounds good. What time?"

He smiled. "How about seven? That should give me more than enough time to solidify things and take care of all the regular business around camp. Maybe we can even have dinner together again. What do you say?"

"I'll be there, but this time dinner is on me." She stood from the table and squeezed his shoulder as she walked past.

Chip glanced over his shoulder, admiring the view as she walked out of the kitchen tent. Seemed like things were back on track with Zoe and tomorrow night couldn't get here soon enough.

• • •

Zoe heard a scratching at her tent flap. It might have taken two weeks, but the noise no longer startled her. Now she knew it was a production person popping by to say hello or to ask her a question. And with no real door on a tent to knock on, scratching the thin material was the next best thing.

"Coming," she said, not even needing to raise her voice to be heard. She quickly checked her makeup and unzipped the flap. "Hey—"

Her voice caught in her throat as a hand clamped across her mouth and a body pushed its way into her tent, forcing her backward. Alex glared at her. Fear and guilt swelled inside of her as she stared into the face of her past.

"I'm going to take my hand away from your mouth and you're going to stay quiet. I'm only here to talk, not to hurt you. I didn't want you to give me away when you found me on your doorstep. We good?"

She nodded.

He dropped his hand and she quickly stepped away from him. She couldn't go far in the little tent, but anywhere was better than right beside him. He turned and peeked out of the tent flap in both directions then zipped it up, enclosing them. She suddenly felt claustrophobic.

Alex faced her. "It's been days since we talked and you still haven't told me what the challenges are, Andrea. I need to know. I can't go home looking like a fool from this stupid show and that's exactly how I look after my team's crap performance in the first two weeks. So you're supposed to be helping me. And I really thought after our little chat in the woods that you'd see things my way, yet you haven't come to visit with me. Why is that, Andrea?"

"Stop calling me that. It's not my name." She forced her shoulders back. He might have the upper hand in this situation, but she'd never cowered away from anything as Zoe Oliver and she wasn't about to start now. Andrea might have been weak, but Zoe was strong. She just had to keep reminding herself of that every time Alex was around.

"But it used to be your name, didn't it? Andrea Miles. I was in the same grade as your brother Jack. How is he anyway? I watched him on that show last summer. What was it called? Treasure something."

"*Treasure Trekkers*," she said. How no one had ever investigated her real relation to Jack Miles after that show, she'd never really understood. But then she hadn't minded either. Come to think of it, the cameras hadn't been around much whenever their relationship had been brought up so the information hadn't actually made it onto the show in any way other than a passing casual comment. She'd been lucky.

"You were on it too, only I didn't recognize you. You're a sneaky one, aren't you? Changing everything about you. Becoming a new person."

"I prefer to think of myself as resourceful."

He laughed. "That's a good one. So how resourceful will you be when I share your little secret with the national viewing audience at the next challenge?"

"You won't have to. I'm working on getting you the information."

"You are, huh? And when do you plan on telling me because I'm kind of running out of time?"

"I'm having dinner with Chip tomorrow and he's supposed to tell me what this week's challenges are."

"Oh, a date. How nice for you. Meanwhile, I'll be eating rice and beans again with a bunch of guys who smell like gorillas."

"I hate to break it to you, but you're not smelling so great anymore either."

He stepped toward her and she instinctively stepped back. "I'd watch my mouth if I were you. You really don't want to piss me off, *Andrea*." He raised his voice when he said her real name.

Fear spiked through her. The tent walls were so thin. She whisper yelled at him. "Shut up. Stop calling me that. I told you I'd get the information and I will, but it takes time."

"I'm sure it takes more than time, doesn't it? Are you on his menu for dinner too?"

"Chip's tent is seriously ten feet away, so unless you want to get kicked out of the game when I scream and they find you in my tent, then you should keep your thoughts about Chip's and my relationship to yourself and get the hell out of here."

"Go ahead. I'll just sell my story to the tabloids then."

She grit her teeth together. "Listen, I'll give you as much information as I can, but you have to promise me you won't go blab about me to anyone, here or after the game. Otherwise there's no point in me playing along with this little blackmail game of yours."

Zoe held her breath, fearing what he might decide to do.

"If you make it so my team wins, then deal."

"That's not fair. I can't control how well your team performs even if I tell you exactly what each challenge is."

"That's the deal. Take it or leave it."

The chances of this deal actually working out in her favor were slim, but she didn't see any other choice. This was her best option to keep the information about her past safe.

"Deal," she said, her shoulders slouching in defeat.

"Good. Meet me tomorrow night in the clearing where we had the first challenge. I'll be there until midnight, so you better take care of your boyfriend's needs quickly. After midnight, I'm gone and the world finds out your story."

Alex peeked out of the tent and bolted toward the woods without giving her a chance to negotiate the terms, not like it would help her any. This was a risky deal no matter how she looked at it.

Sinking to the ground, she put her head in her hands. Now all she could do was pray this deal turned out the way it was supposed to. She wasn't going to hold her breath.

Chapter Seventeen

Zoe stood outside Chip's tent with her arms full of plastic containers and took a deep, steadying breath. This was it. She had to get the information Alex demanded or it was over for her.

And somehow she had to manage it without ending up in Chip's arms.

Or worse, his bed.

"Knock, knock," she called out, hoping she sounded friendly and warm and not so nervous she could throw up from anxiety.

Chip opened up and stepped to the side, allowing her room to pass by. "That seems like a lot of food for the two of us. Can I take something for you?"

"I'll set it down here." Just like last time, Chip had arranged a blanket on the floor in the middle of his tent for their picnic. She set the food into the middle of the blanket then opened the containers.

Chip sat opposite her. "This looks delicious."

"It's just sandwiches and salad, nothing fancy like the pasta you made. But I did warn you in advance I can't cook."

"You did. I think I'll survive this. I'm pretty sure you're not as bad a cook as you fear."

She glanced up to find him smiling, that now familiar hint of something more twinkling in his eyes. She instantly flashed back to their night by the waterfall and her pulse quickened. She forced a deep breath into her lungs. She couldn't go back to that moment again. She needed to say focused on the task at hand, which was finding out about the challenges.

Besides, being with Chip again would just lead to one of them being hurt and she didn't want that for either of them. As much as she didn't want to, she cared for Chip and she didn't want to be the source of pain in his world. There would be far less pain if she stayed away from him now. For good.

"Let's hope we both survive. There wasn't much in the kitchen tent for me to swipe for dinner. Well, that's not true. There actually was lots of food but most of it I didn't think I could cook. So we ended up with avocado chicken salad sandwiches and citrus salad with herb and lime dressing."

Chip chuckled and her nervousness rose.

"What's so funny? I know it doesn't look like much but I did the best I could."

She put a sandwich on his plate. As she reached for her own sandwich, he grabbed her hand. Startled, she peeked up at him through her lashes.

"I'm not laughing because you're funny. I'm laughing because I'm constantly amazed by you. I don't understand how you can continually doubt yourself when you're incredible in so many ways."

"I'm not incredible." She tried to pull her hand back but he held on tight. His touch made her feel more things for him than she wanted to—deeper things.

"You are and I wish you could see yourself the way I see you." He squeezed her hand then let it go. She pulled it to her chest protectively. "One day maybe I'll find a way to make you realize that you're awesome exactly how you are. For now, you should work on taking a compliment. I never realized it was a problem for you to accept one."

It wasn't a problem until you started being the one to offer them. She didn't understand how he could believe those things about her. How could a guy like Chip think a girl like Zoe was awesome? It didn't make sense.

"I'll work on it, but if you knew the real me and not the person you see on your shows or in the tabloids, I guarantee you wouldn't think or feel the same way about me." She dished out the citrus salad.

Chip groaned after his first bite. The noise was distinctly similar to the sounds of satisfaction he'd made for another reason at the waterfall. "Holy shit, Zoe. This is amazing."

"Wow. That's some colorful language over a little chicken salad." She laughed, happiness filling her with the thought that Chip enjoyed her meal that much. She liked his sounds of satisfaction more than she should.

"It's so good. I could eat this every day. Seriously. I think you may have to amend your thoughts on only being able to make desserts because you can definitely make a mean chicken salad too."

"Thank you," she said, trying to take the compliment and not dispute it. Chip grinned at her.

"Better," he said. "So there's something I've been meaning to ask you."

Her palms instantly grew clammy. Nothing good ever came from that conversation opener. What could he possibly want to know?

"Oh?"

"I've heard you singing in your tent as I walk by sometimes. Other times I hear you humming in the shower. I know in your original screen test for *The One* you said you wanted to be a singer but since then I haven't seen anything about you pursuing it anymore. Why haven't you done anything with it? I'm sure you could use the fifteen minutes of fame you've had with the shows to your benefit."

She swallowed her bite of food and took a few sips of water while she decided how to answer the question. Honestly or with her typical "things are coming along" answer? When she looked at him, she didn't see any hint of malice. He seemed genuinely curious. Chip deserved her honest answer whenever possible and this was one she was willing to give him.

"I did try after *The One* ended. And I was laughed out of a bunch of producers' and record label offices. Seems I have the look, but not the voice." She shrugged and bit her lower lip to stave off the tears suddenly prickling her eyes. She hadn't told anyone she'd tried to get a record deal. And thankfully, the producers she'd pitched her work to hadn't been cruel and sold her failure out to the tabloids.

A new realization settled into her chest like a lead weight— they hadn't even thought she was interesting enough to sell her story to the media. How depressing.

Chip was the first to hear this from her and surprisingly, it was harder to talk about than she realized. It was just another one of those things she'd experienced then pushed to the back of her mind where she wouldn't have to deal with it.

"I'm sorry to hear that. From what I've heard, you sound pretty great. I think the music business is a hard one to break into. Maybe you could try again in a few years and see what they say then."

She shook her head. No way would she put herself through that humiliation again. "No, I'm good with singing because I like it. I'm not sure I'd like living on tour. And after being in the tabloids for your reality shows the last couple of years, I've had my fill of the spotlight already. After this show airs and the excitement cools off, I think I'm going to enjoy going back to being a nobody again."

"As long as you're happy, that's what's important."

Was she happy with her life the way it currently was? Happy was a big word. Maybe she wasn't fully happy, but she was content. Wasn't she?

Before being on the first show, she'd been struggling to make ends meet as a personal shopper for a few high end clients and attempting to start a singing career which would hopefully one day save her from having to be a personal shopper forever. After the shows aired, she'd spent her time and earned money making appearances and doing interviews. It had helped pay some of her bills and had kept her in enough income that she hadn't had to return to work.

Once this show was over and the appearances stopped, what would she do? Singing wasn't an option she wanted to pursue anymore. She couldn't take that rejection again and she was looking forward to leaving the spotlight for good someday soon.

So where did that leave her? She had no real employable skills and the one thing she was passionate about had already been shot down. Would she be happy going back to a life that didn't include these shows or her singing?

Would she be happy going home alone after getting used to seeing Chip everyday around camp? After learning what it could feel like to be with someone like him?

"I'm happy," she answered attempting to add a cheerful tone to her voice. But she couldn't force a smile to her lips.

They finished their meal in silence then cleaned up and put away the leftovers. After she was done here with Chip, she'd drop everything back off in the kitchen tent before sneaking out to meet Alex before midnight.

Chip stood and stretched. "I don't know about you, but the lack of furniture around here is almost enough to drive me completely crazy. I've never been so sick of sitting on the ground before." He moved to the cot and sat on the end, patting the spot beside him. "You can't find that any more comfortable than I do. Join me up here. I promise I'll be good unless you ask me to be bad."

Something inside of her squirmed at his insinuation, but she shook off the feeling as she joined him on the bed. She was only here for the information, which they hadn't spoken about at all yet, and she wasn't going to let herself get distracted by anything else.

"Did you manage to finish your planning for the week before I got here? I hope I didn't interrupt you."

"I did. It's going to be a great week for ratings, but maybe not a great week for the last three teams." He laughed and looked very pleased with himself.

"You really enjoy tormenting your contestants in the name of ratings, don't you?" She didn't want to encourage him, but she couldn't help smiling in spite of herself. It was way easier to enjoy the twists and turns of the show as the host than as a contestant.

"I'll admit it. I do take a little enjoyment from watching them struggle through the challenges. But in my defense, it's my job to do this and if I didn't try to do it to the best of my abilities, I'd be out of work just like anyone else. My job is to keep viewers tuning in each week and every single week it gets harder and harder to do that. The contestants should blame the viewers for getting bored with the usual and demanding more drama."

"Sure, take the blame off yourself," she teased. "Meanwhile, you're here in your tent, plotting. So how did you decide to make the contestants sweat it out this week? What crazy competition do I have the honor of presenting to them tomorrow?"

"Reward is pretty easy this week actually."

"You're actually going easy on the contestants in week three? I don't believe you," she said. Chip never went easy on contestants. Easy didn't equal good ratings.

"Reward is a hot, well, lukewarm camping shower like the ones we use as well as towels, soap, toothpaste, and shampoo."

"That will be a pretty coveted reward after a couple of weeks of nothing but the icy cold stream. So what do they have to do to get it?"

"Mud wrestle. The winning team takes all. Easy."

She laughed. "Oh, you are cruel. So you make them get filthy but then only one team gets to really clean off with a shower."

"Well, when you put it that way it sounds bad. It made perfect sense in my head."

"I'm sure it did. So what's the elimination challenge then?"

Chip's smile grew. He really did enjoy this power he had, regardless of the reason behind it. "This week they're going to have to face their fears if they want to stay."

"What do you mean? What do they have to do?" She felt nervous for the teams even if she didn't have to compete with them. She wouldn't want to face her fears on national television and she couldn't imagine being forced to. A shiver shot up her spine at the thought of her biggest fear—the world seeing her scars and finding out about her accident.

"I have this crazy obstacle course set up for them and each member of the team will have to complete a part of the course. They'll have to swim across the current of the river, climb a fifty-foot tree, eat a bowlful of crickets, and go exploring in a cave of spiders." He laughed in a way that almost sounded sinister.

Her heart pounded. Okay, so maybe she had a second big fear—spiders. "Where exactly will they be doing these things? Do I…um…do I have to be near each part of the course as it happens or do I get to stand somewhere safe? Away from the spiders."

He rubbed her knee, the smile falling from his face. "I didn't realize you were afraid of spiders. Don't worry, you don't have to follow the contestants through the course, the cameramen are there for that. And I'll make sure the contestants don't have to come near you after they've been in the cave either."

"Good. I have the creeps just thinking about a cave full of spiders out in the woods somewhere. It's not near base camp, right?"

"Nope. But if I told you it was, would you let me be the one to keep you safe each night?" His voice dropped low and seductive, sending a spike of heat through her body. "I promise nothing would touch you but my hands…Well, maybe my lips would too."

He cupped her jaw in his hand and pressed his lips to hers. His kiss was soft and when he pulled away a second later, it left her wanting more. So much more. She fought the urge to climb into his lap and have her way with him.

"I'm happy the spiders won't be an issue."

"You didn't answer my question. There are many other things out in these woods that could wander through camp at night. Maybe you're tired of being alone. I know I am." He kissed her neck below her ear and she closed her eyes, unable to resist him.

"Are you trying to tell me a big strong guy like you is afraid of the dark? I might have a night light you can borrow to chase away the boogieman." She swallowed hard, trying to keep her emotions under control. Her pulse beat beneath his lips and she wondered if he could feel it too.

I will not jump his bones again. I will not.

The mantra didn't quell her growing desire for him. Especially not when he did that thing with his teeth and his tongue against her skin as if he were barely stopping himself from completely devouring her.

She wanted to be devoured by him. Damn it.

"I don't need a night light to keep me company in the dark. I need you." He slid his hand down her chest to cup her breast in his palm.

Zoe needed him too. More than she realized.

She arched into his hand unable to stop her desire as it boiled to the surface. When he touched her, kissed her—hell, when he looked at her—it felt as if the world tipped on its axis and nothing made sense anymore. Everything she thought she'd wanted…to be alone, to keep her heart safe and secure…all of it flew out the window the second his lips and hands found her quivering body. He made her feel all the things she never thought she'd get to feel.

He made her want things she never knew she wanted.

She wanted to be loved by someone. She wanted to feel desired by someone. She wanted to be accepted exactly as she was, flaws and all, by someone.

But not just anyone.

Zoe wanted all of that from just one person. Chip.

Chip pressed into her until she found herself lying on his cot. He kissed her hard on the mouth this time, his need for her shining through. His fingers brushed against her stomach as his hand snuck under the edge of her shirt.

No matter how hard she tried to force her eyes open so she could refocus her mind, her eyes wouldn't listen. Instead, she was trapped in the darkness and wrapped in the sensation of Chip's mouth on hers, his tongue teasing hers with little licks.

Instead of pushing him away like she should, she grabbed the bottom hem of his shirt and pulled it over his head. She wanted to see him in the dim light from the lantern.

The other night at the waterfall, she'd been able to feel his perfectly flawless skin, but now she wanted to see it in the light. The urge was too much to ignore. Her eyes popped open and she scanned his sculpted chest. His muscles flexed as he hovered over her, his breathing coming out fast and hard as he watched her examine every inch of him.

Rolling to the side, he propped himself on one elbow and left his hand resting on her hip while she turned toward him and studied him more. He was so gorgeous. Sleek, tanned, toned. She'd forgotten how beautiful the human body was when it wasn't tarnished with scars.

Pressing her fingers to his chest, she traveled the line of his pectorals then down to his belly button and over to the edge of his hip. Every line of muscles was exactly how it should be.

She brushed her lips against his chest and he took in a deep stuttered breath. The thought she could make him feel something so strongly that it took his breath away made her feel powerful and more beautiful than she'd ever felt before. She gazed up at him through heavy lashes as her tongue darted out for a quick taste of him, flickering across his skin. He moaned and she almost let a matching sound escape her mouth.

Zoe shrieked as he suddenly flipped her onto her back and his legs straddled her hips. He pulled the bottom two buttons of her shirt open before she realized his intentions.

"My turn to see you in the light, Zoe," he said, his voice heavy with desire, lust glazing his eyes.

Fear instantly cleared the fog settling in her head from his kisses, his touch. *No. Stop! It's too bright. He'll see too much.*

Tears clouded her vision as she struggled to get her hands on the next button before Chip got to it first. "Stop." Her voice came out too quiet and strained.

He bent his head and kissed her belly button, laughing as she squirmed beneath him. He probably thought it tickled. But it didn't. It hurt like a knife to her gut. A few buttons and Chip would find the scar she never bothered to cover with makeup unless she was in a bikini, which wasn't very often. Certainly she hadn't prepared for tonight.

Her body shook as the feeling of being trapped overtook her. She rolled to the side and pushed against him with all her strength. Chip tumbled off the side of the cot, landing hard on the ground with a grunt.

"I said stop. I have to go." Standing from the bed, she pulled her shirt back down into place, fastening the two buttons he'd managed to get undone, and fled from his tent out into the cold dark night air. She didn't stop running until she was almost to the clearing where she had to meet Alex.

When the stitch in her side finally forced her to stop running, she collapsed to the ground, her body shaking as tears came. This time she didn't fight them.

Chapter Eighteen

Zoe stood with a forced smile on her lips and clapped as the rowing team—Alex the blackmailer's team—crossed the finish line first, having successfully completed the obstacle course ahead of Rick's team in second and the doctors in last place.

She gritted her teeth together at the thought of having to look at him—be used by him—for one more week before the show would finally culminate at the final challenge. Of course in the meantime, she still had to find out what Chip had in store for them at the finale. Alex would give away her true identity if she didn't make sure he had enough advance information to win.

Just like he had this week.

While her dinner with Chip had basically destroyed their friendship after she tossed him to the ground and bolted from his tent as if he were a rapist, it had ultimately been successful in gathering the information Alex requested. And with the information, Alex and the rest of the rowing team had been victorious in both the reward and the elimination challenges.

He was here for another week because of her. And she was held to the fire for another week because of her relationship with Chip.

Lack of relationship.

Chip hadn't said more than a few necessary words to her during the setup for filming since the incident in his tent. Not that she could really blame him.

She rubbed the pendant on her necklace. She'd hurt Chip by running away that night. Actually by running away two nights—she'd done the same thing to him by the waterfall too.

She sucked.

She didn't deserve someone like Chip to talk to her, want to have dinner with her, or any of the other things he'd wanted to do with her.

She only deserved people in her life like Alex—people who used her, because that was exactly the same thing she'd done to Chip.

Alex was going to demand she do it again to find out what the final challenge was. But she'd never be able to get the information out of Chip now. Not the way she had this last week. Hell, she'd be lucky if she could even get him to have a civil conversation about the weather at this point.

She was royally screwed.

As if to prove her point, Alex sauntered over to her as his team started down the path that would take them back to their camp. The noise of lights being taken down from trees and production people chatting was all around them, masking their conversation.

"Chip said the final challenge is in four days. So you officially have three days to find out what it is. Meet me in the usual place and time the night before with the information or the finale will become all about you."

She glanced around. "I don't know if I can get the information from Chip again. I sort of burned that bridge last time."

"Trouble in paradise?" he whispered in her ear. "I don't care who you have to sleep with to get me what I want. Make it happen."

Alex walked away. Zoe's shoulders slumped with the weight of this new task. It wasn't as easy as spreading her legs to someone on the production crew. And she'd never stoop to that level anyway. She was a lot of things, but a slut wasn't one of them. Kissing and flirting was one thing, but sleeping with someone was completely different and out of the question.

Any way she looked at it, she was totally screwed.

• • •

Chip stood near one of the production bags, checking to make sure everything that was supposed to be inside actually was. Not like last week's challenge when one of the production assistants left some mics behind after the challenge. Luckily they'd gotten back to them before the rain had and the mics were fine, but he didn't want the same to happen this week. Not when they still had the big finale to film in a few days.

He almost couldn't wait for filming to be over. Usually he really loved every aspect of production, especially when it got to be around finale time, but this show was different. Zoe made it different. She occupied his every thought, distracting him.

And he also wouldn't mind a proper shower one of these days. He'd thought that a show filmed remotely would be a lot of fun, but he was wrong. So, so wrong. Bugs, weather, and the lack of personal hygiene from some of the crew made the experience less desirable than he'd expected.

The only desirable thing about the situation was Zoe and he wasn't even speaking to her at the moment. He didn't have anything to say. It wasn't as if asking her why she felt the need to get all hot and heavy with him only to ditch him constantly would do any good. He'd been pushing her pretty hard, putting the moves on, hoping she would reciprocate his feelings, but it was obvious now that she didn't or wouldn't let herself. Whatever it was she felt for him, it wasn't the same as what he felt for her.

He peeked up at her and found her face to face with Alex. He wouldn't have been surprised if it was Rick talking to her, but Alex was a little unusual. She didn't look especially happy to be speaking with him either, judging by her body language of crossed arms and pulled back shoulders.

As he watched, Alex leaned in and said something into her ear before walking away to join the rest of his team who were already celebrating their victory. Zoe's shoulders rolled forward as she stood there alone and her expression was one of exhaustion and stress. What had Alex said to her? Why the hell was he talking privately with the host of the show anyway? They should know it was against the rules.

On the other hand, it appeared Rick had finally started playing by the rules. He hadn't made any inappropriate comments to Zoe during the entire filming today and even now he was already with his team and heading back to their camp.

Chip relaxed. Finally, he could stop worrying about Rick and Zoe getting together.

Now he had to figure out what to do about Zoe. It was perfectly obvious in her kisses she had real feelings for him; the question was why did she keep pushing him away instead of giving into what she clearly wanted. And how could he help her overcome whatever the obstacle was so they could finally be together?

. . .

Zoe sat on a boulder, staring at the view as the sun set through the trees. The third week of filming was finally done and she'd never felt so exhausted. She really had thought hosting would be easier than being a contestant. Maybe it was easier on a typical show when the host could show up on set after a good night's sleep in a comfortable bed and eat normal meals and take regular showers. But out here in the wilderness, her experience as host had been anything but easy.

Of course, that could have something to do with the men on the show too. Rick, Alex, and Chip were not making her life easy. In fact, they were the main cause of her stress.

The sound of a branch breaking under someone's foot pulled her from her thoughts and the beautiful view. Rick strode down the trail with purpose. Surely he was lost and not looking for her.

Having another discussion with Rick about anything was the last thing she wanted to do right now.

"Hey, Rick. You're not following me are you?" she asked. She really could care less where he was headed as long as it didn't involve her.

"I need to talk to you, but I didn't want to do it back there with everyone else around. You alone out here?" he asked, glancing around.

A private conversation? Just what she didn't need right now.

"Just me and the bugs. What's up?" she asked, trying to sound casual and friendly. She stood from her boulder as he approached.

Rick stopped directly in front of her, his body brushing up against hers.

"Personal space, Rick." She started to take a step back, but he pulled her into his arms. One hand snaked around her waist while the other tangled in her hair. The next second, his mouth was pressed to hers, his tongue on a mission to reach her tonsils. She squirmed against him trying to get free, only to feel his arms wrap tighter around her.

Without seeing any other choice, she brought her knee up between his legs hard and fast. He instantly let go of her and went down on one knee, sucking in gulps of air.

"What the hell was that, Rick?" she yelled, wiping her mouth with the back of her hand as if that would remove the memory of what had just happened.

"I wanted to show you what you were missing now that you're fooling around with that little piss-head producer instead of me. I didn't expect you to go all defensive on me." He groaned and got to his feet.

"First of all, Chip is not a 'piss-head,' as you so elegantly put it. He's a good guy and a great producer. And we aren't fooling around, not that it's any of your business either way. And of course

I went defensive on you. You forced yourself on me without so much as saying hello. What did you think I was going to do?"

"I don't know. I thought maybe you'd kiss me back since you flirt with me the way you do." He shook his head. "You're not really sending me clear signals here, you know."

A wave of guilt washed over her. True, he shouldn't have assumed anything and kissed her, but she had been flirting with him pretty heavy the first week or two of the show. She was partly to blame for her predicament.

"I'm sorry. I know I flirted with you a lot at the beginning, but I thought I'd made it clear recently that I wasn't interested after all. I shouldn't have flirted with you to begin with, but I really did try to tell you I wanted it to stop and I thought you understood."

"I understood that your boyfriend was trying to use his power to persuade me away from you, but I thought you'd still be able to make your own decision if he wasn't hovering around watching you."

"He isn't hovering, he's working."

"He's hovering. And marking his territory. Don't think we haven't heard what's going on with you two. I think you're only with him because you think you can't be with me because I'm a contestant. But I'm only a contestant for another week. So the way I see it, baby, is that we do whatever we want and by the time anyone figures it out, the show will already be over."

He scooped her into his arms again as if he'd already forgotten the pain she'd caused his brain a few minutes ago. She must not have kneed him hard enough the first time. She'd have to be careful not to make the same mistake the second time.

She pushed back against his chest. "Let me go. I said I'm not interested anymore and I meant it."

"You're playing hard to get. You must need a little more convincing." He kissed the side of her neck, but instead of it making her weak-kneed like it had when Chip had kissed her there, it made her nauseous.

Her patience at the situation vaporized. Rick had gone too far this time and obviously wasn't going to listen to reason. She slid her hands up his chest and pressed against his throat. Trying to push against his chest had been like a mouse trying to move a mountain, but everyone had the need to breathe and right now Rick couldn't do that with her hands pushing against his neck.

He stepped back from her and she let go. His eyes were hot with an anger that matched her own. "I told you I wasn't interested. What the hell is with the men in this God forsaken forest? I've had enough of all of you."

"What are you talking about? Did Chip hurt you?"

"Chip is probably the least of my concerns right now. At least he cares about my feelings and tries to watch out for me. I can't say the same for you, Mr. Kissy Face. And don't even get me started on Alex and his threats, which is really the last thing I need thrown into this whole mess."

Her breath caught in her throat when she realized what she'd said out loud.

Shit.

"I, um, I think we're done here so I'm gonna go." She turned and managed two steps before Rick grabbed her by the arm and spun her around.

"What did you say?" he demanded.

"Chip sticks up for me and you should take a hint and stop kissing me."

He shook his head. "Not that part, the other stuff about Alex. Has he threatened you? Why?"

She sighed and rolled her eyes as if what he said was exaggerated. "Threatened, discussed. Maybe I used the wrong word. Either way it's none of your business. What is your business is keeping your hands and your lips off of me because I'm not interested in you. Got it?"

His eyes narrowed and his jaw set into a hard edge. "Looks like I need to have a little discussion with Alex."

"Please don't. Just pretend I never said anything and let it blow over. Okay?"

Rick slammed his fist into a nearby tree trunk. "Nope. Not a chance. I can't do that, baby. You think Chip is the only one who will look out for you? Well, you're wrong."

Zoe stood silently as Rick disappeared into the woods the way he'd come then made her way back to base camp. She stopped into the kitchen tent and fixed herself a cup of tea and grabbed a granola bar before going back to her tent. She was balancing everything in one hand to unzip her door with the other when Chip came around the side of her tent.

She stood and flipped her hair out of her face. "Hey, Chip. Were you looking for me? I stopped to grab a tea on my way back."

The thought that maybe he'd been hanging out, waiting for her to get back to her tent tonight, caused a stirring of something warm in her chest. Somehow the idea of coming home to Chip felt strangely welcoming and wonderful, even though she didn't want it to.

"Nope. Passing by." His voice was cool and clipped, the one she'd heard him use with crewmembers who annoyed him.

Great. So that's what she'd been reduced to in his mind. At least now she knew.

A pain unlike anything she'd felt before buried itself in her chest. "Oh, okay then. I'll head inside." She bit the inside of her lip trying to keep it together in front of Chip. This was all getting to be too much stress. "I thought you might want to talk."

"Not really." He shrugged. "I mean, what could we possibly have to say to each other when you keep running away from me every time we get close? You're a pro at sending mixed signals."

First Rick said it and now Chip did. Maybe they were right and she should keep to herself for the rest of the show so she couldn't send any more mixed signals to anyone.

"I'm sorry." Zoe was taken aback by his reality check. "I guess I thought you might want to hang out and chat like we did the first couple of weeks here. I guess not."

"Hanging out involves two people *not* running away from each other. So I guess that's it unless you want to tell me what's up with you."

"I can't explain it. You wouldn't understand."

Chip sighed. "I think I would, but you'll never get the chance to find out, will you? You'll never let me get close enough to try. At least now I understand where I fit in to your world...I don't."

"Chip, it's not that easy. It's not so black and white in my world."

"It is easy if you let it be, but you never will, will you? Your life is only as complicated as you make it and you've done a great job at making your life more complicated than anyone else's." Chip sighed, then left her standing alone while he went and joined a group of production people hanging out at one of the fire pits.

Zoe tried to think of something to say that would make him understand where she was coming from, but nothing seemed right. How could she explain her feelings when they were making less and less sense even to her? Since coming on this show and being with Chip, nothing seemed to be as easy as it had been before.

Keeping people at a distance used to come naturally to her, but staying away from Chip got harder every day. Keeping her feelings to herself used to be as normal as breathing, but now she felt herself struggling with the notion of telling him her whole story.

Instead of going after him, she zipped herself into the safety of her tent—away from Chip and the discussion he wanted to have with her.

Maybe he was right. Maybe her life was only complicated because she'd made it that way. Maybe she could tell him about her past and have him still want a future with her.

Or maybe he'd get one good look at her scars in the light and hear about how damaged she really was and realize that being with her had no real future. Being with her was a mistake.

Was she willing to risk that kind of rejection from him?

Chapter Nineteen

Zoe felt panic rising in her throat as she paced the clearing waiting for Alex to show up. He was going to flip his shit when he heard what she had to say about the final challenge. This wouldn't go well.

Alex stepped into the clearing. Under normal circumstances, he wouldn't have been intimidating. But these weren't normal circumstances and he held her fate in his hands. What he chose to do with it after she told him was completely up to him. And judging by the look of annoyance on his face, he wouldn't be kind or considerate of her feelings.

"Let's not waste time with pleasantries. What's the final challenge?" he asked, folding his arms across his chest.

Zoe wrung her hands together. He wouldn't like this answer. "I don't know. I wasn't able to find out. The production people aren't told anything in advance other than specific equipment they need to bring, if any."

"That shouldn't be a problem for you since you've been getting into bed with the producer. Surely you were able to sweet talk your way into the information I needed."

"I don't know what you think is going on between Chip and myself, but I wasn't able...we aren't speaking. I couldn't just ask him what the challenge was either. He doesn't really share that information with anyone. It was a fluke that I was able to get it for you last week."

He raked his hands through his hair and looked up at the stars. "Are you seriously telling me you didn't even try to find out?

Seriously? So I guess you don't care if I tell the world you're not really Zoe, but Andrea. Ugly Andrea is back. This should be fun."

"Don't call me that." Zoe's hands shook. She squeezed them together tighter, hoping to steady them.

"You left me no choice, Ugly Andrea. This is your fault." He practically spit the words. "I don't want to look like a fool tomorrow. I don't want my team to lose this stupid game so we go home looking like a bunch of chumps instead of champs. If I have to go home looking bad, so do you. It's that simple."

"I said don't call me that," she said through gritted teeth. "I'm not Andrea anymore and I'm done being threatened by you. Win the show under your own merits or don't, it's not my problem anymore. But you keep your mouth shut about my life tomorrow or I'll find a way to make your life miserable."

"Are you actually threatening me now?" He laughed, clearly shocked at her change of heart.

Well that made two of them. She didn't know where this new fire came from, but she wasn't going to let him or anyone else take away everything she'd worked for all these years. No one was going to take away this life she'd created for herself.

"It's not a threat. It's a promise. Leave me alone. I'm done being blackmailed by you."

"We'll see about that. You better find a way to help my team win because if we lose, your secret is out."

"Well that's great. And fair too. My life has to change based on whether or not you suck at the challenge. Thanks." Zoe stormed out of the clearing not bothering to wait for his response. There wasn't anything he could say to make her feel better about the situation anyway.

Tomorrow her entire life could be thrown into chaos and there wasn't a damn thing she could do about it. For the first time since her accident, she felt completely helpless.

...

"Here's the incident report from the other day," Frank said, handing Chip a standard form. He was one of the cameramen assigned to Rick's team camp.

"What incident report?" Chip asked around a bite of protein bar. It really was the breakfast of champions. That and coffee. "No one mentioned anything about any incidents recently."

"Well it wasn't really a big deal so I didn't feel the need to report it verbally. I figured the form would be enough. So there you go." Frank pulled a bottle of orange juice out of a cooler and chugged half of it.

Chip scanned the form. It involved Rick and an injury that occurred after the last challenge outside of his camp.

Description of incident: verbal argument resulting in bodily injury.

Who the hell was he fighting with and why? Physical violence against anyone at any point in the game was strictly against the rules in his productions. This should have been reported sooner.

Description of injury: bruised groin.

Ouch. Poor bastard.

Persons involved: Rick Morton, Zoe Oliver.

What the hell?

"Frank, get over here and explain this."

Frank pulled out a chair across from Chip and straddled it, hanging his arms across the back. "I thought it was pretty clear."

"What's not clear is why this wasn't reported to me earlier."

"I didn't think it was a big deal. He got kneed in the groin and was sore for a couple of hours. Nothing medical could do about it and not bad enough to be removed from the game. Besides, I kinda thought he deserved to suffer for a night. Maybe he'd think twice, you know?"

"Think twice about what exactly? This form doesn't spell out what happened to cause his injury."

Frank smiled. "Rick messed with the wrong girl is all. That Zoe is a firecracker. Why anyone would want to put the moves on her to begin with is beyond me, but when she refuses and you still insist? Well, I say he got what was coming to him."

Chip rubbed his hand across his forehead while he tried to take in this information. "Exactly how hard did he *insist* with Zoe?" If Rick laid his hands on her, forced her to do anything she didn't want to do…Holy hell, screw the finale, he'd have Rick taken away in handcuffs. "I need details."

Frank shrugged looking unconcerned. "He says he kissed her and then her knee connected with his junk. That's all I know."

"And did you follow up with Zoe to make sure that's all there was to the story?" Chip couldn't keep the concern from his voice. Anger at his incompetent cameraman quickly escalated.

"Not personally, but I radioed to the production assistant here and asked if Zoe seemed okay or not. She said Zoe was her usual Zoe self so we didn't bother with any further investigation."

"Well thanks for really half-assing your job. I'll be sure to remember this conversation when it's time for performance reviews."

Frank leaned back. "I did what I was supposed to do. It's not my fault Zoe didn't report the incident herself. Perhaps it was such a little deal she didn't feel the need to bother anyone with it. So maybe you shouldn't get so bent out of shape, boss."

Chip sighed. Frank was right. He was getting more upset than the situation called for because it involved Zoe and Rick. "You're right. I'm just anxious for the finale tomorrow. And I'm ready to get the hell out of these woods. I won't hold this against you at reviews."

Frank stood from the table and patted him on the shoulder. "Glad to hear it, boss. Now go have a beer before you accidentally fire someone."

"I might do that." Chip still had a few beers left in his personal cooler in his tent. Of course, they would be warm by now since he hadn't had new ice for them in days. But at this point, a warm beer was better than no beer. He needed a little something to take the edge off.

But first he had a pit stop to make.

"File this for me, would you?" Chip asked, dropping the incident report at a table of production assistants on his way out of the tent. He really didn't care if they wanted to or not. He knew they would do it because he told them to. Right now he had more important things to worry about than filing some stupid form. He had to find out from the source if things were okay or not.

It was still pretty early and since he hadn't seen Zoe at breakfast, she must still be getting ready for the finale. He stopped outside her tent door. "If you're in there, open up. We need to talk."

He heard scuffling from inside the tent as she came to the door and unzipped it. Her hair was pulled up into a twist in the back and secured with a clip, makeup expertly applied as usual. He stepped into her tent without waiting for an invitation and spun her around in a circle, examining any area of flesh he could see for visible bruises that Rick may have caused.

When he was satisfied that he couldn't see anything obvious, he turned her back around to face him. "Did he hurt you?"

She scrunched her eyebrows together. "Good morning to you too."

"Answer me," Chip demanded, barely keeping calm. Damn it. Why did she have to be so infuriating all the time? Why couldn't she answer his question so he knew if his day would include filming the finale or filing a police report?

"I don't know what you're referring to, but no one hurt me."

"I'm talking about that shithead Rick. I was given an incident report about an injury he sustained at the will of your knee sometime after the last elimination challenge. Imagine my surprise at not having heard about it from you or the production team earlier. So tell me, are you okay or do I need to call the police and have Rick strung up by his balls?"

"It really is amazing that no one told you sooner with how rationally you're taking the news now. I can't imagine why anyone would keep this from you." She smirked and he suddenly wanted to kiss that smirk right off her face. He'd been so worried she had been truly hurt and here she was laughing at him. "I'm fine. I handled it and I think Rick will finally leave me alone."

Chip didn't actually want to hear the details, but he had to know. "What did he do to you?"

"Nothing. A kiss. That's it. I'm fine, really."

Rick's lips had been on hers again. But thank God that's where it had ended. He couldn't handle it if Rick had done anything more to Zoe. A kiss was already bad enough.

"A kiss is not nothing, but I'm glad to hear it wasn't anything more and that you're not hurt. If you had been..." He trailed off.

"If I had been, then what?" she challenged, crossing her arms. "Last I checked you weren't too happy with me, not that I blame you."

Chip stepped closer to Zoe and cupped her jaw in his hands, his thumb brushing against her lips. They parted with a gasp and he wanted nothing more than to taste her. But he wasn't going to make the same mistake again. She'd told him she didn't want him, even though everything about her body language, the way she looked at him, and her instantaneous reaction to his touch told him otherwise. As much as he hated it, he'd try his best to respect her wishes until she finally admitted it to herself that she wanted him as much as he wanted her.

Didn't mean he couldn't still *want* to kiss her though, and damn it did he ever want to.

"It doesn't matter how I feel about you or whether or not you want me in your life. If Rick put his hands on you against your will, I'd break every one of his fingers. And probably his nose. And maybe a couple of ribs."

He dipped his head, brushing his lips against hers softly, unable to resist their allure any longer, but he quickly pulled himself back before she could run away again. This time things would end on his terms, not hers.

Chip hovered over her, peering into her eyes. "You can push me away if you want to, but I'll never stand by and let someone push you around."

She tilted her chin slightly as if asking him for another kiss. He dropped his hands and stepped back out of her tent, taking a deep breath of cool morning air into his lungs. "See you at the finale."

Chapter Twenty

Zoe cringed as Alex took another hard fall at the hands of Rick. Or in this case, the feet of Rick, since he'd been tripped. Alex grunted as he hit then quickly popped back up onto his feet again and took off down the wooden bridge after Rick. When Alex caught up to him, he jabbed him in the ribs causing Rick to lose his balance and stumble forward.

They'd been going at each other the entire finale and it didn't look like either of them planned to stop any time soon. It was as if they were purposefully after each other to prove something. This was more than just about winning the finale. This seemed personal.

Chip's production crew had outdone themselves this time. They'd constructed a giant apparatus twenty feet off the ground consisting of various rope and wooden bridges, ladders, and barriers. The contestants had to race around the setup gathering a variety of tokens that represented different moments in the game and then place them on a board in the right order. All of the team members had to work together to collect them, organize them, and hang them. The team who did it the fastest, successfully, would be the winners of the show.

The teams were evenly matched, both having collected roughly half of the tokens already. Of course, not many of those tokens could be attributed to Rick or Alex's efforts. Their efforts in the finale seemed to lie directly in making the other person feel as much pain as possible before the show ended. It was unnerving to watch.

"What the hell is going on with those two?" Chip asked, coming to stand beside Zoe while they peered up at the apparatus and the grown men acting like school kids.

"I have no idea. It's like they're out for blood instead of winning."

"Did either of them say anything to you?"

You mean besides Alex threatening me to help him win?

She shook her head. "Nope. No one said a word to me about anything."

Alex cursed loudly as he tumbled over the side of one of the bridges and landed in the net hanging beneath the entire apparatus. Now he had to crawl to one of the ladders and climb back up, easily losing time to gather tokens. From somewhere above him, Rick cackled as if he really enjoyed seeing Alex fall.

Where had all of this animosity between them come from? It wasn't as if they'd been living together recently to get on each other's nerves. At last week's challenges, they hadn't batted two eyelashes at each other. But now they acted as if they were archenemies.

Zoe's slip up to Rick about Alex threatening her flashed through her mind. Shit. Another disaster that was her fault. If she'd only been able to keep her mouth shut, this wouldn't be happening right now. Instead, Rick looked as if he wasn't going to stop until he made Alex pay.

"Get up here, we have the tokens!" Justin yelled from the platform where they would hang each of the tokens in the order in which the event happened on the show. They weren't allowed to start until each member of the team was accounted for on the platform and currently Alex was still in the net making his way to the ladder.

"Get your ass up here," Dale called down to him. "We can't start without you and the other team is almost to their platform."

Alex let loose a string of profanities and scurried to the ladder. He hoisted himself up onto the first wrung but his grip must not have been good enough because a second later he landed spread-eagled on the net again looking up at the sky.

Rick peered over the edge to gawk at Alex. "You get what you deserve!" He laughed again then joined his team on the platform so they could start hanging their tokens.

Zoe held her breath watching as Alex climbed the ladder. He'd better hurry or the game would be over before he even got up there. Then how angry would he be?

Alex pulled himself onto the wooden bridge then sprinted to the platform, collapsing when he reached it, attempting to catch his breath. The rest of his team jolted into action, arranging the tokens on the ground in order then hanging them on the hooks.

Zoe looked back and forth between the teams trying to see who was closer to winning. She didn't have to wonder for long. Rick's team hung their last token then cranked the lever that would only move if the tokens were all in the correct spot. The crank moved, raising a flag into the air, and declaring them the winners.

A loud cheer went up from Rick's side of the apparatus and then the entire team jumped off their platform together to land in the netting below. Curses came from the rowing team's side as a token slammed to the wood at their feet.

While Rick's team lay in the net for a few minutes celebrating and enjoying their victory, the rowing team climbed down the ladder and stalked over to where Zoe stood waiting to film the final wrap-up. They stopped a few feet in front of her on the mark production had indicated for their final positions.

Alex, however, didn't stop with his team. He stormed up to Zoe, anger etched into every surface of his face. "How could you let this happen?"

She stepped back, startled at his outburst. Glancing past him to the rest of his team, they looked as shocked as she was. Off to the side, Chip moved forward as if to come to her rescue, but she held up her hand, motioning for him to stay put. She would handle Alex on her own. "I don't know what you mean."

"Don't start with me. Don't stand there acting all high and mighty when you know full well what you did. You sent him after me, didn't you? It's not enough you've had the producer in your bed, you've probably had Rick in your bed this whole time too."

"I don't know what you're talking about. I never asked Rick to go after you." She glanced to the side to see the cameras aimed at her and Alex instead of the teams. Crap. Just what she needed—to be thrown under the bus at yet another finale. Awesome.

Not that it was against the rules or anything, but there was a huge part of her that didn't really want her fling with Chip broadcast on national television. Was it too much to ask that some aspect of her life be allowed to remain private?

"Get the hell away from her," Rick said, shoving Alex back away from Zoe.

"Rick, don't," Zoe pleaded. She didn't know what the hell was going on with Alex now, but physical violence wasn't going to help.

"You don't know what I'm talking about?" Alex laughed and shook his head. "How stupid do you think we all are? Look at him. Protecting you like a jealous boyfriend. You sent him after me, didn't you? You couldn't seduce the information about the challenge out of your lover boy producer anymore so you sent your pit bull Rick after me to put me out of commission."

"What the hell is he talking about, Zoe?" Chip asked, joining them.

She bit her lip. Great. Now Chip had broken his own rules and was in the shot when he was supposed to remain behind the scenes. He never stepped in front of the camera. Ever.

So much for wrapping up the finale and getting out of here.

"It's nothing, Chip. Can we get the finale over with already?"

"What's wrong, Zoe? Are you worried your little producer boyfriend will find out the truth about you?" Alex smirked, but anger still flared in his features. "Are you worried your pit bull will find out he's been sharing you this whole time?"

"That's enough," Rick said stepping between them. "Zoe never asked me to go after you. I decided that all on my own once I heard about you threatening her. I wasn't going to sit around and let some little shit like you get away with that. Someone had to put you in your place."

"You told him I threatened you?" Alex narrowed his eyes at Zoe. "Did you really think he could stop me from ratting you out to everyone?"

"That's enough, Alex. Join your team so I can announce the winners." She tried to sound as forceful and authoritative as she could, but Alex didn't move or attempt to hide his amusement. Her pulse pounded in her head as her nervousness increased. She had to end the show before Alex told everyone her secret.

"I agree. I think it's enough too." Alex smiled.

"What's going on, Zoe? Threats from Alex? You and Rick? Someone better hurry up and tell me what's going on here." Chip clenched his jaw, barely keeping his cool.

"If you really want to know the truth, maybe you should ask Andrea to tell you." Alex crossed his arms, looking smug.

The trees around her spun as she sucked in a quick breath. He'd done it. He'd sold her out on national television. Now everyone would know.

"Who's Andrea?" Chip and Rick asked in unison.

"I am," Zoe said in a quiet voice. Her breathing came quicker now, unable to hold back the fear and embarrassment as it spiked within her.

"That's right. Your sweet Zoe Oliver is actually Andrea Miles. Ugly Andrea Miles. Andrea here seems to have gotten a new face and a new name since the last time I saw her, but she's still the ugly girl on the inside, aren't you? No amount of plastic surgery can change the person you really are."

"I told you not to call me that." Zoe clenched her hands into fists at her sides and tried to fight the overwhelming urge to punch him in the face. She fought to focus on her breathing so she wouldn't pass out, her dizziness almost consuming her. "I only had those surgeries to fix my scars from the accident and you know that."

"But it didn't fix all of the scars did it? You still look like a monster under all that makeup, don't you?"

She willed Alex to shut up, but it was too late. The damage was done. The truth was out. Now everyone would know she'd lied and she wasn't really who they thought she was. She would be Ugly Andrea again.

Zoe swiped at the tears on her cheeks only to realize that they were mixing with raindrops. Seemed the sky had opened up above them with the news as if mirroring her mood. Good. Then maybe they wouldn't be able to tell she was crying.

"You're not Zoe? You're Andrea?" Chip shook his head in obvious disbelief. "I don't understand."

"I...I changed my name to get away from people like Alex. But it doesn't matter who I was before because that's not who I am now."

"So you had a whole other life I knew nothing about?" Chip's voice trailed off.

"That life was my past. No one was supposed to know the truth. Ever. Alex just couldn't keep his mouth shut when he recognized me." She glared at him and wished looks could kill. Or at least hurt him as much as he'd already hurt her, past and present included.

"I warned you I'd take you down with me," Alex sneered.

"Zoe, what is he talking about? Did he threaten you?" Chip asked.

"Not physically. More like he gave me a compelling ultimatum," Zoe said, not wanting to get into details here in front of everyone. Best to gloss over as much as possible so that maybe she could salvage some kind of dignity after all of this was over.

"Sounds more like blackmail, doesn't it?" Rick added. "Now people don't feel so sorry for you getting beat up in the finale."

"You didn't beat me up," Alex yelled, lunging for Rick.

Chip stepped between them, holding them off long enough for their respective team mates to grab their arms so they couldn't pummel each other. When they were both controlled, Chip turned to Alex. "You blackmailed Zoe? What did you want from her?"

"The same thing I wanted from her last week—information about the challenge so that we'd have an advantage. But last week she was more successful at getting the information out of you, wasn't she? Seemed she couldn't get back into your bed a second time." Alex faced Zoe again. "You must not be very good in the sack. Bad in bed and ugly too. Sucks to be you."

"I..." Zoe started to defend herself but before she could, Chip punched Alex in the face. Blood poured from Alex's nose as he cried out and fell to one knee.

"You knew about this and didn't tell anyone?" Chip yelled, turning on Rick next. He threw his fist out to clip Rick too, but Rick saw it coming and dodged.

"I only knew that Alex had made some kind of threat to her, not that he'd forced her to get information out of you. At least that explains her unlikely attraction to you now. And besides, I did do something about it, in my own way," Rick shot back.

"A lot of good that did," Chip said. "Maybe if you'd told someone on the production team, we could have done something, but now it's too late."

Zoe cringed when Chip turned to her next. She didn't want to answer the questions she knew he'd ask. What could she possibly say to make him understand?

"Zoe—Andrea—whoever you are...How could you let this happen? How could you let yourself get blackmailed and not come and talk to me about it? Why didn't you trust me with the truth so I could help you?" Chip paused, an expression of pure pain flashed in his eyes. "Was I really just a pawn on your blackmail game? Is that all it was to you?"

"I didn't mean for this to happen. I thought I could deal with Alex on my own." She glanced from one man to another wondering how her life had suddenly gotten so complicated. "I couldn't tell you the truth about me, Chip. I wanted to, but I couldn't."

"You could tell me anything. *Anything* and I would listen." Chip raked his hands through his short hair. "But you told Rick?"

"I slipped and mentioned it in a fit of anger and frustration. I had no intention of telling him about the blackmail. I swear I didn't send Rick after Alex. And I'd never tell him the truth about me. Never."

"Please tell me you didn't tell Alex what the competitions were in advance last week." Chip's gaze pierced her, making her chest tighten. She couldn't lie to him but telling him the truth would hurt both of them.

"I..." She swallowed the lump in her throat. "I'm sorry. I didn't see any other way. I thought..."

Chip pressed his fingers to his forehead and closed his eyes, sighing deeply. This was bad. Worse than she'd ever imagined. How had she been so stupid to think she could cheat for Alex's team and nothing bad would come of it? She'd been reckless and impulsive.

Chip probably hated her for ruining his show. How could they air it now knowing the challenge last week had been rigged? It might not have even been these two teams in the finale if she hadn't told Alex what the challenge was. She'd screwed up Chip's entire production.

"I'm sorry. I didn't think it through, I just panicked and did what I thought I had to," she said in a small voice.

The tears she'd been fighting back overflowed her eyes, spilling down her cheeks. She'd made a huge mess of everything and now she'd have to pay the price. Now everyone knew she was a liar and a cheat. She'd never live this down in the tabloids. Never. They'd loved her drama before, but this would be the drama to end all drama. Her hidden past, her new identity, her accident and now her ruthless behavior as host—the media would eat her alive.

And she had no one to blame but herself.

"I need a few minutes to figure out how to salvage this game," Chip said, pacing, his expression one of deep concentration. "Zoe, will you be able to finish filming in a little while?"

"Shouldn't you start calling her Andrea since that is her real name?" Alex commented as he moved to stand on his mark with the rest of his team.

Zoe looked down at her feet. She couldn't look at anyone anymore. They all gazed at her like she was some kind of circus freak—just like the others had after her accident. The memory sent a shot of pain into her chest making her breath hitch. She rubbed her hands against her face as if doing so could somehow stop her from turning back into Andrea now that her secret was out. When she pulled her hands away, they were covered in beige foundation.

Shit. She rubbed her hands together as panic rose in her throat like bile. It wasn't enough they all knew she'd lied about her true identity, but now thanks to the rain, they'd all get to see her scars firsthand. She peeked up through her lashes at the cameras still focused on her. If she looked up, the camera would take in her appearance and then the whole world would see how she really looked.

Well she couldn't let that happen.

Her hands shook, but she steadied her voice. "Chip, I need a couple of minutes to freshen up and then I'll be ready to film when you are." She didn't look up or wait for his response. She turned and simply walked away as if there was nothing wrong with her other than needing a few minutes alone to collect herself.

When she was out of eyesight of the contestants and production crew, she bolted into the forest. Chip would never forgive her for this, but right now she couldn't think about that. She had to get away.

Chapter Twenty-One

Chip couldn't understand how his show could get so out of control so quickly. How the hell had this happened? He'd kept the contestants separated from each other and the crew and yet somehow they'd all ended up in some muddled mess. It wasn't enough Rick had been flirting forcefully with Zoe, but he'd tried to take out the competition on her behalf.

Although Chip couldn't say he wouldn't have done the same thing considering he'd just punched the very same contestant in the face. Alex had it coming.

If only she'd come to him, told him about the blackmail even if she wasn't ready to tell him the truth about who she really was. He could have done something to prevent his show from being completely ruined. But she hadn't. She'd risked everything, the show, the other contestants, his reputation…everything, to save her own skin.

No, it wasn't okay to blackmail anyone, especially not Zoe. But it also wasn't okay to save yourself at the sacrifice of others either. Not knowing the reason why she was so set on being blackmailed instead of telling his the truth stung deep. He would do anything for her, but she couldn't even share the details of her life with him. Ouch.

Of course, here he was defending her but if what Alex said was true, then Zoe wasn't innocent in all of this either. She'd lied about her past, which maybe helped to explain why he'd had so much trouble finding information out about her from when she was younger.

Had she really only been with him to find out information about the show's challenges?

Chip felt like he had a knife twisting in his chest at the thought of Zoe only being with him to gather information.

No. Her feelings were real. She couldn't fake those.

Or maybe she could. She was obviously practiced enough at lying about who she really was. Maybe that meant she was practiced when it came to lying about her feelings too. Maybe nothing he knew about her was true.

He couldn't believe that. He couldn't believe Zoe's feelings hadn't been real. The way she looked at him, the way she touched him, the way she kissed him…it had all been real. Hadn't it?

"The light is fading fast, boss. Are we almost ready to finish up?" a cameraman asked, pulling him out of his torturous thoughts.

"Let me go find Zoe while you get everyone into their places." He still hadn't figured out how to save the show, but they needed to finish filming one way or another. Maybe he could edit it in a way that made some sort of sense later.

Chip started off in the direction he'd seen Zoe go early. How long had she been freshening up? Seemed like it had been a long time. The rain continued to beat down on them and the cameraman was right, the light was fading fast this afternoon. The cloud cover made it seem darker quicker. They really needed to get this filming wrapped, announce a winner and be done with it.

"Zoe," he called as he walked further and further away from the filming area. "Zoe, where are you?" He stopped and listened for her response. Maybe she'd wandered further away than she'd realized.

Silence.

Maybe she'd needed to wash her face with all the crying and the rain. Maybe she'd headed down to the stream that wasn't far from here. He quickly found the path that would take him to the stream and started jogging, anxious to find Zoe. Something inside him warned this didn't feel right.

"Zoe," he called again louder as he reached the edge of the stream. Zoe wasn't there and judging by the lack of tracks in the soft mud, she hadn't been here recently. No one had.

Chip unclipped his two-way radio from his belt. "Is Zoe anywhere in the filming area?" he asked the production assistant on the other end of the line. He wandered back down the trail he'd just walked as he waited for a response.

"Nope. I can't find her anywhere," the assistant said.

"Damn," he muttered under his breath before pushing the button to talk into the radio again. "I can't find her anywhere either and I went all the way to the stream. I need you to send a couple of the crew back to base camp and see if she went back to her tent for something. Tell the other production people to fan out and search the perimeter out about twenty feet but no further. I don't want everyone getting lost in the woods."

"Got it. What about the contestants? Should I send them back to their camps?"

"Not yet. Chances are Zoe wandered a little further than she meant to. We need to find her and get the filming wrapped. I'm going to keep heading south and see if I can find her this way since this is the direction I thought I saw her leave."

Chip went back to where he'd originally thought he'd find Zoe outside of the filming area and looked around to see if he could find any hint at the direction she might have gone. A few moments later he noticed some of the soft grass in one area was pressed flat, almost as if it had been stepped on recently.

With nothing else to go on, he jogged down what his gut told him was Zoe's trail. With the rain continuing to fall and the light fading, soon there would be no trail to follow at all. He had to find Zoe. Fast.

• • •

Zoe ran until the stitch in her side was too painful to ignore then continued walking until she was too winded to keep going. Rain had thoroughly drenched every square inch of her body, her clothes now clung to her, making her cold. She needed to stop for a few minutes to think. She sank down onto a large boulder and put her head in her hands.

What had she done? How had she let everything spiral out of control so quickly? This wasn't at all how she thought her easy hosting gig would go.

And now she'd made her situation even worse by running off into the woods without a second thought as to where she was going.

Smart. Real smart.

It wasn't as if she could go back now. She didn't have a bit of makeup left on her face, her hair hung in tangled clumps like an old rag mop, and humiliation burned in her chest. No, she definitely couldn't go back.

Chip would hate her for bailing on the finale, but knowing him, he'd find some way to piece together other audio clips to get the finale finished so the show could still air. He probably already hated her anyway now that he thought she'd used him to gather information for Alex. She had used their relationship… friendship…whatever it was, to get him to tell her what she'd needed to know, but the connection they had between them had been one hundred percent real.

No way would he believe that now.

New tears fell down her cheeks at the thought of everything she'd lost. She wouldn't get paid, her secret was out for the world to hear, and Chip would never forgive her. Everything she'd worked for was gone. Over.

And it was all her fault. Sure, if Alex hadn't figured out who she was, she could have finished her hosting responsibilities without so much trouble. But no one forced her to hide who she really was. If she'd only faced her fears and had been strong enough to believe in herself after the accident happened, Alex wouldn't have had any power to blackmail her.

But she hadn't. She'd lied to everyone. She'd lied to herself.

She'd lied to Chip.

There was nothing left for her here. No reason to go back and try to make things right. Maybe if she walked further on, she'd find some civilization and then she could get a hotel room. She had her credit card number memorized so maybe someone would rent her a room. If not, she could call her brother and beg him to call in a room for her. It would be hard to ask for his help, but it would be better than going back to base camp. She could never face those people again.

She pulled herself up from the boulder and glanced around, not remembering which direction she'd come from. The ground showed no traces of her steps. Or at least none that she could see. Sighing, she picked a direction at random and started walking. Sooner or later she'd either run into one of the show's camps or she'd find the edge of the forest and hopefully people. Either way, she wasn't staying still any longer.

It was dark, she was cold, and the thought of being in the woods alone at night was anything but appealing.

Zoe walked on, listening to the leaves crunching under her feet while trying to shut out the sound of her thoughts. She didn't want to think anymore. Thinking was stressful and exhausting. Right now she needed to conserve her energy and get somewhere safe.

A loud snap of a breaking branch startled her. She froze. Another loud snap of a branch caused her hands to shake. The noise sounded like it was somewhere nearby. Instantly images of snarling bears and growling wolves filled her mind.

A shape stepped out from behind a cluster of trees and a scream caught in her throat. Paralyzed by fear, she could do nothing but stand there with her mouth hanging open, waiting to be eaten.

"Zoe, is that you?"

The sound of Chip's voice hit her with a wave of relief and guilt.

She wasn't seconds away from being eaten by a bear.

Chip was probably going to kill her for ruining his show.

The bear would have been better to find in the woods after all. At least with a bear it would be a quick and efficient death. With Chip it would be slow and painful and she'd only want to die.

"Hey," she said weakly with a small wave as he wandered over to her.

Without a word, Chip closed the distance between them and pulled her into his arms. He held her tight and dipped his head to bury his face in her neck.

"I'm so glad you're okay. I've been looking for hours. My mind started to make up all these different, awful scenarios about what condition I'd find you in. Are you hurt?"

He pulled back and looked her up and down. His concern was obvious and it made her heart ache. He was such a wonderful man and she'd done nothing but use and hurt him. She'd always known she didn't deserve someone like Chip risking his own life to follow her out in the woods but today's events and her recent behavior absolutely proved it.

"I'm not hurt," she said, unable to meet his imploring gaze. "You shouldn't have followed me."

"What was I supposed to do when you didn't come back to finish filming, let you wander out in the woods lost forever?" he asked, his hands resting on her shoulders. She could feel his body shaking with shivers almost as much as hers.

"Oh." She nodded. "I get it. You wanted me to come back to finish filming the finale. Sorry, but I can't do that. I'll record some audio for you or something to announce Rick's team as the winners, but I'm not going back to film. And I'm definitely not going back to camp."

Chip dropped his hands from her shoulders and folded them across his chest instead. "Do you really think I'd come all this way, walk all this time in the woods risking my own safety because I want to drag you back to finish filming?"

Well, when he said it that way, it didn't sound very likely.

"Isn't that why you're here?" She glanced up at him as best she could while keeping her head bent. It wasn't yet completely dark and looking up at him would surely show off the now naked scars running along the edge of her jaw and under her chin.

"I don't give a crap about the finale. I came after you because I was worried about you after everything that happened back there and I couldn't imagine you out here alone."

He reached out for her but before he could touch her, she turned her back and took a few steps away. She might be fully clothed, but she felt far too naked to be near him.

"I'm going to radio back to base camp and get us out of here." He pulled his radio from the waistband of his pants and pressed a button before speaking into it. "I've found Zoe. But I'm not sure where we are. I'm going to need you to check the map and navigate us back to camp."

Zoe stayed quiet while he told the production assistant their current coordinates according to the radio equipped with a built in GPS tracker and waited for directions on how to get back. She didn't want to go back, but she couldn't very well spend the night in the woods with no shelter. And her quest to find outside civilization hadn't worked so well either. Going back to base camp with Chip was her only option.

"I've found your location on the map," the voice on the radio said a few minutes later. "But I'm afraid you're too far out to make it back to camp tonight. Jenny called the closest rangers and gave them your coordinates. They said to sit tight until they find you. They should be there shortly then they'll take you into the nearest city for the night."

"I guess we'll see you back at base camp sometime tomorrow. Make sure everyone is ready to film the final segment tomorrow when we get back."

"Will do. Stay safe out there you guys."

Chip said goodbye then clipped his radio back to his waistband. "Now we wait, I guess."

She nodded, wrapping her arms around herself. Now that she wasn't walking, the cold and wet settled over her with a chill. The rangers couldn't get there soon enough.

"It looks like there's an outcropping of rocks right over there. We'll still be close enough to the coordinates the rangers have for them to find us, but it should help us stay a little warmer if we're out of the rain."

Zoe followed him seeing no other options. She was freezing and any chance at warming up was a welcome one. He brushed off a spot on the rocks and sat, motioning for her to sit next to him. Seeing no immediate evidence of scary spiders, she joined him.

"So why did you run away exactly?" he asked, breaking the silence.

"I couldn't take it anymore. I couldn't stand knowing I'd ruined everything. And…" Her voice trailed off.

"And what?" he asked quietly.

"And I couldn't face the cameras and the final filming with my secret out there for the world to see. It was bad enough that Alex told everyone my real name, but once we started filming again, the entire national viewing audience would have seen the evidence of his words on my face. I couldn't let them see me like that. I couldn't let you see me that way either."

"Zoe, I've known about your scars since you were on *The One*."

She sucked in a breath. "What? How?"

"Your makeup hasn't always been perfectly applied, as much as you think it has been. Every now and then, the camera picked up your scars if the lighting was right."

"But I never saw that when I watched the show."

"I know, because I got the filmed touched up before the episodes aired." He shrugged like it was no big deal. It was a big deal to her though.

"Thank you. That was really nice of you. I had no idea."

"I knew when I saw your file that I'd have to watch for them so I always did."

"What do you mean? What was in my file?"

"Everything. Or well, I guess I thought everything. I know about the car accident and the cosmetic surgery. I knew it was something you struggled with. I didn't realize you'd changed your name though. And I could never make sense of how you and Jack Miles were related. That whole story you told Paige during *Treasure Trekkers* about your parents divorcing never really made sense because I couldn't find your name in connection with Miles's history. But I assumed it was something with the divorce and I didn't dig too hard when it came to you."

"Why not?"

"Because I didn't want to find a reason to keep you off the show."

Oh.

"So you didn't know that Alex was someone from my past? Someone who would have known me before my accident? You didn't put him on the show to cause drama for me?"

Chip leaned away from Zoe and she instantly regretted her words. "Wow. You really think very little of me, don't you?"

"Well, you have to admit you have done some pretty shady things all in the name of producing a show that will earn big ratings. Like the whole finale thing between Cassidy and me. You did do that."

"So you thought I'd bring on an asshole like Alex from your past to humiliate the host of my show during the finale? That's really nice of you, Zoe." He got up and paced out in the rain in front of the outcropping. "I can't believe everything I've done for you and all you can think of me is that I've been out to get you this whole time."

"Chip, you're taking this the wrong way. I don't know what I thought. It's weird that Alex would be here out of everyone you could have chosen. I shouldn't have said anything. I don't really think badly of you, I'm just trying to figure this all out. I don't understand how everything went downhill for me so quickly."

"Everything I've done on my shows concerning you has been with your best interest at heart and this is what you think of me."

Zoe felt her temper rising at the situation. She was cold and tired and not at all in the mood to have this conversation. "Not everything was in my best interest. Dragging me along for Cassidy's humiliation on the finale of *The One* was an embarrassment for me too. But you wanted the ratings. You didn't even consider how being rejected by Brad would affect me, did you?"

Chip stopped walking and stared at her. "You're right. When it came down to the finale for *The One*, I wasn't thinking about your feelings. I did get caught up in the scandal and the ratings and I forgot that there were real people involved. I'm sorry. If I could take back any moment in my production history, it would be that one. But every other thing concerning you has been with you in mind. And honestly, Zoe, I didn't think you'd be so upset over Brad."

"Why wouldn't I be upset about getting rejected on live TV?" She couldn't remember ever feeling so irritated by Chip before.

Didn't he get it? Didn't he understand she wasn't some pawn in his game?

"Because he wasn't the right guy for you and I thought you knew that. I thought you were playing along with the game because you wanted to win, not because you really cared for him." Chip slumped down onto a wet stump, sighing and dropping his head into his hands. When he looked up at her, she saw something in his eyes she hadn't seen before. Sadness, regret, and uncertainty all rolled into one. "And I sort of thought you wouldn't care about Brad because maybe you already had feelings for me the way I already had feelings for you."

She opened her mouth to say something, but nothing came out.

Chip's jaw set into a hard line. "I should have known better. You don't care about anyone but yourself. Certainly you don't care about me. Never have, never will."

That last comment lit a fire inside her so bright she could barely see straight. "Don't you dare talk to me as if you know me. You don't know anything about me. Not really anyway. Sure, you know whatever is in that little file of yours, but that's just facts. Where I live, what kind of things I like to do for fun, and who my friends are. But that doesn't tell you anything about what I think or how I feel. You're so busy trying to be a big shot reality TV producer that you've forgotten how real life really works. You make these 'reality' TV shows and you think that makes you some kind of expert on people. But guess what? You aren't an expert on me or anyone else. You're just some sleazy producer who's looking for the best thing to capitalize on and I'm not going to be that person for you anymore."

"Do you even hear yourself right now? You're so wrapped up in your own insecurities that you can't even see how you are to everyone else. You spend all of your time pushing people away by being a gigantic bitch so no one can ever get close to you. And you've done it again. I can't do this anymore. I could have had any number of people as the host for this show, but I picked you because I knew you had medical bills to still pay off."

"That's none of your business," she said, the sting of shame digging into her chest. How dare he look into her accounts? That was a violation of her privacy for sure.

"But more than knowing you needed the money, I wanted you here. With me. I thought maybe if we were out here together, away from everything else, you might finally let your walls down with me and give into the feelings you've been hinting at this whole time. But you couldn't let that happen, could you? So you ran away and kept me at a distance even when I pushed you to be honest."

"I had to run—"

"No, you didn't," he cut her off sharply. "You didn't have to run from me. I would have taken you any way I could have had you. I would have done anything for you. Including punching my own contestant in the face, risking a lawsuit, and then following you out into the middle of a forest in the dark. But not anymore. I'm done, Zoe. You keep running away from me but you don't need to anymore. I'm done chasing after you."

She stared at Chip, his words cutting into her, her heart breaking with the pain, and her insides twisting with anger. No one had ever spoken to her like that before. It pissed her off and yet she couldn't bring herself to respond. What could she say?

"Hello?" someone called. "Can you hear me?"

"We're here," Chip called back, standing and walking toward the voice.

Chapter Twenty-Two

Zoe sat on the tiny, uncomfortable couch in the middle of the hotel room still shivering even after they'd cranked the heat in the ranger's car for the ride into the nearest city. She couldn't seem to get warm in her wet clothes. She'd have to get out of them soon, but she wasn't sure what else she could put on in their place. And walking around naked wasn't an option she wanted to entertain at the moment.

Chip groaned as he sat on a chair opposite her and bent to take off his shoes. "These shoes were not made for hiking in the woods. I don't think they're going to survive the night."

She tried to smile a response, but her muscles wouldn't cooperate. Instead, she fought the tears flooding her eyes and bit the inside of her cheek, trying to trap the pain inside.

With a huge convention happening, most of the hotel rooms had been booked, leaving them no choice but to room together in a suite. While she was thrilled to have a warm room and a comfortable bed, it was awkward sharing the same space knowing that Chip was more than pissed at her right now.

She'd been pissed at him too an hour or so ago when they were trekking out of the woods with the rangers who'd come and found them. She couldn't remember ever having been quite that pissed at anyone before and she'd fought the urge to pick up a stick and smack him with it the entire way to the ranger's car.

But once she was tucked into the backseat of the cruiser and Chip was busy telling him about the show, she'd had a lot of time to think. And she hadn't liked where her mind had taken her.

Basically, everything Chip had said about her was true. She did push people away so they couldn't get close to her. She didn't want to run the risk of letting someone in, only to end up hurt again in the end. But in doing that, she'd made it so that she was never close to anyone and that made her miss out on things like a relationship with Chip—the only guy who'd ever really taken the time to see past her defenses. The only guy who she'd ever felt like she wanted to be with for longer than one drunken night of fun no one would really remember. The only guy who'd made her feel like she was more than just a face, or body, or TV personality.

The only guy she'd ever loved.

And now she'd lost him because she'd been too foolish to see what was right in front of her all along.

"I'm going to take a hot shower unless you want in there first," Chip said, pulling the bottom hem of his shirt free from his pants.

She shook her head. A hot shower sounded like heaven, but she knew she would never really enjoy it unless she made things right with Chip. Now that she admitted to herself that he'd been right, she couldn't wait another minute to tell him so.

"Okay." Chip shrugged and turned toward the bathroom, pulling his shirt over his head. The muscles on his back flexed as he stretched.

"Wait," she managed to say before he made it all the way to the bathroom.

He turned back to face her, his shirt in hand, his sculpted chest glistening with moisture from his wet shirt.

At the sight of his naked chest, the words that had been on the tip of her tongue were lost. Her throat went dry.

Think. Say something before he leaves.

"You're right," she said, finally forcing some words out of her mouth.

He tilted his head. "I'm right about the shower? I'm not sure what could have been wrong with that statement."

"No." She cleared her throat. "You're, um, right about me. All of it. Everything you said is true."

He looked down for a moment before finding her gaze. "I shouldn't have said those things. They were rude and hurtful and uncalled for."

"They were true. I push people away all the time because of my past. I judge people now because of how other people have treated me before. And that's not fair to anyone."

"Zoe, I—" he started, stepping toward her, his shirt falling from his hand to the carpet.

"Let me finish, please."

He nodded and waited for her to continue.

"I'm sorry for pushing you away the way I did. It wasn't fair to you and it wasn't fair to me either. People treated me really badly growing up. I wasn't the cute girl in school who the boys liked and who the girls envied. I was the ugly kid who didn't really fit in with anyone."

"I can't believe that anyone would say you were ugly. Kids can be cruel to each other and stupid."

"Maybe they shouldn't have said it, but it was true. I wasn't good looking. Then, when I was fourteen, I was in a bad car wreck with a friend's family, as my file must have told you." She paused and took a deep breath, not wanting to go on but knowing it was finally time to tell the whole truth. "Lana and I had been goofing around in the backseat trying to see who could be the most outrageous. We were in such silly moods, acting without thinking. Her parents had asked us to calm down a few times and finally Lana did. But I didn't. I thought it would be funny and make everyone laugh if I tried to scare her dad. And I did. I settled down for a while then poked him in the side and screamed. He startled and the car jerked to the shoulder, hit the gravel and flipped."

"Zoe, I'm so sorry." Chip reached for her, but she pulled away.

"Don't be sorry. I deserved what I got."

"That's not true."

Zoe nodded. "It is. It's my fault the accident happened."

"You were a kid. You couldn't have known the outcome of your actions. It's not your fault," Chip stepped closer but didn't touch her.

"There's more."

"You don't have to tell me anymore. It's okay. I get it, Zoe. I understand now."

It was now or never. "Lana and her family all walked away from the accident with bumps and bruises, but I had taken off my seatbelt. I was pinned under the car for a while. I'm lucky there was a boulder that stopped the car from crushing me completely. I remember the paramedics calling to me, telling me to be calm and not move around. I remember them telling me they were coming for me and to hold on a little longer. So I did my best to listen and I held on until they pulled me free. When I woke up and learned of my injuries, I wished I hadn't been pulled out from under the car at all. The kids had always teased me before and now I really was a monster. Lacerations all over my face and neck, broken bones in my arms and ribs, and road rash down the side of my face made me a walking nightmare. I feared they would tease me more. And they did."

Chip put his hand on her shoulder and squeezed. It was all she could do not to flinch at his touch. This wasn't something she talked about. Ever. To have physical contact with someone she cared about while she told her story was overwhelming and she wasn't sure she could handle it.

"After I recovered from a few surgeries, I went back to school and it was worse than ever. You'd think the kids would have cut me some slack since I'd been in the accident, but they didn't seem to care. I couldn't take it anymore. Finally my mom decided to move in with the guy who became my stepdad. They got married.

I changed my first name and took my stepdad's last name and he paid for more cosmetic surgery. He gave me a new chance at life and I took it. He made me beautiful. But I never forgot what it was like to be that ugly girl who people teased and made fun of. Once in a while, I'm ashamed to admit, it felt good to be the person to make fun of someone else for a change. To take the focus off of my pain by giving it to someone else."

"Zoe, I had no idea."

"No one did. I made sure of that. I couldn't let anyone, especially you, find out the truth. I couldn't let anyone learn the accident was my fault. Everyone thought I looked like a monster, but if they ever found out what I had done, they'd know they were right."

She wiped a tear as it rolled down her cheek. "I push people away because I'm afraid of getting hurt again when someone sees my scars. They aren't all gone. And if anyone ever saw them, I worried that they would think I was Ugly Andrea again and not get to see the real me underneath the scars. I guess it didn't work because people still didn't get to know the real me. I pushed everyone away before they could get too close. Including you."

"I'm still here," Chip said softly.

She nodded, too overcome to speak.

"Aren't you the one who told Ben during the last show that his prosthetic leg was either a scar or a trophy and the choice was his to make? Why can't you take your own advice?" Chip asked. "Shouldn't you look at your scars as a trophy for all you've overcome in your life?"

She shrugged. "It's always easier to say it to someone else than to live the words yourself."

Chip stroked the line of her jaw with the backs of his fingers. "You could be covered head to toe in imperfections and I would still find every single inch of you amazing." He touched the rough edge of her scars and she suddenly noticed how bright the lights in the room were. A pit formed in her stomach.

Chip could see her scars.

And he still looked at her like she was the most beautiful woman he'd ever laid eyes on.

Tears welled up in her eyes again but this time they were the happy kind. "I'm sorry I pushed you away. I've never felt for anyone the way I feel for you, and I got scared you wouldn't like me if you knew the truth."

Chip brushed his thumb across her lip as it quivered. "You're right. I don't like you."

She gasped at his admission, pain constricting in her chest like a vice grip.

"I love you, Zoe. I think I have since the first time I watched your audition tape for *The One*. Something about you stuck with me and I couldn't get you out of my head. Believe me, for a while I tried. But you were always there and the more time I spent with you, the more I knew you were the one for me. I just never knew how to make you realize it too."

"I love you too. I have for a long time. Of course, most of that time I told myself I didn't and that there was no way you could ever love me...the real me."

"I do love you, all of you. Scars, flaws, annoying personality traits, and all."

"Hey, you have annoying personality things too, Mr. Bossy Producer Guy," she teased, hitting him playfully on the arm then wrapped her arms around his neck and peered up at him. "Kiss me."

"With pleasure."

His lips touched hers and she pressed against him harder, trying to get closer to him. The need to be with him—really with him, without any more secrets—finally bubbled to the surface. She had tried to ignore it for as long as she could, but now there was no need to stop her feelings anymore.

Before she was ready, he broke away from her kiss and took her by the hand, pulling her toward the bathroom.

"What are you doing? I wasn't done with you yet," she said, her voice laced with desire she couldn't hide.

"I'm not done with you either. But we both need a hot shower to wash the chill of the rain away. And I don't know about you, but I think those camping showers were crap."

She laughed as he started the water, steam pouring out of the shower enclosure and fogging the mirror over the vanity. "I thought you were a big supporter of the solar heated showers? Weren't you the guy who told me how awesome they would be, how luxurious they were to have out in the wilderness?"

"I was full of crap. You shouldn't listen to me. I'll basically say anything to keep my crew happy so they'll do their jobs without complaint."

He stripped naked in front of her, letting his clothes pile on the floor. She'd thought he looked amazing in the lantern light in his tent, but holy hell, in this lighting he looked like a god. His muscles were toned and tanned as if he spent long hours working outdoors. His stomach rippled with indentations around a perfectly formed six-pack while his breathing grew more labored as he stared at her. The length of him stood at attention, ready and waiting for her, and she suddenly wondered how he had fit so easily inside of her given the massive length she was met with now.

She pulled her eyes from his manliness to meet his gaze. She saw hunger and fire and lust gazing back at her. But she also saw love in his eyes. And a tiny bit of humor too. "What's so funny?"

"I'm enjoying you checking me out. I've wanted to see that look in your eyes for a long time and finally I'm getting what I want." His smile grew. "And I'm wishing I had time to jump in the shower first to do a little grooming. I hate you're seeing me unkempt. Things are usually much more landscaped down there then they are now. Those damn camp showers were too cold to spend extra time in them."

She laughed and stroked a single finger along his length to the base where the tiniest hint of hair grew. "Seems pretty landscaped already to me. Any more and it would go from acceptable manscaping to 'oh my God are you kidding.' Rest assured, I like what I see."

Chip pulled her shirt over her head and added it to his pile of clothes on the floor. "My turn to see you."

He kissed her shoulder while reaching behind her to unfasten her bra.

"Wait," she said nervously. "There are scars you haven't seen yet. The ones on my face are pretty minor comparatively."

He didn't stop working on her bra while he gazed into her eyes. "Whatever they are, wherever they are, I won't care. The only thing that will ever bother me about your scars is seeing how much they bother you."

The straps of her bra slid down her arms and she swallowed the fear in her throat. Chip cupped her breasts in his hands, his fingers skimming the surface of the jagged scar that had long ago turned white. She blinked back tears. No one but her doctors had ever seen it. Whenever she'd had drunken sex with men in the past, it had always been with her bra on.

Chip paused, eyeing the scar while his fingers traced the outline of it as if he were studying it, committing it to memory.

"I'm sorry. I know it's awful," she said, the tears she couldn't hold back falling down her cheeks. She pushed against his shoulders so she could step away from him. He wrapped one arm around her waist while the other hand stayed on her breast.

"I won't let you push me away again. You're mine—good, bad, awful, ugly, or beautiful, you're mine and no matter how you look, you will never be less than incredible to me. I've never been with anyone more amazing than you."

Chip kissed the top of her breast, his lips brushing against her scar. "I love you, Zoe. All of you."

As he sucked her nipple into his mouth, toying with it, teasing it, her tears dried and she wiped the already fallen ones off her cheeks. She arched her back as he caressed her breasts—kneading them, kissing them. Her breathing came faster with his attention. She'd never let anyone touch her this way before. Granting the privilege to Chip was strangely easy.

Feeling a sudden urge to be with him in the shower, she stepped away from him and quickly stepped out of the rest of her clothes. Taking his hand, she pulled him into the shower behind her, shuddering as the hot water hit her chilled body. It had been too long since she'd had a shower that was more than lukewarm.

They stood together in each other's arms under the hot water for a few minutes soaking up the heat. When she finally felt the chill start to subside, she grabbed the little bottle of body wash provided by the hotel and squirted a dollop into her hand. She rubbed her hands together creating lather then ran them across Chip's broad shoulders and down the ridges of his chest. When she stroked his length with a soapy palm, he groaned and closed his eyes, letting his head fall back.

She squirted another dollop into her hands and scrubbed herself clean while Chip shampooed his hair. When they were both done, he motioned for her to turn her back to him so he could massage shampoo into her hair. The feeling of his hands in her hair, massaging her scalp, cleaning her, almost felt more intimate than actually being naked with him.

Almost. The persistent erection pressing against her back was pretty intimate too.

And distracting.

She tipped her head back under the water, washing the shampoo out. It felt amazing to finally be clean again after so long spent in the woods with minimal hygienic luxuries. While she used her hands to make sure the shampoo was completely rinsed from her hair, Chip pressed against her back, his hands snaking around her waist and exploring south. A moan escaped her mouth as he rubbed her sensitive skin. When his fingers found her opening and slipped in, her knees went weak.

"Are we done with the whole 'get clean' part of our shower yet?" Chip asked, running his tongue along the outside edge of her earlobe.

"We're so fucking clean it's scary." She reached behind her back, stroking him while his fingers worked magic on her body. Her climax came quickly, shattering any remaining inhibitions she had with him.

He spun her around to face him. "Let's get out of here and to the bedroom. I'll grab a condom from my wallet along the way." He started to pull her out of the shower, but she held him back.

"You don't need one with me." She looked into his eyes, knowing the next thing she said might be the thing that sent him packing. But she couldn't lie to him. She had to share the truth about herself with him. Every awful detail.

"I know we're both healthy adults and I'd love nothing more than to be with you one hundred percent naturally, but there's still the risk of a baby to consider."

She shook her head and dropped her eyes, unable to say it out loud and watch his reaction too. Her voice came out so softly she worried he might not hear her over the sound of the shower. "That's not a risk for me. Another scar. This one isn't visible, but it's permanent and absolute. I'm damaged goods."

He wrapped his strong arms around her, stroking her back. "No, you're perfect and I'm going to spend the rest of forever proving that to you."

Zoe's back pressed against the cold tile of the shower wall as his mouth claimed hers. His hands slid down her body exploring every inch of her with a growing hunger that could only be satisfied one way. Wrapping her leg around his waist, she guided him into her, joining them.

"Wait a second. Didn't I hear something about Paige and Miles getting condoms out of your bathroom bag when they fooled around during *Treasure Trekkers?*" Chip asked.

She rolled her eyes, annoyed to be pausing their current activities to talk about Paige and her brother, of all people. "They did. It was all part of my act. Every woman should have condoms with her so if I didn't, I might have to answer why. Now can we stop talking about my brother's sex life and start focusing on ours?"

"Hell yes we can," he said, lifting her against him, gaining better access.

She hooked her ankles behind his back. They moved together as the hot water flowed over them, washing away her past and leaving behind a clean slate for their future together.

Chapter Twenty-Three

Chip woke as the dawn light filtered in around the edges of the blackout drapes. He'd been far too preoccupied with Zoe to make sure that the drapes had been completely closed the night before.

Being with her was better than anything he'd ever experienced before and he wanted nothing more than to stay with her in bed for the entire day...week if he could swing it. But he knew that wouldn't happen right now. They had a show to finish filming and base camp to pack up. Then he'd be free to steal her away for a while.

And he seriously couldn't wait to have her all to himself with no distractions, no obligations, and no other guys around to flirt with her. He might not go back into the office for a month. He could oversee the editing of the season via email, couldn't he?

Zoe stirred on his chest, yawning and rubbing her eyes.

"Morning," he said, caressing the valley between her hip and ribs. Her skin was soft and smooth and sent his blood flow rushing south. Maybe they didn't have to get out of bed just yet.

She rolled onto him, kissing his chest and straddling his hips. Apparently Zoe had the same thing in mind.

He slipped into her quickly as she settled herself in his lap, rotating her hips against him. "I could stay here all day with you," he mumbled, fondling her breasts while she moved on top of him.

"But we can't do that, can we?"

"I'm afraid not. We have to go back and finish filming."

Zoe stilled. "I don't know if I can go back there. I can't face them. What will happen with the show? I cheated for one of the teams. I probably ruined everything for you. The contestants will never be okay with what I did."

He sat up and held her, wanting to ease her anxiety. "First of all, you can't just stop once we start. It's unfair and cruel." He moved his hips, thrusting into her to prove his point. She squirmed against him, instantly driving him wild. "Secondly, I'll fix the problem. Give me a little time when I'm not otherwise occupied and I'll think of a solution. Everyone will understand what you did and why once they learn the truth. I'll make sure they do."

Zoe kissed him. "You would do that for me? You'd risk your own reputation as a producer to save mine?"

"Of course. You're worth any risk." He tangled his hand into the hair at the nape of her neck, tipping her head to the side so he could nibble on the sweet skin of her neck. He loved the taste of her skin below her ear and the way licking there made her squirm in his arms. This morning was no different, only the sensation of her body moving around his while she sat on his lap was more intense than ever.

Chip lost himself in the sounds of her breathing as it grew heavier in his ear.

• • •

Zoe let out a shaky breath while she waited for the production crew to finish setting up the final shot of the show. She'd changed back into her clothes from yesterday. They felt dirty next to her shower-cleaned body but she wore them anyway so they could film the rest of the finale as if they'd done it at the same time and not the following day. The contestants had also been instructed to wear the same clothes. The film from the day before was reviewed and small details were matched like Pam's hair coming loose from its ponytail on one side and the streak of mud on Justin's shin.

Once everything looked as close to how it had yesterday as they could get it, then they would begin the last few moments of the show where she would announce the winning team.

The only difference today was Zoe's lack of makeup.

Chip tried to convince her that she needed to apply it as she normally did, but she refused. The fact was the rain had washed her makeup away. But it was Chip who had made her realize she didn't need it anymore. Alex had shared the truth about her yesterday and today she would face it head on. It would not be edited out of the final film and therefore, she would address it today *without* her makeup but *with* her dignity.

"We're ready for you," Chip said coming to her side. "Are you sure you want to do this now, here?"

She nodded once, resolute in her decision.

"Just another example of why you're so amazing." Chip kissed her quickly then walked away, yelling to the cameramen to start recording.

Zoe took her place before the teams, watching as they noticed her makeup-free appearance. To her surprise, no one cringed at her scars. Maybe she had hidden herself for no reason after all.

"What an exciting finale we've had here today," she said, clapping for the contestants. "Before we wrap this all up and I name our official winners of *Wild Expedition*, I'd like to address something quickly."

The contestants remained quiet, far more patiently than she would have been in their position. She cleared her throat and kept talking not wanting to drag this on any longer than necessary, since the sooner she was done filming, the sooner she could be with Chip without any other distraction.

"Alex brought up that my name is not really Zoe Oliver. He's half right. That is my legal name, but it was not the name I was born with. I was Andrea Miles until I turned fourteen and was involved in a terrible car accident. Recovering from the accident was painful, but nothing compared to the viciousness I faced when I returned to what I thought would be my new normal life. To say kids can be cruel is an understatement.

"I was horribly scarred and eventually wanted a fresh start at life along with the fresh face I received thanks to the multiple cosmetic surgeries I needed to undergo to minimize my scarring. So I picked a new name to go with my new face and started over." Zoe swallowed hard. Tears threatened her eyes at the pain of revealing the truth, but she pushed through them.

"I let people like Alex dictate how I should live my life for a long time, but thanks to this show and to Chip the producer and Alex's revelation about my past, I can finally live my life as myself. So if you want to call me Andrea or Zoe or any other name, you can. But I will always just be me. I'm done hiding my scars and I'm done hiding from my past."

Zoe squared her shoulders feeling lighter and more alive than she had in years. "Now without further hoopla, let's get to our winners. Because of Alex's actions and his attempted blackmail, his team has been disqualified from the show. It seems Alex will now have to face his past as I've had to face mine."

Zoe nodded to Chip, signaling she was ready for the next announcement. From out of the trees walked the doctors, the team eliminated after the last challenge. Their smiles showed their happiness at being brought back onto the show, though they hadn't been told exactly why they were there yet. That was her news to share.

"Edward, David, Joseph, and William, you have been asked to come back to the game because the other team has been disqualified. Therefore, you are now the second place team. While it would be unfair to run the final challenge again since one team did win fair and square, we would like to reward you with a second place prize of one hundred thousand dollars."

The team cheered and high fived each other, apparently not caring that they didn't get to compete in the finale since they were awarded a prize anyway.

Zoe smiled before continuing. "That means that Rick, Pam, Todd, and Roger are the winners of a million dollars! Congratulations! You've proven you can survive the wilderness living on little more than the land itself and a few extras. You met each challenge with strength and determination. And you persevered through four long weeks of this to leave with a lot of extra money in your pockets, and a good amount of dirt under your fingernails."

Zoe turned to speak directly to the camera focused on her. "Thank you for going on this journey with us. We hope you enjoyed the ride. And if you'd like to be a contestant on the next season of *Wild Expedition*, send in an audition video and application to the email address listed on your screen. Good night!"

She held still for a moment, smiling at the camera until she saw the red light flicker off then she walked over to congratulate the winning team. Pam pulled her into a hug and squealed happily in her arms. She shook hands with Todd and Roger. When she got to Rick, he threw an arm around her shoulders and pulled her close.

"I know you're with that producer guy. I can see in your eyes when you look at him. Something changed between you two. So I ain't gonna flirt with you this time. But if you ever get tired of that pretty boy, you come talk to me and I'll show you how an outdoorsman does it." He laughed and she wiggled out from beneath his arm.

"Thanks for the standing invitation, but I don't think I'll be taking you up on the offer any time soon."

"We'll see about that, baby." He winked and went back to celebrating his victory with his family.

"Zoe, I'm sorry for what I said about you," Alex said, stopping her by putting a hand on her arm as she walked by. "I hope you'll forgive me for airing that all on TV."

"What you did finally brought me out of hiding after all of these years, so for that I will always thank you. But if you don't remove your hand from my body in a nanosecond, I'll break your fingers. I don't like you as a person and I never will."

Pulling her arm free, she strode out of the filming area and into the quiet of the surrounding forest. It was hard to believe she'd been itching to leave the entire time she'd been here, but now that the time was coming, she might actually miss the woods and the peacefulness they provided from her regular, crazy life.

Arms wrapped around her waist and a mouth nuzzled the crook of her neck. Chip's cologne drifted on the breeze, greeting her with a scent she hoped she'd get to smell for the rest of forever. It made her head spin and her heart flutter in her chest. His warm breath on her neck didn't hurt either.

"I was looking for you," he said quietly into her ear. His voice sent heat through her body.

"You found me," she answered, turning in his arms to face him. She kissed his lips. "I mean it. I was lost without you in my life, but now I feel whole again."

"And I'll spend the rest of forever making sure you always feel that way, if you'll let me."

Zoe brushed her fingers across his cheek and down his neck, coming to rest on his chest. His heart beat beneath her hand. She took comfort in knowing that if what he said was true, then he would always have room in there for her. "Marry me?" she asked. "I can't imagine ever going back to the way my life was without you in it."

She held her breath as her heart pounded in her chest. She hadn't planned on asking him that question, it just sort of popped out of her mouth as if by its own will.

"Did you seriously just ask me to marry you?" His tone was light and joking.

"I think I did." She laughed.

"And did you buy me a ring too? Are you going to get down on one knee?"

"No I didn't and no I'm not." She smacked him on the arm. "I didn't exactly plan to ask you. It sort of came out of my mouth without me thinking."

"So you've really thought this question through. Well, that does make my decision a lot easier, knowing you took your time to consider what you wanted from me and asked your question with intent and purpose."

"Stop. Forget I said anything." Embarrassment burned in her cheeks. "Can we go back a couple of seconds in time to where things were still normal between us?"

"Nope, I'm afraid not. Nothing about us is normal and I'm totally okay with that. Yes, Zoe, I will marry you. But first you will let me buy you a ring like a proper gentleman since you took the question out of my mouth before I could ask it myself."

"Deal."

"And you will *never* tell anyone that you asked me."

She giggled and wrapped her arms around his shoulders, feeling completely at home in his arms. "Absolutely. It'll be our little secret."

Epilogue

Chip glanced around the table at his friends as he held up his glass of champagne in a toast. "To us. To great friendships, to forgotten pasts, and to unforgettable futures."

"To us," they said together.

Cassidy smiled down at the baby in her arms, no doubt wondering what amazing things the future would hold for little Jeremy, and took a sip of her sparkling white grape juice. Evan had an arm draped across the back of her chair casually yet protective of his wife and six-month old son.

Chip was happy to see they'd managed to stay together after falling in love on the show *The One*. So often, couples on those shows fell in love quickly while taping then fell out of love just as quickly when the cameras stopped rolling. But then nothing was typical when it came to Cassidy and Evan since only she had been a contestant on that show while he'd been her cameraman. Maybe since their love had started behind the scenes, it stood to reason that it was a different kind of love than the contestants on screen usually found.

He hoped for their sake it was a love like his and Zoe's—indestructible, real, forever.

They made a great couple and he was thrilled to have played a part in Cassidy and Evan's romance, even if it had been the part of the obnoxious producer who threatened to sue them for breaking the show's contracts. Thank God he'd never gone through with the threat.

Zoe laughed out loud at something Miles said and smacked him on the shoulder. Chip chuckled, happy to see he wasn't the only one who got that treatment from her. Paige sat perched in Miles's lap, one arm around his shoulders, the other on his knee. They were every bit the lovesick newlyweds he hoped to be with Zoe in a few months after their winter wedding in Oahu.

"I can't believe you actually convinced my sister to marry you. I didn't think anyone would be able to tame her," Miles said. Zoe balled her hand into a fist as if she meant to punch him this time instead of a playful smack.

"Watch it, brother," she threatened. "I'm not afraid to kick your ass in front of Paige if I have to, thereby ruining your macho image for all eternity."

"I'd like to see you try," Miles taunted back.

"Now, now. Let's not go and piss off my beautiful bride before she actually goes through with marrying me. I don't know how I convinced her to do it either, so let's not draw too much attention to it, okay?" He winked at her knowing their proposal secret was still safely hidden between them.

"So the famous Chip Cormack is actually going to take enough time out of the reality TV market to get married and have a honeymoon? I'm truly amazed," Evan said, shaking his head. Evan and Chip had worked together for a long time and it had been even longer since Chip had taken a break from production.

"I think it's long overdue, don't you?"

"Definitely."

"Any plans for future shows already or are you waiting until after the honeymoon to dive back in?" Cassidy asked.

"Nothing planned yet, but I'm always open to new ideas. For now I thought I'd get married to the most amazing woman before she realizes I'm not as awesome as she believes I am, then take the rest of the winter off to honeymoon and relax. After that, I'll figure it out with the studio. I'm sure they'll have something in the works for me by then."

"I'm so happy you can all come to Oahu for the wedding. I wish you could stay a little longer than the week to hang out with us," Zoe said, glancing around the table at her friends.

"Are you afraid you'll be sick of me by the time they head home? I promise to make every second of our honeymoon mind-blowing." Chip nuzzled Zoe's neck and she giggled.

"Get a room," Miles and Evan called together.

They all laughed.

"Well, since you bring up wanting to spend more time together, I was thinking maybe we should all hang out together next summer. We could rent one of those huge beach houses along the coast, relax...make some great memories now that we're all friends." He looked around the table anxiously. "What do you think?"

"I don't know," Cassidy said. "We'll have a one and a half year old by then. It may not be so much of a vacation for the rest of you with us there."

"I think we could make it work. We'd get a house with a bedroom for him. What kid doesn't love a summer spent playing in the sand?"

"True." Evan nodded. "Jeremy would have a blast."

"Will there be cameras in this house?" Paige asked, one eyebrow cocked suspiciously.

"Maybe." Chip shrugged.

Cameras really weren't as big of a deal as they made them out to be. They just stuck in the corners of the room, out of the way. Of course, he'd never actually been on camera before. He preferred things behind the scenes. But if it meant getting to hang out with everyone for a summer and giving responsibility for production to someone else for a change, maybe he could get used to the idea of being on a show. "There could be. I bet America would love to see their favorite reality TV show stars come together to live in a house for a summer. Think of the fun we could have."

"Think of the ratings, right?" Miles said, sarcasm thick in his voice.

"Exactly," Chip said. "I bet I could convince the studio into big fat paychecks to bring back everyone's favorite reality stars at one time, on one show."

"No thanks!"

"No way."

"Not interested."

Chip laughed. "Okay, I get it. No more shows."

Zoe snuggled into his side and kissed him on the cheek while everyone else carried on about how strange it would be to go on another show and how they were completely over even entertaining the idea in the future.

"It was a good idea, sweetheart," she whispered for his ears only, "but it's never going to happen."

He gazed into the eyes of the woman who had always held his heart in her hand, even when she didn't know it.

The woman he never thought he'd get to share his life with.

"Never say never."

About the Author

Heather Thurmeier was born and raised in the Canadian prairies, but now she lives in upstate New York with her own personal romance hero (aka her husband) and their two little princesses. When she's not busy taking care of the kids and an adventurous puppy named Indy, Heather's hard at work on her next romance novel. She loves to hear from her readers.

Heart, humor, and a happily ever after.

Website: *http://heatherthurmeier.com*

Email: *heatherthurmeier@gmail.com*

Twitter: *https://twitter.com/#!/hthurmeier*

Facebook: *http://www.facebook.com/HeatherThurmeierAuthor*

More from This Author

(From *Stuck on You*)

Paige Anderson stood on the outskirts of the staging area under a clear blue sky trying her best not to hurl on her new hiking boots. She'd made a mistake. She didn't stand a chance against teams like Mr. Muscles and Friend—Team Everest, according to the official game team names—or any of the others for that matter.

Speaking of Mr. Muscles, every time she glanced his way—which seemed to be more and more often—she'd catch him staring at her when he was supposed to be engaging in conversation with his teammate. This time when her eyes caught his, she noted his subtle eyebrow raise and a tiny smirk pulling up the corners of his mouth. Combine that with his light brown hair and sun-kissed skin, and it was hard to look away. Not to mention a little twinkle of something interesting in his dark chocolate eyes she couldn't quite pinpoint but found incredibly intriguing nonetheless. She tried to look away but it was difficult when Mr. Muscles stood there with his arms folded across his chest, biceps bulging against his thin cotton t-shirt.

Poor material doesn't stand a chance.

She swallowed the sudden urge to comfort the pathetic t-shirt that looked as if it were a single pushup away from tearing and forced her eyes to keep moving. She couldn't enjoy the man-candy competition fully while her own teammate was still MIA.

Where the hell was Cassidy? She should have arrived yesterday or the day before like everyone else, and yet Paige hadn't heard from her. Nor had Cassidy answered any of the texts or voicemails she'd left before the show's producer Chip had confiscated her phone. How were they supposed to survive on an adventure show if they couldn't even communicate their whereabouts before the show started?

Cassidy and Paige had become fast friends the year before while on a different reality show—one where they'd both vied for a bachelor's attention, along with eight other women. Out of all the women on the show, Cassidy was the nicest and most beautiful and it came as no surprise to Paige when not only the bachelor, but also a cameraman, had fallen in love with Cassidy during the show.

Of course, Paige hadn't made it anywhere near the finale with bachelor Brad. Nope. She'd been sent packing at the third elimination—humiliated and crushed.

Thank God this wasn't another dating show. No chance of major televised rejection to tarnish the experience. No sexy bachelor to distract her and Cassidy from winning the money and prizes.

Her eyes flickered back to Mr. Muscles again as if to prove her theory wrong right from the start. Damn. He was built to climb mountains. She'd like to climb his mountain.

Yeah, right. In my dreams.

Paige let out the breath she hadn't realized she'd been holding when she spotted Evan, Cassidy's new fiancé, chatting with a few other cameramen. If Evan was here, that had to mean Cassidy was here too. And when Paige finally found her, Cassidy would get a solid reminder about how you're supposed to tell your friend and teammate that you've arrived in one piece so said teammate doesn't worry.

"Gather around everyone," Chip Cormack, the show's producer said, waving the contestants over. "In a few moments we'll start filming. After a brief introduction by our host, Spencer Daley, the competition will begin. Now is your last chance to ask any questions you might have after reading the information packet you were provided."

He paused and looked around the group as if he expected an immediate outburst of questioning to begin. No one said a thing. The packet of information had been very thorough. A list of dos and don'ts for the show, legal obligations and warnings, and health waivers had basically covered everything you could imagine.

Except for one thing still weighing on Paige's mind: What to do if your partner is a no-show.

The main reason Paige stood here to begin with was to spend time with Cassidy doing something fun. Well, that and she really wanted a little time away from the chaos awaiting her back home. Seemed every single guy in a fifty-mile radius of her house had seen her get kicked off *The One* and each claimed to be her perfect man. How could she have a perfect man when she felt like a walking rejection? The bachelor Brad on *The One* hadn't wanted her, so why would any of these other guys?

Cassidy always knew the right thing to say to cheer her up, make her feel more confident, and send her on the right path again—exactly what she needed right now.

Of course, she needed Cassidy to actually show up before any of that could happen.

She cautiously raised her hand, reverting back to her Catholic school days of ornery nuns who didn't take kindly to children who spoke out of turn.

"Yes, Paige." Chip smiled one of his famous smiles that could make any woman agree to just about anything, including being on another reality show when she'd sworn she wouldn't be caught dead on television again. Ever.

"Um." She swallowed, her throat feeling dry as all eyes turned toward her. "My partner hasn't shown up yet. Is that a problem?"

"We'll get to that soon."

Not quite the response she expected considering he'd said they would start filming in a few minutes. Maybe he'd seen Cassidy and knew she was on her way here. That had to be it.

"If there are no other questions, then I think it's time we get started. I'd like to see each of the teams standing together in their groups of two." Chip turned his attention to the camera crew. "Guys, you can take your places with your team now."

Paige glanced around feeling her nervousness escalate. All around her, teams formed, looking eager to get started. She stood alone, quivering in her hiking boots and cursing Cassidy. Her gaze landed on Evan as he took his place a few feet to the left, pointing his camera at her.

"Where the hell is your fiancée?" she asked in a stern whisper as she applied a fresh coat of mint lip balm. In about five seconds she was really going to lose her calm façade and start to panic.

"She'll be here. Don't worry," he said, a silly grin breaking his otherwise calm demeanor.

Great. Evan was laughing at her and the show hadn't even started yet. Awesome.

She turned away from his stupid grin and focused instead on Chip who was now standing with Spencer Daley, the host of the show, talking in a hushed voice. Just behind them, movement from one of the production trailers caught her attention. The door to the trailer opened and out stepped Cassidy.

The butterflies in Paige's stomach calmed to a flutter instead of a full on frenzy at the sight of her friend walking toward her. Finally, she wouldn't be standing alone like a chump anymore. She'd have a partner by her side like everyone else.

She waved Cassidy over. Cassidy returned a weak smile, but instead of coming to stand beside Paige, she joined Chip.

Maybe she needs to explain why she's so late to the filming.

Cassidy chatted with Chip for a few minutes, darting tiny glances back at Paige and Evan. Although a spark of nervousness flashed across Cassidy's face, she looked calm and happy. In fact, she looked radiant. Her hair fell down her back in giant waves;

her light tunic-style blouse flowed loosely over her body, except for where she held her hand to her stomach.

I hope she's not ill. Starting a competition like this—one promising to be high-energy with tests of endurance—would be difficult if sick with a stomach bug.

Come to think of it. Cassidy's outfit, complete with leggings and ballet flats, didn't look at all like what the other competitors were wearing. Certainly she didn't go with Paige's Lycra yoga tank top, slim-fit jeans with just the right amount of stretch in them to make it possible to actually do more than stand still and look cute, and pristine hiking boots, fresh out of the box and laced tightly up to her ankles.

Paige stepped toward Cassidy to find out what exactly was going on, but before she could, Chip held up his hand to quiet the bit of talking that had started amongst the teams.

"If I can have your attention again, please. We're ready to begin. Camera crew, it's time to start recording. So without further ado, here is your host for the show, Spencer Daley." Chip clapped as Spencer turned on his television-worthy smile and waved at everyone to stop fussing over him even though he clearly enjoyed every second.

"Welcome, everyone, to the first season of *Treasure Trekkers*, the show that will have you racing for treasures in caches hidden around the New York metropolitan area as well as the lower Hudson Valley." He paused to smile for the camera a moment before continuing on. "You never know what surprise you'll find in the next cache. Perhaps you'll find money, or a fantastic trip for two. Maybe you'll even find the keys to a new car!"

The contestants cheered. Even Paige who was normally pretty quiet and reserved cheered at the idea of being able to win really awesome prizes along the way without having to win the whole show. Even with Cassidy as her teammate, the chances of winning the adventure show were pretty slim for two girls who weren't exactly athletic or outdoorsy. Winning a few prizes could go a long way to making Paige more comfortable in life. Her salary as a freelance graphic artist covered the bills, but little else. But at least she could take time off whenever she wanted.

"Speaking of surprises, we're starting off the show with a big one." Spencer motioned for Cassidy to come and stand beside him instead of off to the side where she had been next to Chip. "I'm sure most of you have already noticed that one of our teams of two is currently a team of one. But not for long."

Paige felt her insecurity creeping up into her cheeks. She hated being the center of attention. Why had she ever agreed to come on this new show? Was a free trip, an interesting experience, and time spent with her good friend really worth all this?

Spencer gestured to her. "Paige has been patiently waiting for her teammate to show up and here she is with me. Cassidy, why don't you tell everyone why you're here with me instead of over there with your teammate."

Cassidy glanced around the small gathering, smiling as she found the spot where Evan stood filming. Then her eyes met Paige's quickly before settling back on Spencer. "Well, um, there's been a little change of plans."

What change of plans? No one spoke to me about any changes and I've been here all day.

"I was supposed to run the race with Paige." Cassidy caught Paige's gaze again, her expression clearly apologetic for what she was about to say. "But I'm sorry. I can't run the race with you."

Can't run the race? I can't run it alone.

"And why is that?" Spencer asked even though he absolutely had to already know the answer. But America didn't and neither did Paige.

How? Why? What could possibly make it okay for Cassidy to think she could abandon Paige at the last minute like this? Her chest tightened at the thought of having to run it alone. Or drop out before they even started.

Damn. Getting voted out in the third round on *The One* was bad enough, but now she was about to be kicked off in the first episode of a show where everyone was supposed to compete until the end. This wasn't fair.

Cassidy looked away from Paige and back to Evan, a smile coming to her lips. "Because I'm pregnant."

Tears instantly pricked Paige's eyes. Pregnant? Okay, that was a pretty damn good reason not to run a possibly dangerous race. Without thinking, Paige took the few steps separating her from her friend and wrapped Cassidy in a hug.

"A baby? And you didn't tell me," she teased.

Cassidy nodded. "We just found out. I'm so sorry, Paige. I was really looking forward to running the race with you."

Paige stepped back from Cassidy. "Don't be silly. We can't have you putting a tiny Cassidy/Evan baby in danger for some stupid show."

"Hey now." Spencer laughed. "The show is anything but stupid."

"You know what I mean," Paige said, brushing off Spencer's comment and focusing only on her friend—her pregnant and engaged friend. Tears blurred her vision. "I'm just so happy for you both."

"I wanted to tell you right away, but once I told Chip I couldn't do the show anymore, he forced me to wait to announce it here."

"And now that you have made this wonderful announcement, the show must go on," Spencer said, nudging Paige back to her spot. He gave a huge smile to Cassidy. "On behalf of the production company, congratulations and we wish you well with everything." And with that, he motioned for Cassidy to step out of frame.

"The show must go on and go on it will. But not with Paige as a solo team."

Paige felt her pulse race again. So this was it. The moment she was asked to join Cassidy on the sidelines where she could watch the show with the rest of America. Kicked off on day one. And she thought getting rejected by Brad was bad. This was a new low point for her life.

Yippy.

"Paige, we can't let you race alone. It wouldn't be fair to you or the other teams and honestly, it would be dangerous considering some of the caches we have hidden for you." Spencer paused, his hands clasped, fingers intertwined as if he were going to pray for help.

She swallowed the lump in her throat and prepared to take her exit with as much grace as she could. She didn't want to run the race alone anyway. It would be too hard. Too lonely. Too embarrassing. She'd much rather sit this whole game out and be able to keep Cassidy company while Evan was filming the show. They could talk about baby names and buy little tiny clothes and have an excuse to eat outrageous amounts of ice cream.

"So, we've made a decision," Spencer spoke, capturing her attention again. "And we've picked a new partner for you."

Say what now?

Just then, someone stepped out from behind the production trailer. The moment Paige glimpsed platform stilettos and long golden hair, she knew she'd died and somehow gone to hell because there was no way this was really happening.

No. Fricken'. Way.

In the mood for more Crimson Romance?
Check out *California Homecoming*
by Casey Dawes
at *CrimsonRomance.com*.